Why is novelist Pen Elliot's life being threatened over and over? There are a few suspects: her bitter ex-husband Peter and Joe, the abusive husband of a friend, who blames her for destroying his family. But what if the answer revolves around something larger and more global? Set in the seaside town of Falmouth, on scenic Cape Cod, the novel involves a romance as well as a coming out story of a young teen. It also asks how far would you go to protect those you love?

Praise for *Clearly Hidden*

"...On the surface...a straightforward mystery...but it is so much more than that. It is a novel about place, people, and the messiness of life; of the resiliency of the human spirit as it triumphs over adversity and fear. In addition, it is an engaging story that pulls the reader into the twists and turns of an investigation which is becoming progressively more urgent. A must-read which guarantees that you will be reading long into the night.—**Birger Johnson, author of the Amy Lee Mysteries series**

"...a wonderfully written page turner. The narrator, Pen Ellis, has a fighting spirit we could all use a little more of. When Pen Ellis is knocked down, she gets back up again. Faced with death threats and forced to deal with a daughter being bullied, she needs to dig deep to fight back...."—**Ed Meek, author of Luck and High Tide**

"... a taut, suspenseful, and fully satisfying thriller that keeps the reader engaged to the very last word. It's one of those unsettling tales that asks what would you do in this situation...strikes just the right balance of edge-of-the-seat action and heart-felt moments...."—**Michael C. Keith, author Insomnia 11 and Pieces of Bones and Rags**

Excerpt

A deep, gravelly voice said, "I know you're here, because I saw you come in the house." Echoing words she'd heard in a game long ago, he added, "Come out, come out, wherever you are!" He sounded like he was enjoying himself.

Pen had never been so scared in her life. Biting her lip, she tried to remember what Greta, her therapist, had taught her about relaxing: take a breath in to a count of seven, then let it out to the same count. She took in a deep breath and held it, afraid if she didn't do something she would panic. She could feel hysteria lurking right below the surface and that scared the bejeezus out of her.

After a few minutes of deep breathing, she started to feel more in control. She talked silently to herself. *I can do this. If I stay here, I am safe.* She willed it to be so as she took more slow breaths. There was a small plug-in light in the socket next to her, but she felt safer in the dark. Even though Finn has shown her that the light was undetectable from the outside room, she couldn't make herself turn it on. She knew there was a phone charger there, too, but as she checked her pockets for her phone, she felt her heart plummet as she remembered that she had left it upstairs next to her computer.

"Where the hell are you?" the same deep voice yelled with increased frustration. She could hear him now, rummaging throughout the house. It sounded like he was looking in closets, opening doors, then slamming them in frustration. She heard him in Aggie's room, then Galen's.

Clearly Hidden

Lindy Bergin Conroe

Moonshine Cove Publishing, LLC

Abbeville, South Carolina U.S.A.

First Moonshine Cove edition
October 2021

ISBN: 9781952439186

Library of Congress LCCN: 2021918311

For Ken, always.

Acknowledgments

I owe a great deal to my early readers Kathy Morton, Jeanné Giddens, and Bruce Ronan. Their hard work, support, and thoughtful insights are very much appreciated.

Thanks to Phil Temples for sharing his expertise and wisdom with me so often and so willingly.

To my good friend and fellow author, Michael Keith, special thanks for the years of encouragement, mentoring, and belief in my writing. I am incredibly grateful.

And finally, to my husband, Ken, huge appreciation for his reading acumen and constant help. Without his support, there would be no book.

About the Author

Lindy Bergin Conroe graduated with a BA in English Literature from Bridgewater State University in Massachusetts and an MA in English Literature from the University of 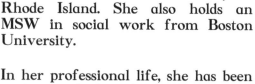 Rhode Island. She also holds an MSW in social work from Boston University.

In her professional life, she has been a junior high school teacher, an Assistant Professor of English, a geriatric hospital social worker, a community social worker, and a licensed LICSW therapist with a private practice. She has written two books for children (*Rockafella Jones and the Hidden Treasure* and *Rockafella Jones and the Journey Home*) published by Blue Mustang Press. Among her hobbies are painting, hiking, reading, and kayaking. *Clearly Hidden* is her first adult novel, and she is currently working on a sequel.

lindyberginconroe.com

Chapter One: Unexpected

Pen pushed away from the computer upstairs in her study and stared out the window at the roiling ocean. Writing this second book was much harder than she ever imagined. Sometimes the words wouldn't come to her, and when they did, they were often the wrong ones. She glanced again out the window, surprised to get a glimpse of movement on the path from the rocky beach in back of her house. When she moved closer to the window, it was gone. *Must have been mistaken,* she thought. There was nothing down that way but the ocean.

At the bottom of the stairs, she turned right toward the kitchen, intending to make a cup of tea and sit on the screened porch while she chewed on a glitch in the plot of the book. Mid thought, she paused at the granite countertop, about to reach for the tea caddy at the far end. In the silence of that moment, she heard the squeak of boards on the back deck. On the other side of the summer drapes, a vague outline of something blocking the sun.

Frozen, she stood still and listened. More squeaks, footsteps on decking.

She became aware that she was alone. Galen and Aggie were at overnights at their friends' homes, and she had planned a quiet night of reading.

The noise again. She remembered Finn saying, "He will come after you. Make no mistake." Finn was the builder who helped her gut, then reconstruct, this sanctuary she had bought for herself and her girls. Because of his background, with a father who ran a large cement business and who sat on the edge between honest and corrupt, legal and illegal, he knew what men were capable of when provoked. He also knew how to thwart ill intention.

"Look," he'd said. "I've designed a safe room in the house." He pointed to the blueprints resting on the dining room table of her old house. "Here," he said, stabbing his finger near the cedar closet in her bedroom on the plans, "Totally hidden. It'll be accessed from the cedar closet in your bedroom and run along the whole wall. Big enough to comfortably fit all three of you. I can put in electrical outlets for charging phones and an overhead light. Could put in a phone jack for a home phone, too, if you want."

Pen remembered rolling her eyes. "No one will be, quote, 'coming after me.'"

"I'll not argue," he'd said calmly, folding up the plans. "You have a few days to think about it. Let me know what you decide. I'll do the work myself, so there'll be no workmen down at the bars talking about the odd plan."

Four days later, she agreed to a modified version, more to appease Finn than because she thought she needed it. He wasn't happy, but as she pointed out in a not-so-subtle way, it was her house. The compromise was half the size of the earlier version and had only one electrical socket. More like a hiding place than a safe room, as plain and functional as could be. But she had liked the idea that Finn was trying to protect her. As a writer, she was alone a great deal, and needed or not, she knew it would probably give her peace of mind.

With the sound of the doorknob being turned, adrenaline finally surged through Pen's blood, overriding her denial and paralysis.

She ran down the hall and entered her bedroom, moving immediately toward the cedar closet. Opening its door, she ducked under the winter coats to the side of the cedar closet. Feeling her way in the dark, she found the right spot to push midway up the wall. The door silently sprung open to reveal an extension of the closet about seven feet long about thirty inches deep. Pulling the coats she had pushed away back into place, she entered the hiding place. Then she gently tugged on the strap inside the door until she heard the soft click that indicated that the door was closed tightly.

Now her head was pounding and she thought she might throw up. As she slid down the wall of the hiding place, she was shaking. *Bless Finn, Bless Finn, Bless Finn*, she said silently to slow her breathing.

Footsteps on the hardwood floor, someone moving about. Footsteps in the bedroom.

Pen scrunched her eyes shut, as children do when they are scared, sure if they cannot see the monsters, the monsters cannot see them.

A deep, gravelly voice said, "I know you're here, because I saw you come into the house." Echoing words she'd heard in a game long ago, he added, "Come out, come out, wherever you are!" He sounded like he was enjoying himself.

Pen had never been so scared in her life. Biting her lip, she tried to remember what Greta, her therapist, had taught her about relaxing: take a breath in to a count of seven, then let it out to the same count. She took in a deep breath and held it, afraid if she didn't do something she would panic. She could feel hysteria lurking right below the surface and that scared the bejeezus out of her.

After a few minutes of deep breathing, she started to feel more in control. She talked silently to herself. *I can do this. If I stay here, I am safe.* She willed it to be so as she took more slow breaths. There was a small plug-in light in the socket next to her, but she felt safer in the dark. Even though Finn has shown her that the light was undetectable from the outside room, she couldn't make herself turn it on. She knew there was a phone charger there, too, but as she checked her pockets for her phone, she felt her heart plummet as she remembered that she had left it upstairs next to her computer.

"Where the hell are you?" the same deep voice yelled with increased frustration. She could hear him now, rummaging throughout the house. It sounded like he was looking in closets, opening doors, then slamming them in frustration. She heard him in Aggie's room, then Galen's.

Footsteps going upstairs to her office. Doors opening and closing. A loud thud, as something fell over.

Now he was back in her bedroom. He opened the door to the cedar closet. Pen bit her lip again to keep from yelping in surprise. He was rummaging around in back of the winter coats and boots, standing literally four feet from her. Only Finn's false wall kept her safe.

"Goddammit!" he shouted. "Goddammit!" She could hear him pacing on the hardwood floor. "I'm fucked!" he said several times. Then there was the sound of footsteps leaving the room.

Pen felt like she was in another world, in a cramped dark place, with her eyes shut and her heart thudding. She couldn't move at all, even to get in a more comfortable position, for fear that he might have come silently back. She sat and waited. Slowly, and silently, she moved inch by inch until she could lay down. She regretted taking off her watch earlier when she washed the frying pan and regretted even more leaving her phone upstairs. *"Dumb!"* she berated herself. *"Dumb."* She could feel tears of fear and frustration prickle in her eyes and run down her face as she lay there silently.

Later, she had no idea how much later, she opened her eyes. She thought, though it seemed unimaginable to her, that she might have fallen asleep. She listened. And listened. Nothing.

Finally, she stood up and pushed on the panel door, holding it by the inside strap to limit the amount it opened. She could see a strip of light under the closet door. Gently, she released the strap more and more, pushing the door slowly open with her other hand. It hit the coats hanging in the closet and she adjusted the pressure so the opening was large enough for her to enter the closet itself.

She listened again. No footsteps, no sounds. She opened the cedar closet door, turning the knob with infinite patience.

Nothing. She could feel it in an intuitive way. No one was in her home. She stepped into the bedroom. Sliding to the floor, sitting against the wall, she sobbed silently, then with loud retching breaths. Relief. Thankfulness. She was alive! She was once again alone in her home, with only the early morning sun streaming into the room from the East and the sound of the rolling waves surrounding her.

After a while, her sobbing subsided. She got up and walked, tentatively, toward the kitchen. Even though she felt sure that the house was uninhabited except for her presence, it felt like an alien space. Since last night, something had changed. Everything had changed.

Only yesterday...but it felt like a lifetime ago. She felt changed in some irreparable way. She had knowledge she did not want to have. People could hurt her. Someone wanted to hurt her.

She realized her vulnerability, she also felt something else well up within her. She could feel it build, like a wave gathering more and more water and grit until it roared up and broke on the beach. Anger was gathering within, anger as well as strength. This would never happen again. Ever. She would be prepared for a next time, whatever that meant. And whoever had menaced her would pay.

She would be goddamned if she would be a victim again. She had had enough of that with Peter, with his sly mental manipulations, his lies, his meanness. "NO MORE," she said to herself, only to hear the words in her mind bounce out loudly in the room, startling her in their vehemence.

For a moment, she thought about dialing the police. But then her common sense kicked in. They would discover her hiding place; the whole town would know in no time. She had no evidence, only her feeling that Peter was behind this. Two of the higher ups in the department fished and played cards with Peter. Nope, not a good idea to call them. Instead, she called Finn's number, but he didn't answer, so she left a brief message. "Finn, it's Pen. There's been an..." She paused as she searched for the right word for what had happened. "...incident," she added. "Call me back, OK?"

He was on her back deck in twenty minutes.

Chapter Two: Later in the Day

Galen came home at three, Aggie at four. They were filled with tales of their overnight visits with friends. Galen went on about the movie marathon she and her friend Lara had watched, and because she was usually so withholding about her thirteen-year-old life, especially with her mother, Pen let her run on. Aggie said less, mostly raving about the Italian dinner she had shared with her friend Angela's parents. "Mom," she said, "there was chicken parmesan, and spaghetti, and salad, and homemade bread, and tiramisu for dessert"

Pen smiled and nodded. "Do you even know what tiramisu is?" Aggie asked.

"Yes, Aggie, I know what tiramisu is," Pen responded. "I have actually been in restaurants and eaten it."

"But not like this one. This was homemade!"

Pen listened as they both recounted more details about their visits and she made suitable comments. She did her best to make sure that the girls couldn't tell she was on autopilot, and she was pretty sure they could not. She had perfected her "looking-interested-but-not" demeanor during her long marriage to Peter. How many times had he gone on and on about what had been wrong with a dinner party she'd just given, or what she should talk about with the head of the law firm and his wife at a company party. She smiled slightly as she remembered all the times he rambled on, directing her and her behavior, criticizing so she could "do better next time." And he'd never known. She hadn't even been there.

She wanted to be there for the girls, as she had always been, but right now she was still too shaken by last night. When they went to their rooms, she walked out to the screened porch and sat down on one of the two chaise lounges facing the water. A breeze had kicked up, but it was warm, and the fresh air felt good.

She sat and watched the waves roll and break, roll and break in front of her. The rhythm was soothing. After a while, she could feel her mind begin to relax and wander.

Had Peter been behind last night's invasion.? She wanted to think "no," but she couldn't. But there was no one else who wished her harm. She thought back to her many years of subservience. Home perfect, meals perfect, body perfect. Stepford wife clone. And the more she tried to be perfect, make everything perfect, the more he found fault. Dishes not put in the dishwasher the right way. Cake for company could have had more flavor. Did she think she'd gained a few pounds?

She'd lived in a constant race to get everything done in a day, before the garage doors opened and he came home. Sometimes he whistled: a good sign. And sometimes he came in and put his briefcase down with a thud, a bad sign. She'd taken to calling him at work in the late afternoon with some made up question, just to try to gauge his mood for the evening ahead. But that had proved fruitless, as she learned how mercurial he could be, changing from normal behavior to silent anger in the time between the call and when he arrived home.

She'd wondered at first where the anger came from. It was always there, a current of unrest, waiting to breach the shore and spew forth. And there was no way to get away from it she'd thought. Irish Catholic, mother of two. Future sealed. This. Always.

Until she'd met Greta.

No, that was not exactly true. The thing that had led to her freedom had started a week before she had met Greta. It was in early May, on a day that held the surprise of warmth. She pulled herself out of bed and got Galen and Aggie off to school. She watched from her bedroom window as they climbed into the lumbering yellow bus and disappeared down the street.

She could remember picking at an English muffin and trying to read the Boston Globe. She just couldn't settle. After fifteen minutes she gave up and started to clean the kitchen, wiping down the surfaces of the counters and the center island. As she finished, she saw more drops of water she had missed. She wiped them away, but then she found more. It was unnerving, and scary. She stopped wiping and stood frozen. What was going on? She stood very still, listening to the sounds of the birds outside the window and the wind blowing through the trees. Her face felt odd and she touched it; it was wet. Those drops of water were tears, her tears. She had been crying and had been totally oblivious.

She put the sponge away and went to lie down on her bed in the master bedroom. Lying down felt good. Lately it was all that she wanted to do. It was becoming harder to get up in the morning or after an afternoon nap. She'd been wondering if she should get her blood tested for an iron deficiency or some organic cause of her tiredness. Now she was presented with still another problem that loomed even larger; she was crying without knowing it. The idea that she might be going crazy flitted through her thoughts like a wild bird. Something was very, very wrong. There could be no debate about that.

It took her several days and a lot of courage to call her friend Vivi. Vivi's husband, Georges Bordot, had died two years before, and she knew Vivi had gone for counseling after that. She'd been crushed, defeated, lost, and almost wiped out by his unexpected death, and Pen had been afraid for her. And then Pen had watched her friend slowly transformed over time from someone who wore her deceased husband's pajamas all day and who never left her home to a new version of her old self, one with a fine patina of wisdom and sadness, but with a regained life force. Vivi had even begun to paint again and had started to sell more and more of her work.

Through Vivi, she met Greta. And Greta started the train moving. Pen discovered that once she started on the road to feeling better, there was no stopping her. Even though many times it would have been easier to stop than to move forward, she found she couldn't do it. Feeling better had become addictive. And Greta, while never pushing, sat by her side, gave her courage when she had none of her own, and helped her battle the dragons that stood between her and a real life. The fear monster was the worst, but she was slowly vanquishing it as well.

"Mom!" The word jolted Pen back into the present. "Are we gonna eat?"

She smiled to herself. The essential needs never quit, she thought.

Entering the kitchen, she responded to Galen's question. "You bet. Aggie, you hungry, too?" The kitchen clock said six.

Starving," Aggie answered, drawing the word out. "And I smell food...or something good," she added, looking around the room.

"Pulled pork!" Galen said. "You made pulled pork?'

"I did," Pen replied. "Now go wash up. Dinner in 15 minutes." Pen gave thanks that even with the trauma of last night and this morning, she had somehow assembled the spices, ketchup, BBQ sauce, and pork butt by rote in her crockpot. She vaguely remembered turning it on after she'd showered. Thank God for small mercies, she thought later, as they ate.

After dinner, she helped Galen with the grammar in an essay entitled," What is Wrong in the World Today." Galen had no shortage of ideas on this subject, so the writing of it had not proven difficult. The grammar was another animal entirely.

Later, she helped Aggie box up a small assemblage she made for art. Interesting. No idea what it was. Too preoccupied to talk much about it now. She'd found the perfect Amazon box to shelter it on its journey to school and Aggie was happy with the results. "Thanks, Mom," she said as she carried the box to the front hall and put it carefully beside the door. "I'm all set now!"

The girls were finally asleep by 9:30, their sleepovers the night before having taken their toll. Another small mercy.

Chapter 3: Finn

Pen was sitting in the screened porch waiting for Finn when he arrived later that night at ten o'clock. She unlocked the door to the porch as he crossed the deck. "Hi," she said. "Thanks for coming this morning."

He nodded and acknowledged her thanks with a nod, then sat down on a green wicker chair near her chaise. In the dim light of the table lamp nearby he looked different than he had in the past. Steely. Cold.

"Sorry for all the craziness," she said.

If possible, he looked even more steely. "Don't ever say that again," he said slowly, enunciating each word.

"What?" Pen asked, taken aback by his tone. "I'm sorry—"

"There. You just did it again." When she remained silent, he said, "Do not apologize for something that is not your fault." His gaze met her eyes. "Ever."

Pen felt tears well in her eyes. She wasn't sure why. "Habits of a lifetime, I guess."

"Bad habits are meant to be broken," Finn said in a slightly gentler tone.

For a moment the only sounds were the crashing of the waves and the calls of night birds. Finally Pen looked at Finn and nodded; he nodded slightly back. A pact of some kind, an acknowledgement of past pain and future changes.

"Here," he said, taking something small from his pocket and handing it to her. She examined the object. It looked like a Fitbit or step counter of some kind built into a silver and black bracelet.

"Thank you?" Pen said quizzically, looking at Finn. It seemed an odd gift, especially right now.

"Do you know what it is?"

"A step counter?"

18

"Not exactly," Finn took the bracelet back from her. "This," he said, pointing to a small window on the front of it, "IS a step counter. We'll sync it with your phone and it will perform like a normal step counter. But this," he said, sliding open a small panel, "could save your life."

He leaned over to let her see better. Inside the panel was a small button, about half the size of the nail on her pinky finger. "Do you see this?" he asked, pointing to it.

"Yeah. OK," Pen answered, with a question in her tone.

"When you push this button, I come. Immediately. Or as close to it as possible. It's set under the sliding panel to prevent you from accidentally setting it off. You push it, I'm on the way. It will give me an address as well, so if you are somewhere else, I will still be able to find you."

Pen must have looked both incredulous and questioning.

"Why?" he asked softly. "Because someone is going to come back again."

Shivering involuntarily, Pen felt suddenly sick to her stomach. She knew in her gut he was right. The visit wasn't a onetime thing.

"And if you are wondering why I would do this, the answer is easy. Because I can. Because I know how to get things like this. Because I hate bullies and targeting. And, because you are my friend. And friends don't let friends be terrorized."

In spite of her herself, Pen smiled, noting the riff on "friends don't let friends drive drunk."

"Thank you," she said quietly, overwhelmed by the gesture, but unable to come up with any other words.

"You're welcome," Finn said. "Now let's have you practice sliding the panel open and hitting the button. I want you to be able to do it in three seconds, without looking or fumbling."

And so, as the night grew still and cooler, she practiced sliding the small panel to the side and pushing the button. She was clumsy at first, but by the eighth time she could do it in one quick motion.

Looking at his watch, Finn said encouragingly, "That's good. Three seconds, exactly."

Then Pen saw his face grow dark again, as he added, "This only works if you wear it ALL the time. Night and day. Understood?"

She nodded.

"If you are in the shower, and this is next to your bed, it's of no help." He looked at her. "ALL the time. It's waterproof, so you can shower in it, swim in it, whatever."

"OK," Pen said. "I'll wear it. All the time."

Finn reached over and attached the bracelet to her left wrist. "Now you're all set. You can use your right hand to slide it open and push the button." He looked at her. "Want to try now?"

She managed it in four seconds. "Not bad," he said. "Remember, though. NEVER take it off."

"No worries," she said lightly, though she meant "Not bloody likely."

They sat for a while in comfortable silence. The crashing waves were lulling Pen into a calm place. "You want a beer," she finally asked.

"Only root beer, while this is going on."

"Root beer, then?"

"Sure."

She got up and got them each a full glass, adding ice, and returned to the porch.

"Life sucks, sometimes" she said, handing it to Finn.

"Yup."

Twenty minutes later they went inside and Finn set up the step counter and synced it with her phone.

Chapter 4: Introduction

The next afternoon Pen was sitting next to Galen in the orthodontist's crowded office. They had gotten the last two chairs and had settled in for a wait. Dr. Ventura always ran late. Galen had come prepared and was doing homework, writing something on her Chromebook.

When Pen had asked what it was, she'd muttered "Personal," and just kept typing.

So much for staying in touch with your kid, Pen thought, but said, "Okay, then."

As she was waiting for Galen's name to be called, she looked idly at the step counter on her left wrist. She wondered if she would ever have to push the button on the front. Then her thoughts wandered to Finn. She could picture him now, always in well-fitting jeans that probably cost four times more than hers. Always in a buttoned-down shirt, usually light blue. Brown belt, Italian leather loafers or Nike sneakers. A uniform of sorts, she thought, offering in its uniformity no clue about what he was really like. Obviously, the way he wanted it.

She thought back to the first time she had seen him. It was at Vivi's house. Vivi, her friend since elementary school, whose house had been a constant for her during her marriage to Peter and later, during the divorce, a sanctuary. Set on a high bluff overlooking the ocean, it was the kind of house most people dream of buying when they win the lottery.

When Vivi had married Georges ten years ago, she had moved in and transformed what had been a cold, sophisticated space into a funky and colorful home. One-of-a-kind pieces of art and furniture. Unexpected colors...like a purple foyer. Emphasis on handmade, extremely comfortable furniture. A nest. Georges had loved it.

Until his death two years ago, it had been the background for art auctions, charity events, black tie dinners, and huge cocktail parties.

Now, with just Vivi in residence, it was mostly empty. Its spirit seemed to have fled along with Vivi's.

On the day she remembered, she had driven down Vivi's long circular driveway, the crushed white shells crunching beneath the wheels of the car. She marveled, as she always did, at the number of daylilies blooming along the driveway and the mounds of blue hydrangeas in front of the house and on the sides of the three-car garage to the left. She'd been preoccupied as she lifted the brass sea shell on the door, announcing her presence. Even though she and Vivi were close, and had keys to each other's homes, for some reason they still observed the formality of knocking. Finn had opened the door.

"Penny?" he asked.

Frowning, she'd nodded, at the same time offering a muttered, "Yes, but I go by Pen. Short for Penelope." She added her last name "Elliot" as an afterthought.

He extended his hand. "Finn," he said, smiling. "Finn Carnavale." Sensing her questions, he quickly added, "Vivi is on the phone. An art dealer, I think. She asked me to answer the door when you came." He beckoned her in, which felt weird. She knew this house as well as she knew her own, but she followed him as he headed to the wraparound porch at the back.

As they sat on two of the green wicker chairs on the porch, he explained that he was a builder and that Vivi had invited him out to give her an estimate on creating a new art studio for her.

"In the house or add-on?" Pen asked.

He smiled. Amazing dental work, she thought. "To be decided later. She's not sure yet."

Vivi started to paint about eight years ago and took to it immediately. It appeared that she had talent, and she pursued it with a vengeance, as if to make up for lost time. Her bright, unusually colored works had just begun to take off when Georges had died. She stopped painting then.

A year later she began again, only now the colorful works of orange and red and yellow and blue were replaced by greys, blacks, ochres, browns and white. Instead of smooth, clean lines, there were chunky brushstrokes across the canvas and rocks and found objects embedded in thick buildups of dark color. Amazingly, they found an even larger audience than the earlier ones. So now, Vivi sold not just locally, but also in New York and Provincetown. For years, she worked in a spare bedroom upstairs, but now it made sense for her to have her own separate customized area in which to paint. *Good for her,* Pen thought.

So," Pen asked Finn, "What are your thoughts on building the studio?"

"If it were up to me, I'd add on," he said, indicating an area off to the left of the house, where the study was. But I'll do whatever the client wants."

"You're pretty sure you can do that?" Pen was surprised to hear the joking tone in her voice.

"Absolutely!" he said, laughing. "No question. It's what I do."

"Good to have confidence," Pen responded, again with that joking-flirty kind of tone. *Where was this coming from?* she wondered.

"What do you do?" Finn asked, changing the subject.

"Write, mostly. Though before that I was a teacher, high school."

"Interesting combination. What do you write?"

"As the saying goes, 'if I told you that, I'd have to kill you.'" She didn't want to talk about her career change or her recent success at writing. It still felt unreal. She changed the subject. "Have you always been a builder?"

He looked at her quizzically, as if acknowledging the awkward swerve in the discussion. Then he told her about his dad Frank, who owned a concrete company. "He's done almost all the concrete work in Hartford, Bridgeport and about ten other cities and towns in Connecticut. Started small, got big." He told her how he'd done his best to be a good Italian son and work the business, take over eventually. Unfortunately, he hated it. Hated the hot, physical work that had over time almost crippled his once active dad, hated the politics of getting contracts. "And there's an underbelly you don't even want to know about."

Now it was her turn to look at him quizzically.

"There's a lot of graft, payoffs for contracts, payback if you don't play by the rules. I learned a lot about life as well as about concrete," he said, smiling sardonically. "But in the end, I left the business. In my idealistic phase, I thought I would work as a cop."

Now it was Pen's turn to smile. "Really? You don't look remotely like a cop."

"Yeah, well, that's probably true. That's why I eventually worked undercover. And that was fun, until it wasn't."

"Why wasn't it fun?"

"Because I decided that I wanted to live." The answer hung in the air and she couldn't tell if he was kidding or not.

Just then Vivi appeared from inside the house, carrying a tray of Pepsi, seltzer water, and chips. The tone of the conversation changed to less personal topics, like the planned studio, and soon Pen had found herself saying goodbye.

She remembered wondering if Finn was the new man in Vivi's life. From what she'd seen, Vivi could certainly have done worse.

Chapter 5: A Discovery

Smiling brightly, sporting new multicolored braces, Galen walked out the door of Dr. Ventura's office. *How nice it was to see her happy,* Pen thought.

After making the next appointment, they walked to the car. Galen was in a good mood, rare lately, and welcome. She said, "They usually limit you to two colors for your braces, but Dr. V. let me have three!" she crowed. She looked over at her mother in the front seat and made an exaggerated smile so Pen could see for herself.

"Cool," Pen said, eyeing the blue, green, and yellow wires in Galen's mouth.

"Cool, Mom?" Galen said, smirking, at her mother's outdated term.

"Yeah, Cool," Pen said, staking her right to use a dated term.

Aggie was ready outside the Richardson Elementary School. "I LOVE Art Club," she stated as she climbed into the white Highlander and put her latest project, a box-like creation with colored knobs sticking out from the top, on the back seat. "The kids are so cool."

Pen looked over at Galen, who had glanced her way at the mention of "cool." They smiled a companionable smile. *Truce then,* Pen thought, feeling for that one moment that all was well in her world.

That feeling changed rather soon after she got home. She dropped the pizza they'd picked up at Papa Ginos on the table. "Wash up, pizza in ten," she said.

Then she filled a large plastic pitcher with water from the kitchen spigot and went out on the deck to water the plant on the back porch railing. It was a geranium Pen prized, a huge one that had elements both of pink and red in it. You could see it from the living room, dining room, and kitchen and the sight of it glowing in the light always made her spirits lift.

As she slid the doors to the porch open, she stopped in her tracks. Standing still, she felt prickles of anxiety run across her shoulders, and she took a deep breath to gather herself.

Moving closer, she saw the remains of the solar-powered hummingbird that had been in the flowerpot. It had been an impulse buy on the same day she'd gotten the geranium. It had yellow and green feathers, and a long beak, and, while she guessed some people would call it 'cheesy,' the girls loved it. "Our new pet," they had exclaimed watching it move around the plant on its thin arc of metal. After debating a name for it, they decided on "Sunny Ray," because it was powered by the sun. Then they had cracked up because it was so silly.

Now it was destroyed, its feathers pulled out, and pushed under the geranium leaves. *Maybe a cat.* The thought went through Pen's mind quickly, as she searched for a relatively benign reason for the destroyed ornament. Then she looked more closely and saw that the stake, with its little solar motor, was lying there as well, slightly under the leaves. It was broken in two places. *Not a cat, then.*

"Mom!" the call came from inside and made her jump. "Dinner time! We're STARVING!"

Pen pulled herself together and went inside. But not before putting the pieces of what she'd found under a pillow in the screened porch. She did not want the girls to see it and to have to explain why it had happened. Especially since she had no clue.

When dinner was over and Aggie and Galen were in bed, Pen called Finn. He answered as he always did, with just his name.

"Hi, Finn, it's Pen." She could almost feel him stop what he was doing and stand up. She could sense his concentrated energy.

"What's wrong?" he asked, knowing she probably wouldn't be calling to chat.

She told him. "I'll be right over," he said. It took her half an hour to convince him that all was well right now, she had her step counter on, she would check all the locks, and call for him the moment she sensed anything else awry. He agreed to wait until the girls left for school before coming over. "I'll see you at 7:45," he said, "sharp." Then they hung up.

Pen lay down on her bed. She had opened the curtains in front of the French doors to the porch, and she watched the moon on the water. Over and over, she reviewed her marriage to Peter: could he possibly be behind all this? On the one hand, she knew he was mean, and petty, and that he held a grudge. She remembered that he had cost George Anson, a colleague at work, his job. George had once questioned a report Peter had done, questioned his data in front of a group of investors. A year later, Peter bragged to her about how he set George up for a fall which cost him his job. "Bet he wishes now that he hadn't crossed me," he had said to Pen over coffee, after the girls had left the room.

Even though she hadn't lived with him for over two years, she could still remember his cruelty. The Christmas he wouldn't get up with her and the girls on Christmas morning because Pen had, after wrapping over 60 presents and preparing for his parents' Christmas visit the next day, dared to rebuff his wanting sex at midnight on Christmas Eve. So, she'd gotten up, told the girls that their father didn't feel well, and carried on. They were unwrapping the fourth present when he wandered into the living room and sat down next to the tree, rubbing his eyes. The girls had both been so happy. "Daddy, you feel better?" Aggie had asked, glad that he was joining them. One of the many times Pen had felt her heart crack.

One night, soon after they had separated, he called just as she had relieved the babysitter who lived one street over and could walk home. She'd been at Vivi's with a few friends, and hadn't even taken off her coat when the phone rang. "I'm coming home," he announced coldly. "Tonight. Enough of this happy horseshit. It's my home and my family and I want it back. I'll be there in 15 minutes."

Months before, she would have been afraid of him and acquiesced. But with Greta's support, she'd grown the beginning of a backbone. "No, you're not, Peter. I'll call the police if you do. I'll tell them I don't feel safe. And they will escort you out, with Galen and Aggie watching." She paused. "Is that what you want?"

His answer was to hang up the phone, muttering, "Bitch!" before the final click.

She had finally fallen asleep in her coat, on her bed, holding the phone in a death grip between her hands. He hadn't come.

He'd had her followed. She went nowhere but the usual visits to the supermarket, doctors' offices, school, Greta's. But she had seen the same man in a Red Sox cap twice in one day, and she could feel eyes on her at weird times. Since there was nothing to find, he found nothing. But she could feel his rage increasing as their separation continued.

She would never forget what happened when she finally told him that it wasn't just 'space' she needed, as she had previously stated as a reason for the separation, but a divorce. He stopped by when the girls were at school. In retrospect, she should have picked a public place to tell him, but she didn't know better then. When she told him, he was holding a large orange mug of coffee. He threw it from the dining room toward the kitchen where she was standing. It hit the granite island and exploded into a thousand shards.

When he stomped out of the house, she was shaking and hyperventilating. "You'll never get a divorce," he yelled out at her as he was leaving. "I will out-lawyer you and crush you. And," he added, "if somehow the divorce did eventually go through, I'd die before I'd pay you alimony."

Yes, Pen thought, he could definitely be behind all this. He had the means and he had the personality and he had the rage. She could easily picture him concocting a scheme where he would have her scared almost to death, thinking that she would be so frightened that she might take him back. A man in the house, and all that. She exhaled a long breath. How wrong he was.

Chapter 6: A Visit

At 7:45 a.m. sharp, just as Pen was starting her third cup of coffee, there was a knock on the back slider. Putting down her coffee on the counter, she went and let Finn into the house.

"Well," she said, looking at him and taking in his unshaven cheeks and chin, his uncombed curls. "You look a little...um...disheveled." She smiled at him. "Sorry, I couldn't resist. You always look so perfect."

"Because I am," he said.

"What's up? Late night at the bar?"

Smiling he said, "Hardly."

"Then what?" she asked, the words out before she could stop them. It really wasn't her business.

"Late night in your woods," he said, rubbing his head. "You didn't really think that I would not show up after the most recent act of intimidation, did you?"

"But you agreed. You agreed to come this morning."

"And here I am, in the morning."

"But you never said—"

"No need. You would have been freaked if you had known that I was out there. And you would have insisted I go home, and there would be an argument. It was easier this way."

"Where were you, out there, I mean?"

"Three quarters of the way up from the water, sleeping bag near the path, but in the bush. I would have heard anyone coming up from the water or in from the front road. I have really good hearing."

"Even sleeping?" she said, half joking.

"Even sleeping," he said, with no sign of a joke in his voice.

"Thank you."

"You are welcome. Now, can you get me some coffee so we can get down to work?"

A few minutes later they were ensconced in the screened porch, she on the couch, he on a large cushioned chair nearby. They shared the end table for their coffees.

Finn took a pad and paper from the duffle he had retrieved from outdoors. The sleeping bag itself was rolled up next to the door.

"You're up first," he said. "We need to find out who is doing this stuff. I've given some thought to it, and I have some ideas. But I want to hear what you think."

Pen took in the sunshine outside the screened porch door. It colored and lightened the deck porch floor to almost white. She could hear the waves, and some bird songs she didn't know. It was peaceful. She was reluctant to start telling Finn her thoughts, as she knew they would crack the peace pretty quickly. She drew in a deep breath, then started to relate her suspicions about Peter, the ones she'd reviewed in her mind last night.

Finn's face tightened as she did so. "He's a piece of work, isn't he?" Finn said when she'd finished.

"I guess so. I think he might be trying to scare me, thinking that alone here, I might be really scared and be open to taking him back. Especially if he started acting nicer."

"And is he? Acting nice?" He was very still.

"Maybe. He asked me to join him and the girls at the yacht club dinner last Friday, and he hasn't made me chase my child support payments lately."

"Did you go? Finn asked. "To the dinner."

"No, I couldn't. Not even for the girls. But I was polite about it, claimed some art thing I had to go to."

"Why not just say 'I don't want to go anywhere with you?'"

"You ever been married?"

"No."

"Well, it's hard to explain. We share kids, and we once shared a life."

"And, you're afraid of him."

30

She was going to get all defensive and do the "that's ridiculous" thing with a vengeance, but then she felt the wind leave her sails. Truth was easier.

"Yes," she said, "I am." She sighed and tried to shrug the stiffness out of her shoulders. "Old habits die hard."

"This is really important," Finn said. "You are the best person to evaluate this, because you know Peter so well. Do you honestly believe he could be behind all that's been happening?"

Pen could feel her eyes filling with tears and she bit her lip. Her eyes met his as she nodded yes.

It was quiet for a few minutes, and Pen got them more coffee.

"New topic," Finn announced. "When is the new security system going in?"

"What new security system? "

"The one we talked about and you agreed that you would get—"

"Oh," Pen said a little sheepishly. "Well, I did talk on the phone to Jim Sparks, uptown. Said he could do it next week, maybe Thursday."

"Really?" Finn said, and Pen totally missed his tone.

"Yeah, he said that was the earliest he could do it."

"Did he now?" Finn continued.

"Yes. He said the latest would be Thursday."

"Not today, then?"

"No, no he can't do it this week at all."

"Well then," Finn said, smiling an odd smile, "he won't be doing it at all."

"But he's the best in town, there isn't anyone else. And it's not so long to wait—"

"It's too long!" Finn exploded. "TOO LONG!"

"But, but, I don't want to—"

"What? Make Jim Sparks mad?"

Pen flinched. And her face flushed. She wanted to lash out, ask him if he knew what it was like to be a woman, especially a woman alone, dependent on the good will of men. But even as that thought flashed through her mind, she saw the foolishness of it. Finn was on her side.

And, ruefully she thought, he was right. She was afraid to piss people off.

"Yes," she said.

He relented. "Do it by email. Just write a note and cancel the project. You can say 'for now,' if you want, to soften the blow." He looked at Pen's face straight on. "Can you do that?"

"Yes."

"OK, now we're moving. With your permission, I'll make a call. The system will go in tomorrow."

Pen nodded again. It was good to have that settled. She was so tired.

They sipped their coffee and watched the waves. It was a peaceful, quiet time. She thought it odd that they could sit together in such peace and be comfortable without words. Odd in a good way. So few people she knew could do that.

Finally, Finn looked at his watch. "Gotta go in a while to check on a house I'm rehabbing in Marstons Mills. It's going to be fun...a total gut job."

"One person's fun...." Pen said, smiling.

"Yeah, I know, not everyone's idea of a good time. But I love a blank canvas. Make it all new in my own way."

Pen stood up, realizing from looking at her own watch that it was going on ten o'clock.

"Last question," Finn said before he got up. "Is there anyone else who might wish you harm, want to scare or hurt you?"

She shook her head, as he added, "Anybody at all?"

She went to shake her head no again. But then one memory came flooding back. "Oh, shit!" she said, "Oh, shit!" And she all but fell down on the couch again.

Chapter 7: Possibilities

Finn looked puzzled. "What?" he said. "What?"

Pen shook her head back and forth, as if jogging her brain. "I just thought of someone else who might want to scare or hurt me. I haven't seen him in a long time, and I consider him kind of crazy, but basically a coward. As in 'all bark and no bite.' It happened a year ago. Oh my God! I'd forgotten."

"Slow down," Finn said. "Slow down. Start at the beginning."

As she started to talk, Finn interrupted again. "Hang on for a sec." He dialed his cell phone and Pen could hear him talking, changing his plans for the day. "Yeah," he said. "Close up there and go back to the Berrigan project. There's plenty of cleanup there. I'll be there by three at the latest." After a pause, he laughed and hung up. "Love that guy," he said. "Always has my favorite response to whatever I say."

"Which is?"

"Whatever you say, boss."

That even made Pen smile.

Then the moment passed. Finn looked serious again. "OK, start from the beginning. I'm all ears," he said.

"Two years ago, after I separated from Peter, I started seeing a therapist named Greta. Mostly one-on-one sessions, but also in a group for a while. We met on Thursday evenings, which worked for me, as Peter had the girls then. Anyway, the group was made up of all women, most of them getting a divorce, some not that far along. But all of them from troubled relationships." After a minute, she took a deep breath and continued. "There was this one woman, Fiona, used to come and not say anything. Just listened. She was polite but didn't talk. I wondered what she got out of the group, as she didn't participate at all. But then I decided that wasn't my problem and if it was a problem, Greta would deal with it."

"One day, after about six months in the group, Fiona showed up in the group and something was different about her. Little by little she started to talk. And it was apparent from what she said that her husband was abusive. He was a middle management guy who worked for that new discount department store Berklins, angry that his gifts and potential weren't fully recognized. Even worse, a fellow employee had filed a complaint against him for being verbally abusive. And he'd brought it all home."

"Anyway, she kept coming to the group. Sometimes she talked, sometimes not. Two things about her were consistent, though. She always sat with her arms crossed in front of her, almost like she was hugging herself or protecting herself, and she always wore long sleeves, even when the weather got warm."

Finn was listening intently. She was waiting for him to say something like "Get to the point" or "How long is this story going to be?" the way Peter would have, but he said nothing. The stony look on his face said it all.

"Then three months after that, she showed up for a meeting with her kids."

Finn frowned.

Pen continued," Well, you really can't do that. I mean, it's an adult meeting. The issues would be disturbing to kids, plus there is the confidentiality thing. "

"What happened?" Finn asked.

"Well, Greta found some crayons and coloring books for the kids and put them in an adjoining room in the old senior center where we met. She pulled me aside and asked if I would sit with them and color while the meeting was in progress. When the meeting was over, Greta asked Fiona to stay. Then she came and got me, and we joined Fiona in the next room. We could watch the girls coloring through a large observation window in the wall. "I remember Greta saying, 'I hate to involve you, but I'm out of other options.'"

Pen shivered involuntarily, even though it was warm on the porch. "Fiona told us that her husband Joe had been physically abusive for years, and it was getting worse. We weren't terribly surprised, because of a few things she said during the meetings. Then she pushed up the sleeves of her shirt. Her arms were black and blue. She pulled her shirt up and turned around, and there were red welts on her back. She started to cry. 'It's getting worse. And last night after he beat me, he grabbed Maeve and picked her up...like he was going to throw her. I thought he would dash her to the floor. I yelled at him, told him he was disgusting, a failure, a pathetic human being. I'd not fought back like that before; I'd usually try to reason with him and beg him to stop. Told him I loved him to placate him. But this time, when I saw him pick Maeve up – the first time he'd touched the girls – something in me broke.' She told us this in fits and starts, sobbing and stopping. She was shaking like a leaf. She pulled herself together and said, 'He left after I yelled at him. He came back later, and I think he'd been drinking. I made believe I was asleep.' She started to cry, huge wracking sobs that shook me to my core. I'd never seen anyone cry like that. Greta was comforting her. I was sick."

Pen stopped and sipped her coffee, now warm. She wondered what Finn would think when he heard the rest of the story. "Shall I continue?" she asked, looking at him. He nodded, barely.

"What happened next came after she said the words that changed everything."

"What did she say?"

"She said, 'If I go back, I know he'll kill me.'"

She paused and looked out at the ocean ahead. "You know the expression 'My blood ran cold?'" Pen asked him.

"Sure."

"Well, my blood did run cold. We all felt it. Greta, Fiona, me. We knew she was telling the truth; we could feel it. She knew this man, this beast, and she knew she had crossed a line last night. And he wouldn't have it. He wouldn't have it. The next beating might well be her last. And she said her daughters would be left motherless in his care. And then she wailed. She wailed, like an animal caught in a trap, like her heart would break, like she was dying." Pen was fidgeting, moving her heels up and down, opening and closing her fingers. "It was the worst thing I've ever seen," she said, as her eyes filled and tears ran down her face.

Chapter 8: Saving Fiona

Finn just stared at Pen. "What happened then?" he asked.

"We made a plan so that Fiona didn't have to go home," she said, shaking as she relived what happened next. "Fiona and the girls came home with me. We hid her car in the garage across from the old senior center. Greta had a key because she works part time in the center and uses the garage in the winter. Fiona and the kids got in my Highlander and we started toward my house. The plan was that Fiona would contact her brothers, Liam and Jack, who lived in North Carolina, that night and tell them what was happening. One way or another, she felt sure they would come and get her." Pen started breathing faster, as if someone were chasing her. She felt scared, just as she had felt in that moment.

"And did that happen?"

She nodded. "But first, we had to get to my house. Fiona knew that her husband would be home at five, as usual, and it was already six thirty. She knew he would be able to tell that something was not right because no one was home. In fact, she had checked her phone earlier and had seen the texts and phone calls. It was clear that he was escalating. The messages were getting more frantic. 'Where are you, Fi?' he'd say. Then he'd lose it and yell, 'Where the fucking hell are you, dammit?' The texts were the same, cajoling in the beginning, then abusive when he couldn't find her. She knew he was already on the warpath. And she knew he would come looking for her."

"But how would he even know where to go?"

"When she first started to attend a meeting once in a while, she told her husband she was going for a women's group thing."

"Yeah, I imagine that went over well. He allowed her to go?" Finn sounded incredulous.

"He did," Pen said. "Because she told him it was a meeting for wives who were looking for ways to be better spouses, to share recipes and child raising tips. All he knew was that it was held in the old senior center on Thursdays."

"Hence, her fear he would come for her when he thought the meeting was over."

"Exactly. That's why Greta ended the meeting early. Time was important. She needed Fiona to get out of the center." Pen made an effort to slow down, to take deep breaths, and to undo the sense of panic she was once again feeling. "Fiona thought he would ride around for a while, just letting sheer anger direct him. But she thought that sooner or later, he would remember those meetings and end up at the senior center."

"So, you all got in your car and took off. And took her to your house?"

"Not exactly. Not at first." She shrugged her shoulders, hoping to diffuse the tightness she was feeling there. Taking a deep breath, she said, "We weren't quick enough."

Finn's eyes met hers. "And?"

"He showed up just as I was pulling out onto Main Street. I can remember Fiona saying, 'Oh, my God, Pen! That's him, in the silver Camry. It's Joe! I think he saw us!' Then she started in, 'Oh my God, oh my God, oh my God. Oh my God.'"

Finn shook his head, not in disbelief, but in puzzlement that such a thing could escalate the way it had. "If she was that afraid of him, why didn't she call the police?"

Pen had a momentary flash of annoyance at his typically male response. She tried not to show her feelings of "Duh, you don't get it!"

"He had a friend there, David Wise, a dispatcher. She knew he would let Joe know where she was. And she had nowhere safe to go. Once Joe knew where she was, he would follow her once she left the station. She had no relatives near, and she didn't want to endanger her few friends. And who would believe her when she said she was afraid for her life? Joe doesn't look like the slime bag he is; he's employed, goes to work in a suit, looks normal. She was afraid he would minimize what she said as 'She gets hysterical every time we have an argument, threatens to leave' and that the cops would believe him. According to Fiona, he can really turn on the charm when he wants. She was too scared."

After mulling that over for a bit, he asked, "So, when you saw him in the car, what happened?"

"I just drove like a madwoman. He had to turn around to follow me, and I used that time. I've lived in this town for a long time, so I know my way around. I headed out towards Wood's Hole and I knew he would follow. After a mile, I took a left onto Cumloden Drive. I was fairly certain he would see me take it, but then I took the next left, too. I pulled into a driveway next to a For Sale sign and parked in back of some giant rhododendrons. We were there for maybe ten minutes. By then, I figured Joe would have passed the street and wouldn't have thought to turn around yet. Those ten minutes were like a day. Fiona was sobbing with both fear and relief, the kids, Kathleen and Maeve, were crying. It was bedlam."

And you?"

"It might be hard to imagine, but I felt like I was the adult in the car. It was my job to protect them and beat that bastard. Don't know where that came from, but I got the strength to get calm and to make a plan. I took back roads to my house. All the shortcuts, no major roads. When I got home, I hit the garage opener and pulled the car in. Then I shut the door. We all sat in the car for five minutes before we got out. Fiona was sobbing and the girls were crying."

Pen was spent from telling the story and from the adrenaline that had rushed into her system as she told it. She hoped never to repeat the experience.

After several moments, Finn said, "That's quite a tale."

Pen nodded as she got up and stretched her arms. She needed to move. When she had stretched for a few minutes, she said, "Do you want to hear the rest?"

"You mean there's more? Well, you sure can't stop there."

Chapter 9: Vengeance

Pen told him how Fiona and the girls had stayed at her house from that Thursday until the following Sunday when Fiona's brothers Liam and Jack came up from North Carolina for her. They all stayed over on Sunday; it was Peter's weekend, so Aggie and Galen were gone until Sunday night. She called Sunday and begged Peter to keep them until Monday morning, pleading a stomach flu. She knew he wouldn't do it for her, but he would to spare the girls getting sick.

On Monday, after they checked to make sure Joe's car was parked at Berklins, both brothers and Fiona went over to Fiona's house one last time. Fiona packed up most of the girls' things and what she could of her own, throwing them into six trash bags. She also took the computer, her family pictures, and her address book. She added another two full bags of toys and stuffed animals.

They had barely started moving away from the house when Liam stopped the car and backed up. He looked at Jack and some understanding flew between their eyes. "Forgot something," Liam said, getting out of the car and going back into the house with Jack. Tired and wanting to be gone, Fiona said nothing. Later they told her they had trashed the house, including the new large screen tv in the living room. They had poured ketchup and mustard all over the queen-sized bed in the master bedroom and milk over the living room furniture.

Finn raised his eyebrows. "Wow, a little vigilante justice."

"Yeah, wow. I wouldn't have done it, but I was glad they did."

After getting the key from Greta, they picked up Fiona's car from the garage at the community center, took it back to my house, and crammed both cars full of all the belongings. Jack drove his car and Liam drove hers. They had lunch, then they all left. I can still see Maeve and Kathleen waving out the windows as they turned out of my driveway onto the street.

"Have you heard from her?" he asked.

"Once a month since then. Fiona sounds like a new person. She's found work, lives in a rental near her brothers' families, and is so much happier. She started divorce proceedings last week."

"Any sign of Joe?"

"Nope. Without the address book, he has no idea where her relatives live. He never kept in contact with her family or paid attention to where they were. And he doesn't even know it was family that helped her. Could have been local friends, anyone."

"Good ending, then," Finn said.

"Well, not really an ending, not yet."

"There's more?"

"More on my end."

He raised his eyebrows.

"Not long after that, maybe a week, I bought groceries at Stop and Shop. When I went to put them in the car, Joe was waiting." Pen looked at Finn and saw the coldness come back into his face, along with a kind of flat look. " He said he had taken my license plate number the week before, when he was chasing us. He had 'friends,' he said, who traced it. He'd evidently gotten my address, and was on my street when he saw me leaving to shop, so he followed me." She took a deep breath as she recalled the day. "Boy, was he pissed! He was yelling about where were his wife and kids, and what a bitch I was, and I'd better tell him where they were."

Finn was staring at her, no expression on his face.

"I told him I didn't know what he was talking about, made up a story about my car being missing for the two days he was talking about, while I put the groceries in the trunk. He was screaming and waving his arms, and my heart was pounding like a bass drum. I think I surprised him, though, when I got in on the passenger side of the car, hit the locks, climbed over to the driver's side, and took off."

"You did?"

"Yeah, me! He had to run to get into his car, and I got a head start. I started to drive home, then decided better of it and drove to Vivi's house. I used the garage opener I'd borrowed when I lived with her, opened her garage and put my car in the second spot. Then I went into the house in search of a drink and Vivi."

"Tell me that was the end of it," Finn said, sounding like he knew it wasn't.

"It was for that day," she said. "I stayed at Vivi's for a few hours, and then she followed me home to make sure I was safe. "

"And after that?"

"That's when I think he really lost it," she said, cracking her knuckles as she had when she was a kid. "I'll be right back," she announced, abruptly standing up. Once inside, she went to her bathroom and splashed cold water on her face. Over and over. Telling the story had upset her and her body was on overdrive.

"So," Pen said after she'd returned. "Everything was quiet for maybe ten days or so. I was careful coming home, driving right into the garage and closing the door before I got out of the car. Everything was normal."

"Until it wasn't?"

"Exactly," Pen said, explaining the part that had been the scariest. "I came home from Vivi's one afternoon while the kids were in school. I didn't pull into the garage because I was going out again for an appointment with Greta."

"And he was there?"

"Oh, yeah, he was there. He'd been waiting somewhere nearby, on the side of the road, for me to come home. And he'd gotten lucky, because I had dropped my guard and hadn't gone into the garage. He parked in back of me, blocking my exit."

He nodded for her to continue.

"He looked like a mad dog. His face was red, and he'd started yelling as soon as he got out of the car. I was really scared. It felt like I was in a bad movie."

"What did you do?"

"I called 911, told them my address, then left the line open so they could hear his yelling. He kept telling me to get out of the car. He wanted to 'talk.' Said I had helped his family leave him, and I was gonna pay. He said I would tell him where they were, or I'd be sorry. He kept yelling "Fucking bitch!"

Pen found herself starting to breathe quickly and shallowly as she relived that day. Finn didn't push her, waiting until she was ready to continue.

"It was a long fifteen minutes before the police showed up," Pen said finally. "I waited in the car, and Joe paced around it, yelling, sometimes banging on the windows. Scary as hell."

"I'll bet."

"The police finally arrived," she said, "and they made him get back in his car. I told them I only knew Fiona from a women's group we were in, and that I didn't know what he was talking about." She glanced at Finn. "OK, I know that was a lie, but no one had any proof and I wasn't crazy. I wasn't going to admit to anything. Joe was clearly beside himself. He wasn't even thinking of how crazy he sounded, or paying attention to the fact that the police were there. It was like he was nuts. He told me it wasn't over; I could count on that. Called me some more names. Said I would pay for helping his wife leave. Actually, he said, 'ex-wife' and spit out the window of his car after he said it."

"Then one of the policemen, Jamie Douglas, I think, told him to stop with the words. He also told him that if he got another complaint about his harassing me, he would pick him up. Then he and the other officer, didn't get his name, told him to get moving or they would cite him. After he'd backed out of the driveway, he gave me the finger as he drove away."

"When was this?" Finn asked.

"About three months ago," Pen said. "He never came back," she added. "Unless...the other night..."

"Definite possibility."

"I did take out a restraining order," Pen said.

"Read the news much?" Finn asked her, which was confusing.

"Yeah, every day," she said, puzzled.

"Then you know how much of a deterrent they are. Women killed every day who were 'protected' by a restraining order."

"I know. It was three months ago. I guess I was in denial, wanting it to be over so much I didn't think that he might come back. And I was so sure at first that whoever was here the other night was Peter's doing." She paused. "And now I don't know what to think or who to blame."

She glanced over at Finn, who was watching the waves intently, no expression on his face. She wondered what he was thinking.

Chapter 10: Remembering

Just then, Pen's phone rang. Walking into the kitchen, she picked it up off the kitchen counter.

When she looked at the caller ID, she saw that it was Vivi. She braced herself; she had so much to tell her friend that she didn't know where to start. Plus, she would rather tell it when she was alone. She didn't answer it.

Going back to the porch, she said, "Vivi."

Finn looked at her and said, "You have to tell her, Pen. She's your best friend."

"I know, I know. But talking about it makes it even more real. Plus, she will want us to move in with her for a while, and I don't want to do that. I love my house, and the kids are finally settled."

"Are you sure that wouldn't be a good plan? To leave for a week or two, until we figure this out."

As scared as she had been, now she was angry, a slow burn kind of anger that strengthened her resolve. "I will not let whoever it is scare me out of my own house. I won't do it!"

"OK, then," Finn said, rising and taking his cup to the kitchen. "But you should at least tell Vivi."

"I know," Pen said, nodding wearily. "I know."

When Finn left a few minutes later, she called Vivi back. "Got a minute for a quick visit?" she asked.

"My dream come true. I just finished a major piece and I wanted your reaction."

"I'm on my way," Pen said, ending the call and grabbing a fleece out of the closet. Vivi's deck could be chilly.

As she drove to Vivi's she remembered how wonderful Vivi had been when she had been separating from Peter. Vivi had been a shoulder to cry on so many times. She'd supplied a warm place to land when Pen had almost been broken by Peter's petty cruelties and her own overwhelming anxiety about her financial future. Vivi had shored her up, telling her what a fine writer she was, that her first book was no flash in the pan, that she would write others and earn more than enough to live well. And through all the pain and fear and terrible anxiety, she had somehow believed Vivi's voice. It had been so sure, so outspoken, so absolute that it had drowned out the doubt in Pen's mind. For the millionth time, she was aware of how much she owed Vivi and how grateful she was for her presence in their lives.

As she passed the marshes on the way to Vivi's house, she thought of the peace she'd felt while living there. There'd been a very bad two months when she and the girls had moved in, right after she'd told Peter she wanted a divorce. She was afraid, and Vivi insisted they all move into her giant house. "It's not like we'll be squished together here. For God's sake, Pen, I have sixteen rooms. You and the girls can have your own wing, your own bathrooms." She'd smiled her brilliant, too-many-teeth smile. "And I'd have the best company I know." She added, "Please, Pen, indulge me."

And so she did. It was a peaceful time, even with the upheaval and uncertainty hanging over their lives. Aggie and Galen adjusted to the huge house and found nooks and crannies where they could curl up with their books. They had their own rooms and had grown to love the sound of the sea crashing on the rocks outside their windows as they fell asleep.

Pen particularly missed the lonely beach walks she took whenever her anxiety would take a romp through her mind. She would walk and walk, sometimes at dawn, sometimes at dusk, alone but for her thoughts and the waves. She found the sheer cliffs at the base of Vivi's house to be a worthy adversary, and she'd spent hours working her way up their rocky handholds. She was rewarded when she found a small cave near the top, in an almost inaccessible spot. Sweating profusely and panting from exertion, she rested at the outermost edge, then went about fifteen feet into it when her breathing returned to normal. Beyond that, it was too dark to see. She was surprised to see cigarette butts near the front, a sign that someone else had been there, too. She stayed a while, feeling a sense of safety, somehow comforted by the earlier presence of someone else.

Twice after that she returned to the cave, and twice after she saw signs that someone else had been there. Once there was a partly burned candle in a squat wooden holder and another time there were more cigarette butts and scuff marks in the sand floor.

She was surprised at Vivi's reaction when she finally mentioned the cave. She hadn't told Vivi about the cave at first. It had felt like her own special place, a place no one but she and another person knew about. It was so hidden she was sure that Vivi didn't even know it was there. One afternoon when they' been sitting on the deck high above the cliffs, she brought it up. "It was so cool," Pen said, describing her climb and what she'd found. "Like a secret world. Well, mine ...and someone else's, I guess." She'd shrugged.

When she glanced at Vivi, she'd seen a look she couldn't decipher.

"Don't worry. I think the other person only goes later in the day, because of the candle. I don't think I'll run into anyone."

Vivi still looked odd, unreadable. She finally said, "Pen, I didn't even know that was there. But as you described it, it's so high up. I'm scared to death of you climbing up those rocks, or falling. Good God, Pen! The last thing you need is an accident. Besides, who would even know if you fell?"

Pen felt her balloon totally deflate. She loved the feeling of accomplishment when she'd finally ascended to the small cave, and the way the isolation and view of the ocean gave her peace. But, she thought, in a way she hadn't thought before, it WAS Vivi's house. Vivi's cave. But before she said any more, Vivi added, "Please, Pen, please! Tell me you won't go there again. I'd be worried all the time if I thought you might try it and fall, or meet someone weird at the cave. It's just too scary." She waited a bit and then added in as somber a voice as Pen could remember, she added, "Pen, think of the girls. What would their lives be like if something bad happened to you?"

Pen suddenly felt cold, even though she was sitting in the sun.

Vivi's voice cut straight through to her heart. "Promise me, Pen. Promise me you won't climb the cliffs again."

And, feeling sad with another loss, albeit a small one, she promised.

She would miss the sense of adventure she had gotten from climbing up to the cave as well as a burgeoning sense of self she felt from doing something she wanted to do for the first time in a long time. But, she thought, it would be worth it to lessen Vivi's anxiety. And she had to concede that her points about safety were pretty much on the money.

Pen sighed and started paying attention to the road again, back in real time. She was almost at Vivi's house.

Chapter 11: At Vivi's

As Pen drove into Vivi's driveway, she considered how she might begin her conversational catchup on the recent nightmare. Then she discarded the idea of planning. She would wait for an opportunity and just tell it like it was. She knew Vivi would be upset, but there was no getting around that.

Vivi was sitting on the front porch as Pen got out of the car. "Hurry up, hurry up," Vivi said by way of a greeting. "I can't wait to show you something." She had already turned and walked through the door as Pen got to the porch.

Pen followed her to the remodeled den on the first floor that now served as Vivi's studio. Vivi and Finn had decided to do a combo approach, using an already existing space and then adding footage to it. He had knocked down the walls and added another five feet on one side with a large bump out storage area. It worked perfectly now. Vivi was standing in it, waving her hand, then pointing and saying, "Voila!"

Pen was transfixed. Before her, dominating the one free wall Pen used to display finished work, was a huge piece of art, easily 6 feet by 10 feet. "Well, what do you think?"

"Uh...uh."

Vivi's face looked defeated. "You don't like it?" she asked, more softly this time.

"No, Vivi, it's not that," Pen responded. "It's just...so massive. And so unusual." Then she added, "And so freaking beautiful. I don't have the words...."

"Yay! You do like it!"

They both stood and looked at the piece. It was an abstract of sea and sky and land, done all in whites and greys and beiges and blacks. But while it was definitely an abstract piece, it gave a definite sense of space and water... and somehow, of possibility. It was magnificent.

"It's actually a commission," Vivi said. "I didn't want to tell you until it was done. It's for a Bank of America bigwig who has an incredible house in Chatham. Before Pen could ask more, she added, "Met him and his wife at a big art shindig in Chatham. A gallery opening for Georgia LaCoste, you know, the artist? "

Pen shrugged and shook her head.

"Really successful artist out of Boston and New York. Nice person, too. I went as a favor to a friend. The more the merrier at openings, right? Anyway, Mr. Bigwig and I got talking and it seems they needed a huge piece for their foyer. They came and looked at some of my pieces, didn't see anything big enough, and commissioned this." She looked overwhelmingly happy. "My first LARGE commission! Ten thousand dollars' worth!"

Now Pen really took notice. "That's amazing!!" She looked at her friend and added. "And well deserved." Pen knew that it wasn't just the money that was exciting Vivi; she actually had lots of that, inherited from Georges. It was the feeling of being vindicated as an artist.

After Vivi crowed some more about her accomplishment, they moved to the deck with some coffee and croissants. The sea was roiling today, throwing huge waves toward the shore, and crashing on the base of the rocks on the cliffs below the house. It was overcast, with patches of light and dark clouds, without even a touch of blue.

Pen knew it was time. She began her tale, starting with the invasion of several days ago.

Vivi was mesmerized, hanging on Pen's every word. She didn't even interrupt the narrative, which was unusual for her. By the end, when Pen told her about the most recent find in the flowers on the deck, she had turned pale. Whatever light had been in her eyes before had been extinguished.

"Oh my God, Pen. Oh my God."

"It's OK, I'm OK," she told Vivi. "And so are the girls."

"No, it's NOT ok!! Not even close. You could have been hurt, who knows what else."

"The hard part, "Pen said, "is that I don't know who is doing it. Or why."

"Peter!" Vivi spat out the name. "It has to be Peter. Who else would it be? He's never gotten over your leaving. Or the way you worked the divorce so he wouldn't get any of your earnings. He HATED that his poor little stupid wife out-thought him and made more money than he did. Plus rejected his wonderful self as a husband. It has to be him."

Pen reminded her about Joe and that whole episode. "What about him?" she asked.

Vivi looked thoughtful. "Could be. He's mad as a hatter. Might be murderous. Depends on how unhinged he really is." There was another pause. "My money? Peter all the way."

Pen nodded her head. "Yeah, that's what I think, too."

They got more coffee refills in the kitchen and went back to the porch.

"So, Finn has been helping you?" Vivi said.

"Yeah. You can't imagine. He's been a brick. He came as soon as I called. And he is helping me get a state-of-the-art burglar alarm installed." For some reason, she did not tell her friend about her new step counter or it's other functions. It seemed too intimate, and she knew Vivi would pounce all over it as a lot of trouble for a 'friend.' Then there would be more questions about Finn, and Pen didn't want to talk about that right now.

But Vivi went there anyway. "So, with Finn? What's that about?" she asked, looking sideways at her friend. Seems like he's really invested in helping you...maybe more than a friend would be?"

Pen didn't know what to say. It was true, Finn seemed really invested in her. And she herself wondered why. It had something to do with the feeling she'd had when she met him, she thought. And which she still felt. He was unlike anyone she had ever met. And it wasn't just his looks. She'd seen, and dated, even more handsome men. No, it was something else. Something primal. She'd known as soon as she'd shook his hand. Even though they had just met, she felt connected to him, as if he were a life-long friend or a member of her family. It had been disconcerting. And even more disconcerting was the feeling, no, the certainty, that he felt the same way.

There had been no acting on it, however. They had become actual friends over the time since they'd meet. At first, that was at Viv's house, as he started work on her studio.

Later, Pen had hired him to design the new version of the house she'd bought. He'd gutted the inside of the house and put it back together in a totally different way. And in the process, she'd seen him almost every day over the course of a year. Often, she would stop over for coffee midday to see what progress he'd made, anxious and excited to see the plans she'd made with him come to life. She marveled as large open spaces became actual rooms, rooms with big windows and beautiful hardwood floors. Rooms with views and with the light off the sea bouncing around in them. Something in her heart had been released then, something she hadn't realized she'd been holding onto: some dark place, full of fear and anxiety. She began to believe that in this space, this place of solace and new beginnings, she might actually be happy. Happy. A word she had stopped thinking about a long time ago, when her focus had stopped being on happy and become about getting by.

They had become friendly enough that Finn would occasionally come over and watch a movie and have a pizza. A few times even with Aggie and Galen there. Once in a while they would grab a quick lunch if he were between his work sites during the day. But nothing more came of it. A good friendship...but. A line was always there, and they never even ventured close to it. She had wondered why she hadn't moved closer. A lot. But it was comfortable, and her life was just settling down, and until now, at least, she hadn't been willing to rock her now becalmed boat.

In some ways, Pen was sorry for that. She wondered what it would be like to have someone love her without cost or cruelty. What it would be like to embrace someone, and be embraced by a person you could trust. And for whom you felt an almost a dizzying attraction. She usually stopped thinking about this before she got to the fantasizing stage.

Because she was not ready to move forward yet, to even begin to let her guard down, to risk more injury. She knew she was too frail still, too beat up and shaky to move toward the possibility of love. And she ventured to herself that while Finn may have been ready, perhaps he could read her internal state. He knew she was not there. She wondered sometimes if she would ever be there, in a place where she could throw caution to the wind, and embrace possibility and hope. And she wondered how long Finn would stick around to see.

"Pen?" Vivi cut into her thoughts. "Earth to Pen. Where are you?" she asked, grinning now.

Brought back by Vivi to the subject of Finn, Pen made up some story about his being the best friend she'd ever had, after Vivi, of course. And that she didn't think of him in any other way, and that maybe he just needed a friend as well. It was all bullshit, and it sounded like bullshit, but Vivi didn't challenge it. She only said, quietly, "I don't know, Pen. It seems a shame to waste a perfectly good man on friendship." Then she looked at Pen and smiled, content for the moment to let the subject, or secrets, lie.

Chapter 12: Finn's Report

Two days later, Pen was upstairs in her office trying to craft the shape of her new novel, *The Man in the Fat Dog House,* so that it made sense. The words to her first book had mostly come when beckoned. This one, not so much. About once a week lately, she would have a brief moment of real despair when she would explore the possibility that her earlier success had been a fluke. Then she would gaze unseeing out the window at the sea for half an hour. Finally, she would turn away and just start writing again. That's what she was doing now, when her cell phone rang. She wished she had turned it off, but she was afraid to do it during school hours, in case there was a problem and Aggie or Galen was trying to reach her.

This time, though, it wasn't Aggie or Galen. Caller ID said: Finn. Just Finn. She picked it up.

"Hate to bother you, Pen," he said by way of hello.

"Oh, no problem. I'm just sitting here writing a book, trying to make a living." She smiled as how uncharacteristically snarky she sounded. Must be she was feeling better.

"Well, I suspected as much. And I'll let you go in a minute. But I have some news, and I was wondering when would be a good time—"

"News about?" she asked, intrigued.

"Peter, you know, your ex."

"OK, now you have my interest. Let me finish some work here. Do you want to stop over or meet me in town?"

"I'm actually at a work site near town, so why don't we meet at Killer Coffee? Maybe an hour and a half?"

"OK, that works. See you then," Pen said, hanging up and turning her swivel chair back toward her computer.

When she next looked at her watch, she said, "Oh shit!" It was an hour and fifteen minutes after Finn's call. She still had to change out of her shabby 'writing clothes,' as she called them, and brush her teeth. Her few makeup ministrations wouldn't take long, maybe ten minutes. With the fifteen-minute drive into town, she was definitely going to be late. She texted Finn, then moved quickly downstairs to her bathroom. Her hair was mercifully short and her minimal makeup went on quickly after she washed her face and put on sunscreen. Eyebrow pencil in light brown, eyeliner in dark brown, makeup in what was called "neutral beige," Revlon lipstick in Ultimate Wine. She used the later to make two spots on her cheeks and spread it around. One of these days she'd remember to buy regular blush makeup for her cheeks. The reflection in the mirror didn't please or displease her. It was what it was. She would pass.

A quick change into cropped white jeans and a blue striped T-shirt completed her preparations for facing the world.

Grabbing her purse, she exited into the cellar and through the garage to get to her Highlander. A minute later she was on her way down Wild Oak Drive and into town. Right before she turned off her street onto route 128, she thought she saw a car she recognized and for a second, she froze. Joe, she thought. It was Joe's car. But it went by so quickly she couldn't be sure he was driving. And what if he was? It was a public road, and Falmouth wasn't so big that people didn't drive all over town. And, she reminded herself, it wasn't as if silver Toyota Camrys were rare.

As she pulled into Killer Coffee, she tried to get the calm of the morning back. She was angry at herself for letting a glimpse of a silver Camry rattle her so much and wondered if she should even mention it to Finn.

He was waiting toward the back of the shop, in the last booth near the outside window. It had privacy as well as good light, and they had met there a few other times, both with Vivi and without.

She moved right into the topic of the day. "So," she said," what's the news about Peter?"

"Well, hello, Pen. How nice to see you." He smiled.

"Sorry. My mother would go crazy if she ever realized that I've forgotten almost all of my manners. Let me start again. Hello, Finn. How are you?"

He laughed. "I guess that's better. I'd feel better if you had led with that, but oh well." He started to get up as she settled into the booth. "Let me get us both some coffees and then I'll spill."

A few minutes later, he told Pen about the plan he'd executed last night.

"You met with Peter in a bar? What the hell, Finn."

"Yep," he answered. "He sure is a charmer."

"Where? How did that even happen?"

"There are two upscale bars near Peter's condo. I knew you said you had the kids on Mondays and Tuesdays, so that meant that he was at loose ends. I didn't picture him as one to stay home and read a best seller or watch Netflix alone, so I scoped out both The Dancing Bear and Murphy's. Found him at the second one. Sitting at the bar with his third glass of scotch."

"That sounds about right," Pen said. "Peter likes to be known, likes to be a regular. We always went to the same restaurants, so when we walked in, they greeted us by name and sat us at a good table. I suspect it's the same now. Go often, tip big. Big whooping deal."

"Yeah, well to continue," Finn said, sipping his coffee. "I sat down next to him, ordered a Sam Adams lager, and just remained quiet. Made a comment or two about the baseball game on the TV in back of the bar. Before I knew it, I had made a new friend." Their eyes met and Pen shook her head.

"You are bad!" she said.

"You have no idea. After a while, we got to talking about our ex-wives."

Pen almost spit out her coffee. "Oh, that's rich. Interesting, no doubt." Then she thought to add, "Do you even have an ex-wife?" For some reason she expected him to say, "No," but he didn't.

She noticed that he did not answer the question, but said, "I made believe I had the bitchiest of all exes. And he really got into it, almost as if it was a contest. On and on and on. So much bullshit all at one time. Poor Peter. Such a great husband, good father. And his ungrateful wife actually divorced him. After all the ways he took care of her: great house, vacations, jewelry." He snorted. "Zero self-awareness. Totally convinced that he's been wronged. 'Blindsided,' was the word he used. She, that's you, Pen, 'broke up his family. Ruined his life.'"

Pen looked mildly amused, but was wondering where this was going. She could tell by Finn's manner that there was more to it.

"And then, as he drank more, the talk got dark. And darker. Said he'd love it if his ex-wife had, and I quote, 'something bad happen to her.' The thought actually made him smile. I asked if he would ever orchestrate 'something bad' and he said in a whisper. 'Don't think I haven't thought about it.'"

"Holy shit, Finn," Pen said under her breath. "This is scaring me."

"Shall I continue?" Finn asked, knowing the answer.

As he did, Pen's eyes got wide, wide and serious. Finn told her how Peter had explained all the ways that Pen had done him wrong. "I was particularly impressed with your financial moves in the divorce," Finn said, eyes dancing.

"Like what?" Pen asked, wondering how much Peter had told him.

"Like signing off on Peter's plan to pay child support but no alimony. He thought when he agreed to no alimony on his end, he'd hit the lottery. And no doubt his lawyer told him that as well. Probably said something like, 'Well, you know these independent women, they don't want handouts. And then later, when they can't make a living, they do. But by then the ink has been dry for a while and it's too late to fix.' On his fourth scotch Pete all but told me that's what his lawyer said. He was stoked to have no alimony to pay. Which, he added, was why he was so easily persuaded to sign the form that said he was not entitled to any of your assets, made before the divorce or after. 'Assets my ass!' is what he said. But he wasn't laughing then."

"I said it sounded good to me, better than the deal I'd gotten with my blood sucking ex-wife. And that's when he explained what really happened, how you unfairly out maneuvered him. How you had actually written a book under a pseudonym the year before the divorce, and then sold said book, a BIG book, the year after. It was a huge hit, and you were paid a LOT of money for it. Not to mention foreign rights, film rights, and so on. The part that sent him into the stratosphere was the fact that he couldn't get a red cent from any of it. Said so in the divorce agreement that he and his lawyer had drafted and laughed about."

They looked at each other. Pen didn't know what to say. All her secrets, well, mostly all, were on the table now. She wondered what Finn would say next.

What he said was, "Master play. Checkmate!" Then he laughed out loud, long and hard. "I had no idea, Pen. You're Katrina Savage? Even I know that name, dammit." He smiled broadly. "And with that said, I think we need seconds on the coffee. There's more."

Chapter 13: Bad News

Once they had started sipping their second coffees, and before Finn could begin whatever more he had to say, Pen decided to tell him her news. She moved her neck around in circles for a minute with her fingers to work out the tightness she was feeling. She took a deep breath. "I think I saw Joe's silver Camry on my street yesterday." She didn't think Finn looked too impressed with her information. "I know it's a public way," she added. "But it's on the other side of town from both his house and his work. There's no reason he should be over here." She looked at Finn to gauge his reaction.

"I agree. And I do believe you saw him on your street. I've seen him twice in the last several weeks."

Pen felt like her head would explode. "WHAT?" she said, loudly enough that several customers looked over at them.

"Didn't want to tell you and freak you out until I had proof."

"Do you have proof now?"

"I do. I put a tracker under his car when he was at work. Then I removed it and got the data from it. Absolutely clear he takes your road several times a week."

"A tracker?"

"I was an undercover cop for a while, remember?"

"Has he stopped by the house? Like, gone in the driveway?"

"Doesn't show that. It appears that he just drives by. Sick bastard. Probably imagines he's terrorizing you."

Pen's eyes were huge. "Because he is..." she said quietly. She felt a kind of despair descend on her, like a gossamer covering of grey. It was all too much. Peter wishing her ill, wanting to do her harm, then Joe driving by.

"There's one more thing," Finn said.

"What's that?"

Finn slid some pieces of a picture across the table at her. As she looked at them, she felt herself recoil and turn cold. Moving the pieces together like a puzzle, the picture became clear. It was of Fiona's family, Joe and the girls and Fiona. It had been torn in two pieces, with Fiona and the girls on one half and Joe by himself on the other. "Where did you get this?" she asked.

"In your mailbox," Finn said grimly. He put a tattered white envelope on the table. It had the name "Penelope" on the front in block print letters. "The pieces were in this," he added. "It was unsealed. I wouldn't have opened it, but one of the pieces fell out."

"When?"

"Yesterday," he said. "I thought I would drive by and see if all was well. I was taking out my phone to call you and see if I could drop by when I saw a silver car flash by. About a mile from your house. I thought it was Joe so I followed him. I passed him slowly and saw what happened in my rearview window. Then I circled back and took out the envelope."

Pen looked stricken. "Why didn't you stop him?" she asked, incredulous. "And confront him?"

"Because I didn't have a plan. I never do anything without a plan. And I didn't have one then." He let his words hang in the air.

"And you do now?"

"I'm working on it," he said and smiled at her. "I think I need a Bear Claw first. For energy. Want one?" he asked, sliding once again out of the booth.

At the same time Finn slid away from the booth, Pen's phone rang. She glanced at it and answered. Finn could tell from the frown lines on her forehead that whatever it was, it wasn't good. He slid back into the booth.

"Yes," Pen said, "I understand. Yes. Yes. I'll be there in twenty minutes. Yes. Thank you." She set her phone on the table and took a huge breath. Finn waited. "Galen was in some trouble at school. Something about fighting." She looked puzzled and sad and diminished.

"Galen?" Finn asked softly. "No mistake?"

"No, mistake. It was definitely Galen. And another girl, Patty something." She gathered up her wallet, phone, and sunglasses. "Gotta go. I'll call you later." She wore a look she couldn't peg. "I'll tell you later what's going on, and you can tell me your plan with Joe." Then she was out the door.

Pen wondered why she was so calm. Normally, a call from the principal's office would have freaked her out. She felt detached, going through the motions. Maybe there was just too much lately. But she would deal with this, too. She was learning that she could deal with anything. Didn't want to, but could.

Ten minutes later, she was on her way into the main building of the junior high school. It was mostly red brick, and had been renovated. It looked bright and shiny inside while still reminding those approaching from the outside that this was a venerable institute that still had old school charm. And money.

She found Sally Crawford behind the office desk, where she seemed to live. "Hello, Pen," she said with a neutral smile that belied her real personality. Sally had been a member of Marta's support group when Pen had belonged, and she knew Pen's struggles almost as well as her own. "Mr. Dockery will be with you in a minute." Then she moved closer to the counter and to Pen. "I took Galen to Mrs. Delaney's office to wait. She's upset, and it was more private there."

Pen knew Mrs. Delaney as a warm, motherly type nurse, and she was grateful. "Thanks, Sally," she whispered quietly.

Suddenly the door was open and Mr. Dockery stood there, beckoning her in. He shut the door behind them.

"Please take a seat," the tall man said, waving her to a chair in front of his desk. In truth, he wasn't just tall, maybe around six feet three, but he was also skeletal. And his propensity for dark greys and blacks did not flatter his sallow complexion. She imagined him to be about fifty and a runner. No one could be that thin normally. *Maybe he doesn't eat*, she thought, nonsensically, as she heard his voice and was brought back to attention.

"I hate to have called you in," he said, "but there's been a problem today, and I thought we should talk about it."

Pen nodded remotely, like a bobblehead doll. She had the sense that she was on overload right now and a little spacy. But she was IT. There was no backup here.

"As I was saying," Mr. Dockery continued, not seeming to have realized that Pen was not herself, "there was a problem today after fourth period involving your daughter Galen and Patty Bueller."

Pen stopped bobbing her head and asked, "What kind of a problem?"

Mr. Dockery cleared his throat. "Well, actually, there was a fight." He paused for a moment. "Involving the girls."

Pen tried to keep calm. "A fight?"

"I'm afraid so. What we do in these situations," he said, warming to the topic because there was obviously a protocol for dealing with it, "is that we suspend both students. Two days. Then we get together with the students and their parents to discuss what happened. We try to reach some resolution and to have students take responsibility."

Pen was bobbing her head again, in shock. Neither of her girls had ever been in a situation like this before. She had no idea what it entailed. Gathering her thoughts which were going in wildly divergent directions, she managed to ask, "And what if no one takes responsibility? Or they disagree about it?"

"Well, both of the girls are asked questions, and we try to get them to reach a peaceful resolution. Each of the students brings his or her version of what happened in written form and that is what we use to lead the direction of our meeting."

Pen was getting hot, her feelings breaking through her earlier detachment. "And what happens if they cannot 'reach resolution'?"

"Oh, "Mr. Dockery said, smiling. "I think you will find that is the most common result. Usually both participants want it over and will try to find a way to make that happen."

"And if not?"

Mr. Dockery's smile faded rather rapidly. "Occasionally, very occasionally, one or more of the participants has a more severe punishment."

"Such as?" Pen asked, trying not to snap at him.

"Oh, well," Mr. Dockery continued, smoothly. "One step at a time. Let's just concentrate on getting to the bottom of this and worry about all that later."

Pen's face had become steel. "What kind of punishment?" she reiterated, working hard on making her face remain pleasant.

Seeing there was no way out of answering, Mr. Dockery said, "Well, it depends. First offense or second or third. Bodily harm or not. Remorse or not. Hate crime or not. Many factors."

He may have seen Pen struggling to retain her composure, trying to breathe deeply and stay calm, or he may have just wanted to end this, one of many meetings in his daily schedule. "At any rate," he said, "let's take one step at a time, shall we? I know that Galen has not been in any trouble before. This may be a simple problem, easily solved."

But as he ushered her out toward the front office, she knew in some dark and unfathomable mother-wise way, this would not be easily solved.

Chapter 14: Galen

Pen and Galen walked out to the car together. It seemed so much brighter outside than it had been in the school. Galen's head was down and she was trudging along with a full backpack. Since she was going to be out of school for at least two days, Galen had gone to her locker and taken most of her books with her. She was bent under the weight, and she looked like she was carrying bricks.

And she was uncommunicative. As they pulled away from the school and entered traffic on Forge Street, Pen asked, "Do you want to talk about it?"

The answer was a quiet, "No."

Later, at home, Galen had hauled her books into her room and closed the door.

Pen took herself to the screened porch and tried to let the waves and quiet settle her. She knew she would be best able to help Galen if she was calm and in control, and that was not what she felt right now. Her daughter was in some kind of trouble, and she didn't know what. She could feel that she was not going to be able to pry it out of her. She'd have to find another way in.

Taking out her phone, she noticed that Finn had left a text, asking how she and Galen were. She quickly texted back, summarizing the situation and saying she needed to spend some time with Galen at home. While she was anxious to hear about it, his plan regarding Joe would have to wait.

When the school bus dropped Aggie off later in the day, there was still no sound from Galen's room. Pen thought at one point she heard crying, right before the bus had come, but nothing since then. She had knocked earlier and offered a sandwich, but Galen had simply said, "No, thanks."

Aggie had gone into her room and changed, then asked if she could go to Michaels with Abby and her mother to buy supplies for an art project they were doing together. As soon as she'd heard the sound of a car on the gravel driveway, she had waved, "Bye, Mom," and was off.

Finally, Pen approached Galen's door. *Desperate times call for desperate measures,* she silently quoted someone unknown. Taking a deep breath, she said, "Galen, we need to talk!"

No answer.

Then her desperate measure: "This seems serious. I think I should call your dad and see if he can come over for a family meeting."

"MOM, NO!" was the instant response. "Don't do that. PLEASE!"

"I have to know what is going on. What caused all this. Why you are so upset." She paused for a moment. "Either you tell me now or you tell your dad and me together. One or the other." She hated to do this, to hold Peter as leverage, but things had to get cleared up. It wasn't going to happen by sitting by and waiting.

The click of the door gave her the answer. Galen stood in the open door looking utterly defeated and miserable. Her face was pale and she had definitely been crying. She moved away from the door so Pen could enter.

"Would it be easier to sit on the screened porch with some lemonade?" Pen asked.

A minute later, glasses on a tray between them, that's where they were.

They sipped the lemonade for a few minutes without speaking, and Pen was surprised how peaceful she felt listening to the birds and the ocean. "OK," she said finally, breaking the silence. "What's going on?"

"I don't know where to start," a small voice said. It wasn't sullen, just flat.

"Let's go with the old saw, 'Start at the beginning,'" Pen said.

"It goes back a while," Galen said. Then, "OK."

She began by telling Pen about the beginning of the school year and a girl at school. "Her name was Patty Bueller," she added. "And for some reason, she seemed to dislike me from the first day. "

"How could you tell?"

"Oh, lots of small things. She would move if she got put in line next to me in gym. She would get up to move if my friends and I sat near her in the cafeteria. She would giggle out loud if I walked past her."

"Sounds like bullying to me."

"I guess. But it was only little things at first. Then she got worse. I would find notes in my desk. Or in my books if I left them for a minute on my desk. Sometimes things would be stuffed into my backpack."

"What kinds of things?" Pen asked, very still and cold. No answer. "Galen?"

Galen sat still, making no sound. But tears were running down the front of her face. "I can't tell you,"she whispered.

"You have to tell me, sweetheart," Pen said, moving next to her on the outside couch. "Whatever it is, I am on your side. I don't even have to know any more about it to be able to say that. I am on your side. I will stand by you. We will figure this out." When there was no response, she said, "I promise."

Galen was clearly struggling. She was taking deep breaths and tapping her heels on the porch floor.

"OK, Galen, NOW. What?" Pen said quietly but firmly.

Galen took a tissue from her pocket and blew her nose. Then she cleared her throat and drank some lemonade. "Will you let me talk and not interrupt?"

Pen nodded.

"OK. You know how I like to dress? Kind of subdued colors. Plain, dark clothes mostly?" Pen flashed back to the first day of this year, eighth grade. Galen had gone to school in black boots with buckles, black pants, a grey short sleeved top, and a grey and black bandana on her head. Pen had wanted her to wear clothes more like Aggie, who had worn a short-sleeved pastel sundress, but she also wanted her daughter to claim her own style. She remembered how it felt when her mother made her dress in an older, more sophisticated style than her friends, because that was her mother's style. She had hated it. So, she had stayed hands off.

Galen continued. "Patty started making comments on day one. Like, 'Oh, are you training to be a rag picker?' or 'That look went out in the 60s, Galen, haven't you heard?' It was always under her breath, so no one else heard. Then the notes started." Reading her mother's mind she said, "I didn't tell you because you had enough on your plate with dad and the divorce and writing your book. I knew you would freak out."

She looked ready to cry.

"But I'm not freaking out, am I? I'm listening."

"The notes were the worst. Sometimes they said one word: GAY! Sometimes they said, 'We don't hang around with Lezzies!' Once there was a small gay pride flag that someone had poured black ink on. That was in my homeroom desk."

Pen thought she could feel her own heart breaking. "Oh, Galen! I wish you'd told me."

"But I couldn't," Galen said softly.

"And now?"

"Now I evidently have to," she said with the look of someone resigned to marching off a cliff.

"What else went on?" Pen asked, with the sinking feeling that they were just probing the surface.

"Sometimes Patty would elbow me when we faced each other coming down the hall in opposite directions. Or maybe push a little. And hiss, 'Lesbo!'"

"And what did your friends think?" Pen asked, shocked.

"Mostly they didn't see it. Patty was pretty sly. Once or twice Alice and Nora asked what was going on, but I just made out it was just 'crazy Patty' acting out."

"But it wasn't, was it?"

"No." Pen watched her daughter's eyes fill with tears again. "No. It was a vendetta. Evidently Patty hates all kinds of diversity. She calls the LGBTQ+ club a group of perverts. Calls them shit, dirt, disgusting human beings."

Pen was appalled at how out of touch she was. She hadn't even known that there was a LGBTQ+ club at the school. Or that these issues were appearing in her own daughter's school. Her mind whirled. She wanted to beat herself up for getting so caught up in her own issues that she missed all of what was going on in her daughter's life. For allowing her daughter to shoulder this alone.

"Did you save those ugly notes?" Pen asked.

Galen nodded. "Don't know why."

In the silence that Galen's unburdening created, both of them rested. Pen poured more lemonade. They sat.

Finally, Pen said, "Do you want to tell me what caused today's episode?"

Without any preamble, Galen said. "There was a new girl in school, Zoe, came a month ago. Nice. Pretty. Interested in art and writing and drawing. Like Alice and Nora and I. We were all nice to her, asked her to sit with us in the cafeteria, to go to the mall on the weekends. She seemed to be glad to make friends, and she really fit in with the three of us. And she was funny, which was great."

"OK, so far. What happened?"

"At the end of last week, she started to act weird."

"Like?"

"She didn't sit with us much at lunch. Once I saw her turn the opposite way when she saw me coming."

"You're right, that is weird."

"I had a bad feeling about what was happening, that it had something to do with Patty. So today I confronted Zoe in my free study period. The teachers don't bother you if you whisper and don't disturb anyone else. I asked her what was wrong." She paused before getting through the next part. "At first, she said nothing was wrong, she was just busy. But then I pressed her and told her that was bullshit. She got angry then and told me that Patty had warned her that I was a butch dyke and was hitting on her. That I had done that to all the pretty girls in class until they had to put me in my place. That Nora and Alice were lezzies, too, and she should just avoid us all. Patty said that was what all the popular kids did, because we were an embarrassment and really messed up."

"Oh, Galen." Pen exhaled. Galen's pain was her own. She could barely breathe for it.

Galen's sobs started for real then, and Pen moved over and held her. Held her tight, as she hadn't for years, as she'd done when she'd fallen from the carousel in first grade, and when she hadn't won a prize in the writing contest two years ago. But this was different, in some elemental way, unlike anything that had come before.

They sat together like this for some time, even after Galen's sobs had subsided, each seeming to draw some kind of peace or security from being close.

Finally, Galen spoke. "There's more, Mom."

Chapter 15: Truth

"OK," Pen said. Then, with a bit of steel in her tone, conveying that whatever it was, it was their problem, not Galen's alone, she added, "Bring it on...."

"I'm gay. I've always been gay. That part was real."

A small puzzle piece slid into place, and Pen recognized the truth of Galen's statement. Galen had always been her own person, even as a small child. She defied stereotypes, liking pants more than dresses, wearing boots with girly clothes, hacking her hair in angles and gelling it before it was 'cool.' She had marched to her own drummer in so many ways.

Galen searched her mother's eyes with trepidation for a reaction to her truth, and to her amazement, she saw Pen smile. Through tears. "Oh, sweetie," Pen said, exhaling at the same time. "You are who you are. And whoever that is, which you are probably just starting to figure out, whoever that is ... is engraved in my heart. Perfect, as is. You will always be one of the great loves of my life. Nothing can change that."

Galen did not sob or hyperventilate or scream. She sat stone still, and tears flowed quietly down her face. "I've wanted to tell you for a long, long time. But..."

"But?"

"But I wasn't sure that it would be OK. That you would still feel the same way about me."

"Oh, Galen. I'm so sorry you had to keep this to yourself. Had to keep who you were to yourself."

"Looks like the cat's out of the bag, now," Galen said, wiping away some of the tears on her cheeks and sounding a little more like the old Galen.

"Do you feel better?"

Galen just looked at her with a half-smile playing on her lips. "You have no idea."

"How long have you known?"

"Forever. As long as I can remember. I didn't have a name for it, but I felt different somehow. And I kept feeling more and more sure that I wasn't like most of my friends. I didn't want to play with dolls, or dream about some teenage movie star, or want to flirt with sixth grade boys. By the time I'd figured out I was gay, I also knew that it was something shameful to be hidden. That people might not like me if they knew." She shrugged. "Maybe not even my parents."

Seeing the hurt look on Pen's face, Galen added, "I just didn't know. I thought maybe you would be OK with it, but Dad?" She sniffled and shook her head. "Probably not. Not the norm. Not perfect. Not someone he could brag about."

"He might surprise you."

"When pigs fly." Galen sounded sadly older and more jaded than her age.

"Do you want me to tell him?" Pen asked.

"No. When I'm ready, I'll tell him myself."

"With the school situation, maybe sooner than later."

"I can't right now," Galen almost shouted. But then, in a more conciliatory tone, "I'll think about it." After a minute or two, she added, "At least I have you on my side."

Pen nodded. The storm was over for now. But they had more to discuss. "What do you want to do about school?" Pen's mind had been working overtime since she'd picked her daughter up earlier in the day.

"What do you mean?"

"Well, according to Mr. Dockery, you have a two-day suspension because of fighting."

"Yeah."

"I'm not sure that's fair."

"But that's what it is, Mom."

"Will you tell me how the fight started? What finally triggered the argument that got us here?"

"I will, Mom, I promise. But can we take a break now? I am totally exhausted. And hungry."

"Sure," Pen said, as she got up and walked inside with Galen. "Do you want a snack, or do you want me to make you something?"

"Snack's good. Then I'm gonna put in my earbuds, listen to some music, and chill. Maybe even fall asleep."

With Galen resting in her room and Aggie still at Abby's, Pen went into her bedroom to lie down. She was wiped. But she couldn't stop her mind from churning. What caused the actual fight with Patty? Should they fight the suspension? When should Peter be part of this? When would Galen be ready to go back to school? She lay on her bed perfectly still while her monkey mind jumped from topic to topic with a rapidity that almost made her dizzy. The next thing she knew, her phone was ringing. She grabbed it from the bedside table and answered.

"Finn here," said a familiar voice. "I started to get worried about you. And Galen."

"No need. Galen is sleeping, I think, and I was just taking a nap."

"Sorry, didn't mean to wake you."

"No problem. I was just going to get up anyway."

"Are you tied up with everything at home right now, or can we get together for a bit? I want to tell you about my plan for dealing with Joe."

"Man, I would love to hear that," Pen said. "But right now I have to be with Galen. We have Part II of our discussion to go. Besides which, I want to discuss her talking to her father and getting him involved. We might fight this suspension. It doesn't happen until Monday, which gives us tomorrow and Sunday to figure out what to do."

"Yeah, busy time. I hear that. And you really need to step up for Galen. Maybe we'll connect early in the week. I think I'll just work all weekend. That Mallory project is exploding."

"Exploding?"

"Yeah. They want a closet I just put in to be made three times bigger, two huge windows I just installed in the living room turned into a wall of windows, and the new roof changed from light grey to charcoal."

"That's crazy!"

"Yup."

"Does it drive you crazy? When clients keep making changes to already signed off on plans?"

"Nope."

"Why not?"

"One, because I know I'm able to do the work. And two, because I earn a boatload of money along the way. It's all the same to me."

"I see," Pen said, laughing. "Well, good luck with that. I think I hear Galen moving around, so I'm going to go check on her now."

"Sounds good. Still wearing the step tracker all the time?" he asked. When she said "Yup," he said, "Good. Talk soon."

Then he was gone.

Pen marveled at how easy he was. No fits about not being able to see him, or being tied up with her kids. Even Peter, who was the father of those kids, used to be jealous if she spent too much time with them and not enough with him. He would tell her she was hovering, or make fun of how she checked in on them to see if their homework was done or what they needed for school. "No one ever did that for me," he said, "and I turned out fine."

But Finn was a different case entirely. Sometimes she wondered if he was for real, or whether once she got to know him better, she would find feet of clay.

Galen was in the kitchen, getting some milk. Before they could speak, Aggie came in through the front door, moving fast, a bundle of energy. "Mom, mom," she yelled, "Abby's mother's taking her out for dinner at the Cinema Pub. It's one of the new Marvel movies, the throwback one. Anyway, she asked if I can go. Can I? Please?" This last word was extended into a long, begging "Pleeeezz?"

Galen and Pen both smiled at her intensity, as if going to the movie with Abby was the only thing that mattered in the world.

"OK," Pen said. "You can go." She got up and took some money from her wallet. "How about you pay for the tickets," she suggested, "and Mrs. Murphy can get the food if she wants?" Aggie was already tucking the money in her pocket as she moved toward the front door.

Halfway down the granite front stairs, Aggie turned back. "Thanks, Mom," she said, smiling. Then she was moving in a blur toward the road, where Mary Murphy's car idled.

"Guess it's just the two of us," Galen said.

"That sounds good to me," Pen said. "Why don't we order some steak tips and Caesar Salad from Jack's Place? They deliver."

The food came forty minutes later, and, as planned, they set up on the porch, sitting at the round teak table in the corner. Galen brought out two wine glasses and a bottle of Moscato. She poured herself half a glass and put about a quarter of a cup in Galen's glass.

"Mom?" Galen said, puzzled. "What's this?"

"This, my dear, is wine. Moscato. Not champagne or a wine for a connoisseur. But I like it, and I am going to propose a toast."

Galen shrugged, as if to say, "I don't get it."

"Here," Pen said, handing the smaller glass to Galen, who took it with a frown. "I'm proposing a toast on this auspicious day." Then she held up her own glass and motioned Galen to do the same. "Here's to your courage in telling me your truth." She stopped for a moment as her throat closed a bit with emotion. Clearing it, she added, "And here's to both of us being exactly who we were meant to be."

The slant of the late day light as it bounced off the waves in back of the house filled the sun porch. Pen knew she would never forget this moment, or the shy smile and glistening eyes of her daughter as they clinked glasses in their mutual pledge.

After they had eaten all the steak tips and most of the salad, Pen pushed the plates away. "Let's sit on the couch and continue this afternoon's discussion," she said. "We can clean up later."

Slowly, maybe reluctantly, Galen moved toward the couch. The sun was starting to signal that the day was nearing its end, though it was still light out. Pen often thought of this time of day as a magic time. If she had written for most of the day, she would come out and sit on the porch and revel in the peace and sun and glinting sea. Or she would work her way down the path towards the small rocky beach at the base of her property. There she would sit on a large rock to the left and dangle her feet in the water, and offer thanks for the strange and wonderful ways her life had changed in the last year.

Today, though, all that would not happen. Today she would find out what had really happened this morning when the telephone call from the school had interrupted and changed their lives so dramatically.

"So, Galen, tell me what caused the disruption this morning? I mean why today, after all you've been through, did things erupt into a fight?" Seeing the look on Galen's face, she added, "Don't get me wrong. I'm not blaming you. I just want to know what actually happened. And even if it is your fault, I am still on your side."

Galen sat still, looking at the water. Her shoulders slumped with the weight of earlier in the day. Pen could feel her own heart crack yet again. Finally, Galen looked at her mother. "OK," she said, "here's what happened. I was getting books from my locker, like I always do after fourth period. Nora had already gotten hers and she was waiting next to me. When I straightened up from getting a pen from the bottom of my locker, Patty Bueller was there. Her face was inches from mine. One of her friends, Donna Bailey, was with her. Patty started in with the usual, 'Hi, Lezbo girl!' Then pointing to Nora, she said, 'How's your GIRLFRIEND?'"

Pen didn't know what to say. She shook her head in disgust.

"Nora's cool, though. This isn't the first time Patty has been mean or said something in front of my friends. So, Nora said, 'C'mon, Galen. Let's get out of here. We don't need to be around this trash.' Then Patty got into Nora's face and said, 'Who are you calling trash, lezzie?' Nora just ignored her and said, 'Time to go, Galen' as she started to walk away. I had my stuff together by then and I started to follow her. Then I felt someone grab my shirt, from behind. I kept walking; I figured she would just let go of it." Galen seemed to shrink down further as she recalled the scene. "She did let go, but she grabbed the other side of it instead and pulled really hard. It spun me around, so I bumped into my locker and I was facing her."

"Don't you EVER walk away from me when I'm talking to you," she said.

"By then I was really scared, and I could feel my eyes watering. I said, 'Look, I don't want to fight. I don't know what your problem is with me, and I don't care. Just stop. I need to get to class.'"

"But Patty doesn't miss anything, ever. She had seen that I was afraid, and also that my eyes were starting to tear up." Galen looked at her mother as if to apologize for that weakness.

"Galen, I would have been scared to death. Honestly. And I wouldn't have had as much self-control as you had, either. Don't you dare feel bad about that." Pen felt sick, and at the same time, she wanted to scream. *Someone would pay for this*, she thought.

Galen continued. "Once Patty had seen my eyes tearing up, it was all over. She was brutal. 'Oh, poor baby, Gay-len. Are your feelings hurt? Are you gonna cry? Do you need to see the nurse?'"

"What happened then?" Pen asked, breathing shallowly.

Galen bit her lip, hard. After a moment, she continued. "She moved in closer and put her hands on either side of my head. She held it so I couldn't move, and said, 'Poor, pathetic, stupid, scared Baby Gay-len.'"

There were tears running down Galen's face. As she watched her daughter suffer, Pen thought she might kill this girl, this Patty Bueller. Unless she could think of something better.

Fighting through her tears, Galen said, "And I lost it. I lost it, Mom! I went crazy. I pushed her, and then she backed up a step and tripped. When she got up, she went batshit. She slapped me hard across the face." She paused. "It literally took my breath away. And it really hurt." She had tears in her eyes again, but there was a glint of something else in them as well.

Before Pen could say anything, Galen looked at her and said, "I shoved her really hard, and she fell backward again. And then I started to kick the shit out of her until Nora and Donna Bailey pulled me away. And I'm glad I did."

Chapter 16: Dilemma

The next morning, a sunny, warm Saturday, found Pen up early. The girls were still sleeping, and by her watch it was 6:30 a.m. But she had had a rough night, waking and then eventually falling asleep again, only to repeat the process several hours later. She had finally gotten some good sleep after 3 a.m., but then she had awoken at 6. She lay in bed listening to the waves, hoping they would lull her back to sleep. But they had not.

She pulled on some jeans and an old t-shirt and went into the kitchen. After starting coffee, she mixed up some pancake mix and put it in the fridge.

When the coffee was ready, she grabbed a cup, a fleece sweater on the dining room chair, and her cell phone. For a while she sat and sipped her hot coffee, glad for the warmth around her hands as she held the mug. It promised to be a beautiful day in late Spring, but it was still slightly cool in the morning, especially on the porch.

Then she put down her cup and dialed.

Finn answered after two rings. "Hi," she said. "It's me."

"Hi, Pen. What's up?"

"Not much," she said, ignoring her discussion and Galen's revelation of the day before. She might tell him at some point...or not. "I'm still having some anxiety about Peter. And about your having a plan for dealing with Joe. "

"Do you want to get coffee later?"

"I do. But I have the girls and I want to make them breakfast first. I think they both have plans for later in the afternoon. Maybe three would be good. Does that work? Do you want to meet at Killer Coffee and thrash out the world's problems? Or, at the very least, mine?"

"Sure," he said. "See you then." He seemed a little abrupt to Pen, but then he often sounded that way. To the point, no bullshit. And sometimes no small talk, either. There were worst faults you could have in a friend, she thought, as she walked back into the kitchen to warm her coffee.

Later, after a pancake breakfast, Aggie asked Pen if she would drive her to Abby's house so she could play with Abby's new Dalmatian puppy. She was back in ten minutes.

"So," Pen said to Galen. "How did you sleep?"

"Pretty well." She looked at Pen with a strange, almost smug, unreadable expression on her face. After a brief pause, she added, "I think I have some good news."

"I'm ready for good news."

And then Galen told her how she had texted her friends yesterday, bringing them up to date with her suspension and asking them if there was any chance that someone might have caught the fight on a cell phone. She asked them to reach out to their other friends and see. It was a bit of a wild card, as most kids were moving fast between classes, and they were not supposed to use their phones in school. But it was not impossible that someone had filmed the altercation.

"And?" Pen asked, holding her breath.

"Stephanie O'Malley, one of Nora's friends, was just moving her phone from her pocket to her backpack when it started," Galen said. "Her locker is three down from mine. She hit 'video record' as soon as Patty started her stuff." Galen took a big breath. "She has it all, Mom. The whole thing! She sent it to me." She sat back at the table, folded her arms in front of her, and looked intently at her mother.

The video had captured all but the first 5 seconds. Patty's taunts were there as well as her slap across Galen's face. It had captured Galen's actions as well, but it was clear they were in self defense. Except for the last 20 seconds, which showed Galen kicking Patty after the slap. Retaliatory, and not in defense. A human response to what had happened before. Patty had clearly been the aggressor, had started the fight. On the whole, Pen thought, it exonerated Galen.

"Well," Pen said when it was over, "that was hard to watch." She shivered through her fleece.

"Do you think it will make a difference?" Galen asked.

"We can only hope." Seeing Galen's face collapse, she added, "But I think so."

In midafternoon, Pen dropped Galen off at Nora's house on Shore Road and Aggie at the library for a meeting of the science club. Aggie was complaining because she was going to be late. "Why does it take so long to get out of the house? It seems like forever." She jumped out of the car in the parking lot and said, "See you in the parking lot at four?" Pen nodded and Aggie bolted toward the library's entrance.

Pen just sat in the car. Indeed, it did take a long time to get out of the house. She locked and double locked all the doors and checked that the windows were closed and secured. This took a while, because of the nice weather. Someone was always leaving a window open to catch the spring breezes. Sometimes that person was Pen.

It was hard to be on the alert all the time, every time, but she knew she was the adult in charge. Once everything was locked, she engaged the new system that protected the whole house. She had to admit that having that in place changed everything for her. Once it was engaged, even when they were home, she felt safe. Finn had showed her early on that even if a wire was cut in order to disable it, a screeching alarm would sound. On a weekend when the girls weren't there, he had even demonstrated, cutting the actual wire. She had gotten a headache from the horrible sound it emitted, but it was worth it to see that it couldn't be hacked. Finn had rewired it quickly and then proceeded to show her what would happen if a window was opened after it was locked. She'd had to replace one of the locks that Finn broke when showing her this, but that was a small price to pay to believe she could be safe in her home again. The alarm generated a call to the police station automatically. Within seconds of each breach, she had received a call from the station asking for her passcode and if she was OK. She sighed. That system was essential to her mental health. And that was why they were almost late getting anywhere now.

She told the girls that the alarm system was something she'd meant to do when they moved in. Explained that since she worked from home a lot of the time, it made her feel safer. They'd hardly reacted to the news.

But she never told the girls about the home invasion or about Sunny Ray being trashed. She had just hidden the pieces of the artificial bird in a garbage bag and said she had taken him to Vivi's to cheer her up. Sometimes a good white lie was just what you needed. though she suspected that Greta would not agree.

She went back and forth about whether she should show the girls the safe room. But she couldn't figure out a way to do it. To say, "Oh, by the way, girls... look at this," seemed ridiculous and would make light of what was actually serious. But to make it a serious discussion would probably scare them both more than it would reassure them. She knew, too, that if she asked Galen to keep it a secret, she would, absolutely. But Aggie was another story. She was filled with unbridled enthusiasm for everything. Pen could picture her "accidentally" telling Abby about the neat "hidden room" in her house. Maybe even showing her during a play date. Going back and forth in her mind, Pen could not get clarity on it. Could not decide what was the right thing to do, so she did nothing and felt guilty.

She rationalized that because she never left Aggie and Galen home alone, they would never need to use it by themselves anyway. If the room did need to be used again, she would be there. Pen sighed. *That's it for now,* she thought, pulling into a parking spot. Her brain ached.

Finn was already at Killer Coffee when she arrived. He was sipping his coffee and had started a jelly donut, the remains of which were on a napkin in front of him. A cup of what she assumed was black coffee sat across from him with a top on it. She slid into the booth and picked up the cup. "Mine?" she asked and he nodded. "Thanks," she said prying off the top and taking a sip. The coffee was hot and black and it stung her tongue. But it tasted really, really good. Almost like normalcy.

"Can we talk about Joe?" Pen said.

"Sure," Finn said, eating a small piece of the remaining donut before continuing.

Pen found herself jiggling her right foot up and down nervously before she made herself stop.

Finn took a sip of coffee and started to talk. "I had a friend who is good at this kind of thing check into Joe's background. Seems he's always been a bully. Two restraining orders against him in the last ten years, by different women. Right now, he has a job with Berklins, the discount store, in lower management, though God knows how he made that happen. Anyway, it seems he is having an affair with the woman who works as his assistant. Name is Jane Clary. "

"OK?" Pen queried, not understanding where this was going.

"Well," Finn said, "it becomes interesting and useful when you consider that having any type of personal relationship with a subordinate is verboten at most businesses. Especially now. But in Berklins, it's written in blood. They had a big lawsuit several years ago, where a subordinate employee sued them for a lot of money. She reported overtures by her boss several times to HR and they did nothing to protect her. Then her boss started to stalk her. He almost raped her one night when she came home late. Anyway, after a lot of appeals, she was finally awarded over two million dollars because the company knew about the behavior and didn't protect her. So, no relationships between employees and bosses are allowed now. Not even the hint of one. And Joe and Jane are in deep."

"How would you even know this?" Pen asked, shaking her head.

"I have sources," Finn replied trying to sound mysterious, and Pen laughed.

"No, really."

"Doesn't matter. But what I said is true. I plan to confront Joe very soon, probably at his house, but maybe in his office, and tell him his scary act with you is about to end."

Pen said nothing.

Finn continued, "And if it doesn't end, or I even see him on a street near your house, I'll submit evidence, including pictures, that he and Jane are 'really good friends.' I will point out that such evidence will no doubt cost them both their jobs."

Pen didn't know what to say. Finally, she said, "It's kind of blackmail, isn't it?"

"Yup. And your point?"

"I'm not sure. In general, I guess I don't think blackmail is right. I was thinking maybe there was some way of going to the police or doing something legally to him."

Finn had an old look on his face. "Pen, if there was some way to do that, don't you think I would have done it? But there isn't. We know he trashed the thing you call Sunny Ray and that he left the photo in your mailbox. He moved so fast on the last one I never got a shot of the car. There is no proof."

"So, this is a backdoor way of making him back off?" she asked and he nodded agreement.

"And you plan to do it by yourself?"

He nodded.

"When?"

"Soon."

Pen didn't say anything. She didn't know what to say.

Finn noticed her discomfort. "If it's ok with you," he added.

"That's just the thing," she said. "I 'm not sure it is."

She could see Finn's face tighten marginally. He spoke very clearly. "Do you want Joe's harassment, or worse, to stop? Or not?"

"Yes, of course I do," she snapped.

"Well, then you have a few very limited choices. You can go to the police with no evidence to present." When he saw her face's response, he added, "No, Pen, you have no 'evidence.' You think you know who is responsible for the Sunny Ray thing. But you didn't see anyone. I saw Joe put something in your mailbox. Could have been anything." No one spoke for a few seconds. "No evidence," he repeated.

"So," he continued, "second choice. My plan, as discussed earlier." When Pen didn't say anything, he added, "And third choice, do nothing, keep looking over your shoulder every time you leave your house, and hope for the best." He seemed to be getting more intense as he spoke. "Which one is it, Pen?"

Pen felt cornered. This was so unlike Finn. She didn't know what to do. He clearly wanted her to say the logical thing, that his plan was the best one. It was a go. But she felt pressured and that made her feel unsure, unbalanced. She said nothing.

Finn gathered up his napkins and cup. "Look," he said. "I have to check out some work sites this afternoon. Why don't you think about it and call me when you decide what you want to do?" Then, as if to soften his tone, which sounded cold to Penn, he added, "Or call me even if you can't decide." He smiled. Then he was out the door.

Chapter 17: Two Calls

After dinner, while the girls were playing in the water at the back of the house, Pen made a phone call. She dialed and waited. On the fifth ring, Sally Crawford answered.

"Hey, Sally, it's Pen," she said. She was comfortable with Sally, a comfort forged from being in a therapy group during tough times. Sally had two boys and was struggling with a difficult marriage. So far, she hadn't called it quits.

"I've been wondering when you'd call," Sally said.

"Yeah, me, too. Have a few things I thought you might be able to help me with."

"If I can, Pen, of course."

They talked for thirty minutes as Pen drank iced tea and watched the girls cavort in the water below.

Later, while Galen and Aggie watched a movie, she climbed the stairs to her study and began working on her book. She knew that Jessie Siddel, her agent, would be checking on her soon, wanting to get an idea about her progress. And she could truthfully say there had been progress. Just less than she had expected, and harder to come by. She was grateful for the few hours she could spend right now and was hoping that today would be one of those days when she could get into the groove early on. Her advance, based on the sales of her first book, had been substantial and she was aware that it had to be earned by the appearance of a finished book in the near future.

She often wondered if the total lack of pressure she'd felt writing *Two Suitcases and a Cat* was the result of having no expectations. The writing had actually been fun, a way out of her life then and a release of creativity. She had had hopes, of course, but no real expectations. Now whenever she sat down to write, she could feel the fate of her financial future looming in front of her. Not for the first time, she wondered how she could tap back into her creativity and get back to the enjoyment of playing with words.

Sitting at her desk, she turned her head toward the window and the panorama of sea and sky spread out across the horizon. Then she turned back to the keyboard. For now, she thought, all I can do is plug away. And she began again to chip away, slowly, at the vague shape that lived in her mind. The one she had named *The Man in the Fat Dog House.*

A hand on her shoulder made her jump. Aggie was behind her, looking startled. "Sorry, Mom," she said.

"No problem, sweetie. I was just lost in ... another world. What's up?"

"Just wanted to see what you were doing," Aggie yawned. "I'm going to bed soon. Galen is reading in her room, I think."

As Aggie headed toward the stairs, Pen said. "Get ready for bed. I'll be down in a few to say goodnight." She didn't dare sit back down at the computer for fear she would lose track of time again, so she shut it down and neatened her desk.

At eleven she made another phone call. "Finn?" she asked, before he could say anything.

"Hi, Pen," he answered, sounding much like his normal self, the coolness earlier in the day seemingly gone. "Everything OK?

"Yeah, for now anyway. Can we talk some more about Joe? And what to do?"

"Sure. What are you thinking?"

"Well, first I want to explain why I was so bristly today." And before he could demur, she added, "I need to."

"OK by me," he said. "Shoot."

She took a deep breath before she began. "I've been taken care of my whole life. First my dad, bless his heart, made decisions for me. Really for the whole family. He ran things; it was just the way it was. Then I married Peter. He ran everything, I mean everything: where we lived, what kind of car we bought, what I should wear to a party." She stopped for a minute, aware that she was starting to wallow in how bad things had been. Off track. Gathering herself, she continued, "The point is, almost all the decisions in my life have been made by men. Well-meaning some of the time, some of the time, not. But I haven't been a part of them. When you started to explain your plan, I started to feel uneasy. Like it was happening again. It was like I was sitting back and deciding to be a spectator in my life again." She paused and he did not speak for several moments.

"Pen, it wasn't my intention to do that to you. To take over your life. None of what I've helped you with has been about that."

Before he could go on, Pen interrupted. "I know that, Finn. I don't know what I would have done without your help these last weeks. And your friendship. But it wasn't even so much what you were suggesting... though I had some reservations about that. It was about how I was feeling. And the feeling triggered something in me, something I had been ignoring. That something is my need to be part of my decisions and actions. From now on, I need to be, as the trite phrase goes, 'Captain of my ship.'"

"Wouldn't have it any other way. I can see where my gangbusters approach to the Joe problem could have been off-putting. I apologize for that." Before she could reply he added, "No, no really. I've been alone for a long time, and I make and execute my decisions without consulting anyone. It's a pattern and a way of life for me. We are talking about your life here. I need to be...a different way. More respectful of what you think." No one spoke. Then he added, "I've been a bit much lately, huh?"

"Well," Pen said. "Yeah. But from the time when the home invasion happened until now, that was what I needed. I couldn't even think straight. And I thank you for stepping in and shoring me up. But now that I've gotten some of the wind back in my sails and some time to think, I need more of a collaborative approach."

"Sounds like business school speak," Finn said, and she could hear a lightness in his reply.

"Can we move back to Joe?" she asked. "I've made a decision about how I want to deal with it."

"Ready. Spit it out. I'm all set to listen."

"I've decided that you were right. The only approach that will stop Joe is to be confronted with some facts that will deter him. Mostly what you suggested."

"Ah ha!" Finn said, and it was hard not to hear the slight crowing in his voice.

"But there's a major difference in what you proposed and what I'm proposing now."

"And that is?"

"That I go with you to confront him."

Chapter 18: Confrontation

Sunday passed quickly, and before she knew it, Monday had arrived. It dawned bright and clean, a day for the beach or a bike ride. Not a day to face down a principal. But that's what it was, so after a half hour huddled in the comfort of her bed, Pen got up. It was only 6:00 a.m. The meeting wasn't until 11am.

Once Aggie left for school, Pen woke Galen. She had been distant the day before, withdrawn. "Whatever," was her reply to most of what Pen had asked. She seemed resigned to her fate, however it turned out. They both suspected that news of the fight and what caused it had spread throughout the school. Pen thought that they should talk before the school visit and said so while Galen was eating breakfast.

"Yeah, OK," Galen said.

"Mr. Dockery might want a written account of what happened from you."

Galen shrugged. "OK," she said without enthusiasm.

"If he starts with that, just run with it. I'll take it from there. I'll introduce the video."

"I don't want Stephanie to get in trouble for using her phone," Galen said firmly, and Pen admired her desire to protect her friend.

"No problem. I sent it to a friend who has computer and internet savvy, and it's been scrubbed."

"Scrubbed?"

"Means it's been sent to another server, or maybe several, and the link to the original site has been removed. It's not possible to tell where it came from."

The look of relief on Galen's face made Pen glad she had asked Finn about doing this. Once again, he knew someone who had a set of skills that fit the problem. The scrubbed video had arrived on her phone when she checked it earlier.

Thinking back, she said to Galen, "You should remove the earlier version of the video from your phone, so it can't be traced that way. I've already done mine."

And then it was 10:30 and they were on their way.

As they got into the car, Pen felt compelled to say one more thing. "No need to be nervous, Galen. There is nothing at stake. If they add more suspended days, who cares? Even if, worst case, they expelled you, no problem. It's near the end of the. year. You could easily go to Daton Academy in town or another school in the fall. My point is, there is nothing they can do to you that matters. I'm going in loaded for bear because of what has happened to you all year and the injustice of your being considered in any way responsible for the fight."

An unusually quiet Galen clicked her seatbelt and sighed. "Thanks, Mom."

At eleven o'clock, they entered the school and opened the door to the outer office of the principal. Sally Crawford looked up from her desk and nodded at Pen. "I'll tell Mr. Dockery you're here," she said, picking up her phone.

When Pen and Galen entered Mr. Dockery's office, Patty Bueller and her parents were already there. They had taken the seats on the left side of the room in front of Mr. Dockery's desk. Pen and Galen took the ones on the right.

Mr. Dockery looked and sounded like he was trying really hard to be easy going and cool. "Glad you are all here," he began, looking from one side of the room to the other. "I would like to begin by hearing from the girls, in their own words, about what happened last week to cause the altercation that has brought us here." The room was silent. Pen could feel the wave of antagonism that was coming from across the room. The Buellers sat with their arms crossed in front of them, matching statues. Patty lounged in her chair, a smug, self-assured look on her face as she looked at them. Pen wanted to slap her.

Mr. Dockery continued. "Who would like to go first?" he asked.

Patty sat up straighter. "I will," she said, clearly looking forward to telling her version of the story. She looked over at Galen, a challenge in the glance.

"That's fine," Galen said, and Pen was proud of the way she sat up and spoke clearly in a calm voice.

"Proceed," Mr. Dockery said.

The next ten minutes were agonizing for both Pen and Galen. Patty's defense was to lie about everything. She was walking down the corridor. Galen bumped into her on purpose. She got mad and told Galen to watch where she was walking. Galen got mouthy back, pushed her again. Then, before she could even defend herself, Galen shoved her one more time, hard. And then started stomping on her. "I have pictures of the bruises," she said, "if you don't believe me." She looked at Mr. Dockery and then at Pen and Galen.

"And why do you think she did that?" Mr. Dockery asked.

"She's always disliked me," Patty said. "Don't know why. Just has. It's not the first time she's shoved me in the hall."

Pen was breathing deeply, trying to keep cool in the face of all these lies. She was half waiting for Galen to explode, to accuse Patty of lying. But, to her surprise, Galen said nothing.

"Are you finished with your recounting of the fight?" Mr. Dockery asked Patty.

Patty shrugged nonchalantly. Then she lounged back in her chair.

"Galen?" Mr. Dockery said. He looked at her and said, "Your turn."

For a moment, Pen held her breath. Then she steeled herself. Whatever happened, happened.

Galen began by addressing Patty directly. "Patty, you know that's not what happened."

Patty yelled back, "You liar! Yes, it is! And I have the bruises to show for it!"

Mr. Dockery broke in. "Patty! Let Galen speak. You owe her the courtesy of listening to her." Patti raised her head and looked defiantly at him. "Or you'll sit in the outer office." A short pause. Then, "Galen, continue."

And Galen did, starting with the abuse that began in the fall. After documenting numerous instances of Patti's harassment, she added, "Patty seems upset by the fact that I'm gay."

Pen couldn't believe what she was hearing. All she could think was, *My brave, brave girl.* Then she looked over at the Bueller's and Patty. The Buellers looked grim, as if they'd heard something distasteful, and Patty's eyes were bugging out of her head. She looked like she'd explode. And then she sat back in her chair and looked over at Galen with a slight smile as if to say, "Gottcha now, asshole!" Pen could picture her retelling Galen's acknowledgement over and over until there was no one in the school who hadn't heard it.

Mr. Dockery broke the silence. "Please continue," he said, looking again at Galen.

And she did. She documented over and over how Patti had made her life miserable. How she had tried to avoid her or to walk away when that wasn't possible. And then she told the story as she had told her mother just days ago. About Patty taunting her, pulling on her shirt, not letting her ignore what she was saying. And about the slap that had stunned Galen into the final push and the stomping retribution when Patty fell.

Patty was shaking her head back and forth and muttering, "Not true, not true, not true," under her breath.

"Patty! Stop!" Mr. Dockery said. But he made no move to remove her from the room. Then he asked Galen, "Do you need more time, or are you finished?"

Sounding resigned to whatever would happen, but with her head up, Galen said, "I'm finished." The words bounced around the room and it might have sounded to Patti and her parents like Galen really was finished. Done, cooked.

"Well," Mr. Dockery said, making an attempt to move forward. "We seem to have two different versions of what happened last Friday. Clearly. Given that fact, I don't know if I will be able to find the truth."

Pen glanced over and saw that Patty was smirking again. Almost as if she knew what would happen, almost as if it had happened before. "So, in light of that," he said, "I believe that both girls will serve the second day of suspension tomorrow."

"And then?" Pen asked.

"And that will be the end of it," he said. "No way to access blame. Either girl might be to blame, given the two versions of the fight, so each will have another day of suspension and that will be that." He must have seen the look on Pen's face, as he added, "Of course, if there is another incident, we might reopen it. Or, if more information were to come forward now, we might proceed differently." He shrugged. "My hands are tied." He started to get up, to bring the meeting to an end and the Buellers stood as well.

Pen remained seated. "What if I have more information?" she asked. Everyone stopped moving.

"I'm sorry?" Mr. Dockery said.

"I have more information."

Momentarily taken aback, Mr. Dockery attempted to make sense of this. "Umm, well, I guess we should all sit down and hear what you have to say."

Once they were all seated, Pen began. "Well, as we've all heard, we have two very different stories about last week's fight." When no one said anything, she continued. "I actually have a way to present the truth."

"Really?" Mr. Bueller asked, sarcastically.

"A video." Pen's words fell like boulders in the room.

Everyone but Pen and Galen said, "What?" at the same time.

Pen opened the large pocketbook she'd been carrying and took out her Ipad. She opened it up and propped it up on its stand. Before she continued, she motioned Mr. Dockery to come over to the front of his desk, so he could watch with the others.

"I've taken the liberty of loading it into my Ipad, so we can all watch it together and see what happened." Her finger tapped the triangle on the screen and the video began.

Since Pen had seen it several times, she concentrated on watching the others. They were transfixed. Mr. Dockery's mouth fell open. Mr. and Mrs. Bueller sat very still. Patty was clenching her jaws and in a different setting, Pen might have feared that she would throw something. Pen glanced over at Galen, who was watching intently. The video ended.

Mr. Dockery spoke first. "Where did you get that?" he asked in a tight voice.

"I'm not actually sure," Pen said, which was technically true. She didn't know the name of the person who sent it back to her once it was scrubbed. "It just showed up on my phone."

"We will look into this," Mr. Dockery said in a slightly menacing way, as if shooting the video was more upsetting than what was on it. "Phones are not allowed to be used in school! It's a very serious rule that we enforce vigorously."

Pen couldn't resist, didn't even try. "Obviously, not vigorously enough." After a brief pause, she began speaking again, and it was as if a new person had joined them in the room.

"Let's cut to the chase here. This video clearly shows who started the fight. It was Patty who was taunting Galen, who spun her around by her shirt, and who slapped her across the face." Patty started to say something but Pen said, "My turn. Shut up!"

She continued, "In fairness, I should give you all the information we are dealing with. Our lawyer has watched this, and just so you know, the acts involved meet the criteria for assault. Patty can also be charged with a hate crime. Both are serious charges." She let this sink in. "She could go to jail, in fact, if this were brought to the police. At the very least, a juvenile detention center."

Again, stunned silence.

There was no refuting what they had all seen

Chapter 19: End Game

No one said anything. Mr. Dockery looked greyer than he had, and Patty's parents glared hard at the wall. "Now, there might be mitigating circumstances," Pen continued, "that would argue for leniency. For example, if this were the first time Patty had ever been in trouble, if she had a spotless record, that might count for something with a judge. Or jury." She watched to see what affect her words had on everyone. In spite of herself, Mrs. Bueller bit on her lower lip, seemingly unaware of what a tell that was. Mr. Bueller looked at Patty with such fire in his eyes that Pen actually had a moment of fear for her. Pen continued, "I can see from your reactions that this is not a first-time offense." When Mr. Dockery and Mr. Bueller started to protest, Pen said, "Cut the bullshit. Easy to find out. Simple as looking at her record. Here, at school."

Mr. Dockery said, "Those records are not available to the public. They are private documents."

"Oh," Pen replied," I wasn't suggesting that we go get them, or even look at them. No, I think that would be a job for a judge or prosecutor. Either one might subpoena them. They'd be helpful in getting a true picture of Patty's character. And help decide what her sentence would be if she were convicted of assault." Warming to her topic, Pen forged ahead. "Obviously, they would talk to a lot of sources and check to make sure that the records hadn't been changed or anything omitted. If that happened, they would be looking for why that had been done. You know, motive. Who would have access, that sort of thing."

Pen waited a bit here, like a cat letting the mouse get almost to safety and then pouncing. After a few beats, she added, "Then they might find out that Patty is, in fact, Mr. Dockery's niece. And that might explain a lot." She didn't need to say more. They all knew what she meant. Obviously, there had been other events like this. And just as obviously, there were few repercussions for Patty. This could be a disaster for four of the people in the room.

Pen almost felt sorry for poor Mr. Dockery who looked like he'd been punched in the gut.

Finally, he spoke. "What do you want?" he asked in a tight, controlled voice.

"I was just going to get to that," Pen said.

She looked at Galen and asked, "What do you want, Galen?"

At first Galen looked uncertain. Then she looked Patty in the face and said, "I want an apology. Written and verbal."

Patty started to say, "I'll never..." when her mother, who was closest to her chair, reached over and grabbed her arm. Hard. "Shut your mouth!"

"A few other things," Pen said. "I want to see some sensitivity training about LGBTQ+ issues, also about harassment and bullying. For faculty as well as students. And lastly, I want to see Patty enrolled in weekly counseling. With a therapist outside of school." After a short pause she looked at Patty. "Look at me," she said to the girl. "Frankly, I'm not inclined to like you very much, or to feel sorry for you. You're old enough to know better. But you weren't born this filled with hate, and I think there might be a chance for you to leave it behind. I'd like to see you have a chance to be a compassionate and decent human being."

At this, Patty almost lunged at her, but thought better and sat down. No one else moved or spoke. Pen started talking again, still looking at Patty. "It goes without saying that I don't ever want to hear that you have spoken to Galen again. Anywhere. In school or out. Or that you've been anywhere near her. If you see her in a corridor, you turn around and go the other way. Is that clear?" Patty's face was red and anger blazed out of her eyes. Pen repeated herself. "Is that clear?" she asked again. The sound of Patty's labored breathing filled the room. No one spoke while Patty faced down Pen, who never stopped looking at her. Finally, Patty nodded her head. "What?" Pen said. "I didn't hear you."

Again, no one spoke. The Bueller's stared daggers at their daughter and she stared daggers at Pen. This meeting had gone so very differently than they could have ever imagined. Finally, Patty said, "Yes."

Then Pen spoke again. "Since all this is a bit of a shock for you all, I'm going to suggest this: think about it. Here are some of my business cards. Call me by tomorrow night. You, Mr. Dockery, and the Buellers. The terms are not negotiable. If they're not accepted, I will have my attorney proceed with the assault charges. I don't want to put my daughter through that, but make no mistake, I will.

As she gathered her things, Pen added, "Galen will be in school tomorrow, Mr. Dockery. Unless she decides she needs a sick day. At any rate, her record will be changed immediately to reflect the fact that she was blameless in starting the fight and that her one-day suspension was the school's mistake." In answer, the tall, thin, grey man stood up and nodded.

Pen and Galen remained seated until the Buellers stood and left the room. After giving them a head start of a about two minutes, she and Galen left as well. Mr. Dockery followed them out and went to his office. As they crossed the outer office, Sally Crawford looked up from her work. She smiled slightly, then continued typing.

As they left the building, and started down the outdoor stairs, Pen somehow caught her heel and missed the last step. As she slid over the last step, she lost her balance and went down. Momentarily stunned, she sat there as Galen said, "Mom!" and moved to help her up. By then, Pen was already half up, muttering, "Oh my God, oh my God" over and over.

"Are you OK?" Galen asked, standing close to her.

Pen answered by laughing. First just a giggle, then a full-fledged laugh. Galen looked at first stunned, then puzzled. Then she started to laugh.

Anyone nearby would have seen them walking slowly to the car, convulsing now and then with giggles. It was the kind of laughter that occurs at funerals occasionally, forbidden, inappropriate, and unstoppable. A response to tension and too much emotion.

Once in the Highlander, they just sat, letting their breathing come back to normal. The laughing jag was over.

"Mom," Galen said. "That was amazing."

"You mean because of the way I almost stuck the landing?" Pen quipped, putting the car in gear.

"No, I mean the way you were in the meeting. You stood up for me, for us, like the best lawyer I could ever imagine. You dominated." She gave extra weight to this last word. "How did you know all that stuff? Patty's past troubles, that she was Mr. Dockery's niece?"

"Better you don't know, actually," Pen said as she eased the car out of the parking lot. She stopped before she was fully in the road and turned and looked at Galen, who was gazing ahead. "Look at me," she said, and Galen turned to head to face her. "I am so very proud of you. You were so composed. And so brave." They both knew that Pen was referring to Galen's disclosure that she was gay.

Softly, Galen said, "You've been brave, too, Mom." As Pen pondered what her daughter meant, Galen said, "This whole last year. Maybe longer. It hasn't been easy, but you did what you had to do. That was brave."

Pen could feel tears gathering in her eyes. She looked back over at Galen. She sniffed a little and cleared her throat. "Thank you for that," she said. Then she added, "We haven't fought all of our wars yet. Not yours, not mine. But we won the battle today." Then she added, "Small victories."

"Maybe not so small," Galen said in a clear voice. She sounded proud.

Later, after lunch at home, they decided that Galen would take Tuesday off as a 'sick day,' before deciding what to do after that. There were only three weeks left in school. Pen told her that Dr. Avalon, their pediatrician, would probably write her a note documenting mental anguish from the recent events. That would exempt her from going to school. She could keep up with the little work expected at this time of year by doing it at home. Or, she could elect to go back for the remaining time. Having Tuesday off would give her a little time to think before she made the decision about what to do.

After their discussion about school, Pen and Galen sat on the porch eating ham sandwiches. There was a sense of letdown and also of relief. "Do you think they'll call?" Galen asked her mother.

"Oh, they'll call," Pen said. "For sure. Too much to lose otherwise."

And they did, shortly after dinner. Both the Buellers and Mr. Dockery. Same phone call, change in speakers. All agreed to the terms Pen had laid out at school that morning.

And that is that, Pen thought, sitting on the porch with a cup of tea. The words, "*For now,*" popped into her head as she leaned back in the chaise and closed her eyes.

"For now," she said aloud.

Chapter 20: Joe

On Wednesday morning, Finn and Pen were in the back of Berklins, Finn looking at men's shirts, Pen picking up and discarding home goods. She fingered one vase and frame after another, waiting for Joe to arrive at work. Finn had said he usually got there around 9:00 and it was now 9:15. She had wanted to confront him at his home, but Finn had argued that it was too risky. Showing up at his house unannounced might cause a physical altercation. Or he might have a gun. No, better at work, he said. There was still the surprise element, but it was unlikely that he would cause a disruption as he would not want to sully his workplace by having a yelling match there. Pen agreed. And here they were, waiting.

A minute later Finn joined her at the summer wreath section. "He just came in," he said quietly to her. "Let's give him ten minutes to get settled."

And then they were walking toward the corridor at the back of the store. On the right was a door that said, "Staff Break Room" and further back, "Bathrooms." On the left was a short corridor with a room on either side. One had a plaque that said "manager" and under it a slot with a typed slip of paper that read "Joseph Farley." The door was closed.

Pen knocked. Someone said "Come in," in a baritone voice that sounded pleasant.

Joe's eyes widened as soon as he saw Pen. She watched him take in the presence of Finn standing next to her. "What do you want?" he said in a voice distinctly not-so-pleasant.

"Mind if we sit down?" Finn said as he and Pen pulled up two rolling chairs near the front of the desk.

"I do, in fact." Joe said. "This is my workplace. I'd like you to leave. Or I can call security."

"Don't think I'd do that right yet," Pen said as Finn got up and closed the door to the office.

Joe looked like he was gritting his teeth and Pen thought how wise they'd been to confront him here, at work.

Sitting back in his chair, Joe took a deep breath. "What do you want?"

"I want you to stop harassing me," Pen said in a reasonable voice.

"Really? But I'm not harassing you," Joe said, a smug look on his face.

"Oh, but you are," Pen countered. "First with the bird ornament in the flower box and then with the picture in my mailbox."

"Don't know what you're talking about."

"Oh, I think you do," Finn said.

There was momentary silence in the room.

Then Finn continued, "And it needs to stop."

"Can't stop something I'm not doing," Joe said, seeming to be feeling more comfortable now and looking, if possible, even more smug.

Pen took the lead again. "Well, here's the deal. We know you were responsible for both things. But you're lucky; we can't actually prove either charge."

Joe smiled. He was relaxed now. "Then you are just asking me 'pretty please' not to bother you, is that it?"

"Not exactly," Finn said. "We don't have evidence, so we can't use those things as bargaining chips. Or go to the police."

"Well, then," Joe said and shrugged, smiling again. Pen had to grit her teeth to keep from either cursing or throwing the paperweight on his desk at him.

Instead, she said, "We do have a chip, though."

"Do tell."

Pen took some photos from her pocketbook. "Here you go," she said, sliding them over the desk and in front of his computer.

For a second or two, Joe looked puzzled; then wariness took over. "What are these?" he said, knowing full well what they were.

Finn said, "Those are pictures of you and Jane Clary going into your house." When Joe didn't immediately respond, he said, "Last Friday night." And when he still didn't respond, he added, "You do recognize Jane Clary, your assistant manager, right? And it's definitely your house?"

"No business of yours." His smugness was gone.

Pen said, "This, Joe, is our bargaining chip." Her tone was chipper. She was obviously enjoying this.

Just then, someone knocked at the door, and opened it before Joe could say anything. In walked Jane.

Joe quickly stood. "Not now," he said gruffly, as they watched the tone on Jane's face turn to puzzlement. "I'll call you later."

Finn continued where Pen left off. "See, what you do on your time IS your own business. We agree. However, when you do it on company time, with a subordinate, especially a female subordinate, it becomes a business concern."

Joe still did not get it. "But it's not your business!"

"Well," Finn continued, "normally that would be true. But since we need a bargaining chip, now it is."

Pen continued his thought. "We checked the employee handbook that Berklins gives out to new employees." Joe had started to get it. The smugness was gone from his face. "You know the one?" she asked. He didn't acknowledge the question. She went on. "It says that employees who work together are barred from having personal relationships with each other."

Joe was no longer lounging in his chair. He was looking daggers at both of them. Finn added, "And we do have proof that you and Jane are 'having a personal relationship.' Bad, very bad. From a personnel perspective. And a really bad move in light of the 'Me Too' movement." He paused for a second. "You do know what that that is, right?"

Joe crossed his arms and put his chin up. He looked pathetic Pen thought.

But she continued. "If Berklins found out about your affair, you might be in a lot of trouble. Probably lose your job. Jane's husband would definitely not be pleased. It might make the papers, get your name out there." Then she appeared to relent a little. "Well, maybe it wouldn't get out. Berklins would want to contain it, for sure. Who wants that kind of publicity, right? But you would have to go, for sure. And without a reference, well, you know how that goes."

His chin had come down now, the menacing pose gone. He looked sick.

"Only a minute more and we'll be gone," Finn said. "Don't want to take up too much of a busy manager's time."

"But," Pen said, "we would be remiss if we didn't give you all the facts." She smiled at Joe. "One, I know you are what they call a 'smooth talker.' But after the earlier accusation of sexual harassment against you - oh, I know the company found you not guilty - this one would definitely seal your fate. Pretty quickly, I would imagine. Management would see you as a lost cause, someone who just doesn't get it. You've seen how they immediately walk people who are fired out to their cars, right?"

Joe looked diminished. He saw who had the power, and it wasn't him.

"But before we go," Finn said, "There is one more thing that you should worry about." He made an exaggerated sad face. "I should tell you, man to man, so you can thoroughly assess the situation." He paused here and let Joe stew. This was fun. "If anyone ever tipped Jane off to all of the above, she could file a lawsuit."

"Bullshit!" Joe said, roused to action for a minute.

"Oh, not bullshit, at all," Finn continued in a calm, practical voice. "She could say that she was coerced into a relationship with you because you were her manager. That you forced her into it and she had to go along with it because she couldn't afford to lose her job."

When Joe started to say something like, "that's not what happened," Finn continued, "You probably don't have enough money to make a lawsuit against you worthwhile. But if Jane knew enough to do it, she could sue Berklins for putting her in a 'hostile environment' when they should have protected her. Most especially after the earlier accusations."

"She would NEVER do that. She loves me."

"With the right lawyer, the suit could be worth millions to her," Pen said. "That's a lot of money."

Pen and Finn both watched Joe as his thoughts ran around in his mind. He appeared distracted and he was jiggling his left leg under the desk. After a long pause he stopped. "What do you want?" he asked. He didn't appear angry or defensive. He had finally grasped the big ugly picture that could be his future.

As agreed beforehand, Pen answered this question. "I want you to leave me alone. No contact with me, in any form. I don't even want to see your car on my street. Use another route."

Joe nodded.

"And if you break this agreement, we will send all the pictures of your affair, and there are a lot of them, to the management of Berklins. We will also advise Jane of her rights and give her the name of a good lawyer."

No one spoke and for the first time, they were aware of the sounds of store bustle outside the office.

"OK, I agree," Joe said, looking at the wall in back of Pen.

"Look at me and say it," Pen said slowly.

He met her eyes and said, "OK." He paused for a moment and then said, "I agree."

"We'll leave you to your business now, "Finn said. "But just be very clear. If you transgress, we will do what we said. And if anything happened to us, a friend would follow the plan to a T."

They got up to leave, but Joe remained seated.

Finn exited first. At the door, Pen turned and said, "Just one more point. Don't even think of firing Jane. That would really be a disaster. Probably add a big motive for her to start a lawsuit." Before she closed the door behind her, Pen added, "Fiona says good luck!"

After getting into Finn's BMW, they high fived. "Now that was fun," Pen said, sounding surprised.

As Finn pulled out of the parking lot onto 128, he laughed. "Yes, it was," he said.

Later, as Pen sat alone on her screened porch, she tried to relax and let the sound of the sea lull her into a sense of peace. As she thought of the last few days, she was aware of how different she felt. She was finally winning some battles. But more than that, she was standing up for herself, fighting for what she knew was right. It felt good, but strange. In a way, though, she felt like she was reverting to a girl she had known a long, long time ago. A girl on the debate team who fought back with words, and won, a girl who confronted the bullies that were making Vivi's life miserable so long ago. She had missed that girl, and right now, she felt like that girl was back.

There was a question, however, she couldn't get out of her mind. Was the old Pen just visiting or here for good? She'd been gone a long, long time. As Pen watched the waves roll in and break and the colors change as the sun hit the water, she tried to give herself over to a celebration of her recent confrontations and wins against the Buellers and Joe Farley. But she couldn't fully allow herself to revel in her changing luck and changing persona. Right now, she was still living with old habits; instead of euphoria, she was instead waiting for the next shoe to drop.

Chapter 21: Thursday

As soon as she woke up, Pen knew that she needed to talk to Vivi. So much had happened in such a short time; she was feeling guilty that she had not had the time nor the emotional energy to bring her friend up to speed. So today was the day.

As she drank her coffee, she remembered the talk she had had on Tuesday with Galen. Galen had actually sought her out after lunch. "Mom," she had said," can we talk?" They sat on the back porch in the quiet of the day and discussed Galen's options about school. "I want to go back," Galen said. "But then I think about it and I don't want to."

Pen knew she was supposed to be helping Galen with the decision, but she was really at sea here. She didn't know which was the right thing, either. "OK," she said to Galen, "I get that. Let's try to figure it out. Why do you want to go back? Let's do that first."

"That's easy," Galen answered. "My friends are all there. It's near the end of the year. It's too late to go anywhere else right now." Then she was quiet, sipping her Coke for a minute or two. Pen was still. Galen began again. "I don't want to feel like a quitter. Like a loser who just walks away."

"Sometimes walking away is the best solution,"

"Yeah, I know. But I would feel like I was hiding, like I was ashamed to be who I am, afraid to show my face. That feels like being a loser to me. And I don't want to be that."

"OK, I think I see what you mean," Pen said. "Tell me about not wanting to go back."

"Well, everyone will know about the fight by now. And the fact that I'm gay. That will be a big topic of conversation. As well as the fact that I was suspended Monday and I didn't go back today." Pen could see Galen thinking to herself as she spoke. "Worse case, someone might say something really ugly. Or kids would snicker. I know people would be watching my every move."

That sounded dreadful to Pen, but she kept her mouth closed. After a minute, she said, "I think you have to think about the two sets of consequences and which one you can live with: one, feel like a loser, like you are running away or, two, having people look at you and maybe judge you. Two tough choices." The birds chirped as if all was good in their world and Pen and Galen listened to them and to the sounds of the sea below. Belatedly, Pen added, "You know I'll support you whatever you do, right? One hundred percent. "

They sat in stillness for a while longer. Then Galen put down her empty glass and said, "Can I let you know later?"

"For sure," Pen said, getting up to give her daughter a hug before she went inside.

Later in the afternoon, Galen came upstairs to where Pen was working in her study. Pen heard her footsteps on the stairs and steeled herself for whatever choice Galen had made.

"I'm going," Galen announced as soon as she entered the room. "For tomorrow. One day commitment. See how it goes." She looked at her mother to see her reaction.

"Sounds like a wise decision," Pen said, meaning it. "One day at a time."

"Yeah," Galen said, "that's what I thought."

As Galen turned to go downstairs again, Pen posed a question to her. "I know this isn't the best time to ask, but I'm probably going to be seeing Vivi soon. Can I tell her what's going on?" It would be hard, but she would respect her daughter's wishes. It was her life after all.

"Yeah, you can tell her," Galen said. "I trust Aunt Vivi," she added, using the honorary title they had always given her mother's friend.

Pen had spent the better part of the next day hoping for the best, anticipating the worst. Hoping Galen hadn't been met by smallness and hate. She ached for her daughter, her firstborn. Not for the first time, she wished it could have been her at the receiving end of this pain that would continue as long as people were small-minded and intolerant.

Probably forever, she thought with a sinking heart, but maybe not. Maybe it wouldn't be forever. Maybe Galen would find her peace, and her people. Maybe there would be support and grace enough to see her through.

And when Galen came home, Pen found that at least some of this prophecy had come true. She looked tired when she came in and dropped her backpack in the corner. But then she looked up and gave her mother a tiny, rueful smile. "Made it through," she said. Before Pen could ask anything more, the words poured out, "Grace and Nora were great. They were with me whenever they could be and we sat together like we usually do at lunch. Zoe actually joined us." She shook her head as if in disbelief. "Patty Bueller was in the cafeteria, but far away, near the windows. I never saw her anywhere else; it was like she was a ghost. I could feel the kids at school looking at me, like their eyes were laser beams. But I decided it wasn't so bad. No one was actually mean. And I found this." She had handed her mother a piece of paper folded into a tiny package. Pen unfolded it and read, "Head up, Galen. We support you." It was signed, "SOME MISFIT FRIENDS."

"Do you know who it was from?" Pen asked.

"Nope. Doesn't matter. Just means there are some other kids, among the 'regular' kids, who are weird ... you know, different." She looked up and smiled at her mother. "Like me," she added, as she walked toward the kitchen and grabbed a banana.

Pen put down her coffee mug to call Vivi. As she heard the phone ring, she prayed her friend would be there. There was so much to tell her.

On this bright Thursday morning, as she drove down the long driveway towards Vivi's house, Pen was struck, as always, by the incredible landscaping along both sides of the crushed shell driveway and in front of the house. The late spring warmth had brought the blue hydrangeas and coral azaleas out of their winter hibernation and into full bloom. In back of them were low growing bushes with white flowers which Pen could not identify. Vinca, startling now with cerulean blue flowers, filled in the gaps between bushes. Across the front of the house were some pink old growth rhododendrons, the kind that presented themselves all over the Cape in front of huge old mansions. Vivi's house was old, too, but because it had been so lovingly cared for and totally rehabbed, Pen never thought of it as old.

Nearing the house, Pen wondered, not for the first time, about the level of income needed to maintain Vivi's lifestyle. As adults, they had never spoken about money, though there was clearly a discrepancy between what they each possessed. Even when she had been married to Peter, who was a high flyer and a high earner, Pen knew their income had never approached that of Vivi and Georges. As she got out of the car, she thought back to the two poor girls who once had a lot of fun with almost no money.

Vivi greeted her by throwing open the front door as she mounted the wide front steps. "Pen!" she said loudly, as she walked toward her friend, arms outstretched. Pen loved that Vivi was and had always been so demonstrative. It was nice to feel so welcome. Even if she had seen Vivi only the day before, she always got the "so-glad-to-see-you" treatment.

A few minutes later they were ensconced on Vivi's back porch, coffee and croissants in hand. As the fluffy clouds passed rapidly overhead and the waves broke against the rocks below them, Vivi was literally spellbound by the stories Pen was recounting. Pen could see her friend's face darken as she told her about Galen's abuse by Patty Bueller, and Pen knew she was remembering her own abuse by bullies who thought because she was poor, small, and Italian, she was fair prey. How Pen had put a stop to it, literally going face to face with Shirley Whipple after school one day. It had started as a verbal exchange and then gotten physical. Pen still had a small scar on the back of her wrist where she had fallen when Shirley pushed her. Before Pen had all but demolished her, a bully who had never learned to fight properly.

"So, then what happened?" Vivi asked. Pen related how Galen had to leave school and how she wouldn't talk about it. Until finally she did.

"And she told me I could tell you what she said." Vivi leaned forward in her chair.

"Which was?" Vivi asked.

"That she's gay," Pen said without preamble.

Vivi said nothing but the shadow of a puzzled look fleeted across her face. "And she'd never said anything before?"

"No," Pen said quietly. "Too afraid of the consequences, of Peter's reaction. Maybe worried about mine."

"Which was what?" Vivi asked.

"You have to ask?" Pen said, looking straight at her friend.

"Yeah, same as mine," Vivi replied, knowing exactly what her friend's reaction had been.

Then Pen told her about the rest of the story, about the school meeting, about the video. After seeing the video, Vivi abruptly went inside. She came out with a bottle of white Zinfandel and two glasses. "I know it's too early," she said, "but Jesus Christ!"

They spent the better part of two hours talking about Pen's recent adventures with Patty and the Buellers, Mr. Dockery, and finally Joe.

"What a kick ass few days you've had," Vivi proclaimed. "I can hardly believe it. Just like the fighter you always were. Only this time with strategy and words." She raised her glass. "Here's to you, girlfriend."

Later, when Vivi went to get them some pretzels and fruit, Pen went to use the bathroom next to Vivi's studio. As she was about to leave the small room, she looked out the window and saw a truck in the driveway. "Vivi," she yelled as she walked toward the kitchen, "there's a big white truck in your driveway, near the garage!"

"It's ok," Vivi yelled back from the kitchen.

Back on the porch, Pen wondered aloud, "What's up with the truck?" Then in a mock accusingly tone she asked, "You aren't doing another house project are you?" After a slight pause, Vivi said, "No, no more projects for now. The truck was from a new service I'm using. I used to bring my finished pieces into the framers on Main Street."

"Bricksley Gallery?"

"Yeah, them. But it was a drag to take them in, pick out each frame, pick them up, and mail them to the buyers."

"I would have thought you would have had fun with that."

"It was fun, in the beginning, when I began to sell," Vivi said. "But believe it or not, I'm selling a lot more now. Sometimes several pieces a week. Once, four. And I can't be schlepping around with framing and also painting at the same time."

"Makes sense, but where does the truck come in?"

"It's from a framer in Hyannis. He sends a truck whenever I have more than five pieces. I put a note on each, with the frame I want to use, and the buyer's name and address. I leave the works in the garage, he comes and picks them up, then does all the rest."

"That's handy."

"Yeah, he's a lifesaver." She laughed. "And a timesaver, too!"

"Big truck. Seems like a bit of overkill."

"Oh, he works with other artists, too. All over the Cape. Usually picks up works from about seven artists."

"Wow," Pen said again. "What a gig. Probably makes a fortune."

Vivi got up from her Adirondack chair. "He does from me, anyway. But it's worth it. Want to see a few of my recent works?"

Pen stood up, too, and stretched. "You bet," she said, genuinely excited to see what her friend had created. "Then I have to get back to the house and the book. I want to call Galen, too, after school and see how it today went." Seeing her friend's blank look, she added, "It's Thursday. Today and Friday are Peter's days. The girls are with him overnight."

"Oh," Vivi said, stopping short. "That's what I was going to tell you about. I saw Peter uptown on Monday."

"Hardly news."

"Yeah, but he was different."

"Different how?"

"Well, we both know he's always disliked me. What did he say to you once? 'Vivi takes up too much of your time. She's not your family!'"

Pen nodded, remembering how she was not allowed to have close friends when she was married to Peter. How he resented any time or emotion she expended on anyone other than himself. She knew deep down that he even resented the kids.

"Well," Vivi continued, breaking Pen's reverie, "he was actually nice to me."

"What?"

"Yeah, it was weird. He did that charming thing he does to people sometimes. Smiled. Asked how I was doing in a solicitous kind of way. Wondered how my art career was going."

"You mean Peter pulled his 'charming act' on you?" Pen asked incredulously.

"He did," Vivi said. "It was really strange."

Pen just shook her head. "Trust me, there was a reason. Maybe he wants to show you that there are no hard feelings after you helped me out during the divorce. Or he wants something from you. Or he was, for some reason, feeling especially happy and he forgot who he was talking to." Pen laughed.

"Last one sounds about right."

Chapter 22: Breach

Pen got up the next morning and started working on her book right after her first cup of coffee. The urge to linger on the screened porch and watch the waves and sun dance together was tempting, but she knew that giving into that urge so often was why she was behind in her writing schedule. She was just beginning to be able to block out life's aggravations and to immerse herself in her characters. Getting herself up the stairs and into the chair in front of the computer was the next step.

But first, she thought, as she put her cup in the dishwasher, laundry. She knew she had two hampers full and was pretty sure each of the girls had at least one full one as well. Using both hands, she carried a hamper with her white wash down the cellar stairs. She had ugly visions of falling which worked to make her super cautious on the steep stairs. Once again, she cursed herself for not insisting that the washer and dryer be put on the main floor. Hard as she and Finn had tried, though, there was really no room for them there. And the laundry room downstairs was fully functional...so, that was that.

Just as she had started to put the clothes in the washer, there was a horribly loud blaring sound. The alarm system. Something had set it off. As she stood rock still, she pushed the button on the side of the step counter Finn had given her.

What to do? Where to go? She stood rooted to the floor of the laundry room, willing herself to do something. She couldn't move. Her breathing was fast and shallow and she could feel her thinking was muddled.

What if someone was upstairs even now?

Her first thought was to get to the safe spot in her closet, as she had done the first time. But. But. If someone had set off the alarm and just broken in – which could have happened – they would no doubt already be upstairs in the house.

Think! Pen commanded herself, trying to cut through the brain fog of fear. Slowly, she left the laundry room and moved through the family room on this level. She scanned the room quickly: TV, couch, chairs, shelves. No place to hide.

She moved toward the garage, thankful that she had put the glass highlights at the top of the new garage doors; they let in the light, but were too high to look through. At the time, she had justified the extra expense by telling herself they would buy privacy and not let Peter see whether she was home or not if he stopped by.

As she scanned the garage, she remembered an article she had read some time ago in the Boston Globe about a woman who had hidden from her abusive boyfriend in the trunk of her car. When she'd heard him pounding on the front door of her house in the middle of the night, she'd quietly called 911 and headed for the car. Saved her life, evidently, as he was drunk, carrying weapons, and later confessed to a plan to kill her.

Pen moved quickly toward the back of the Highlander. She opened the hatchback and noticed the two folded blankets there. Beach blankets. She quickly pulled them out and opened them. Then she climbed into the small space of the trunk, pulling them in with her. Slowly, she lowered the hatchback from the inside, being careful to avoid a telltale click or thump as it closed. As soon as it was closed, she manipulated the blankets so they covered her completely, making it look like they'd been thrown randomly into the car. Then she took slow, deep breaths to try to calm the panic that was racing around inside of her mind and body. Lying in the small trunk, her body shaking, she knew she was totally vulnerable.

She gave silent thanks that the girls were safe at their father's house. Knowing that the break-in would trigger an alarm at the police station calmed her slightly, but she didn't know how long it would take them to come. She also knew Finn would be on his way once he got the alert. But she couldn't remember how far away he was working today. She wondered how long it would be before Finn arrived, and if it would be his face she'd see once the trunk opened, or another's. *"Please God,"* her mind repeated with every breath. *"Please God."*

She'd never been so scared, not even during the first break in. Then she'd been in a place she felt was secure, and while she had been afraid, she had felt reasonably safe. This time she just felt exposed and vulnerable. It was like waiting for someone to find you in childhood games of hide and seek, only the repercussions were so much greater now. As she curled herself more tightly into the fetal position, she realized the faulty thinking behind the idea of the safe place upstairs. If she were anywhere but near her bedroom, it wouldn't work. To get to it from her upstairs study might even be problematical. *Please God,* she thought. *Please God.*

Then, a sound. Nearby. Pen held her breath and listened. Over the blare of the alarm siren, she heard what she thought might be the door from the garage to the family room open and shut. Loudly. Someone was yelling her name. It took a second to identify the voice, but when she did, relief overwhelmed her. For maybe ten seconds, she couldn't move. Then she pushed herself partially up and opened the trunk from the inside.

Strong arms reached in and helped her out. It was Finn. She fell into him with relief and abandon, the release of fear leaving her shaky. Finn held her tightly, strong arms enveloping her, saying, "It's ok, it's ok, it's ok,' as he rocked back and forth as one would with a child.

Pen made no move to pull away. After the terror of the last half hour, she felt safe. Finn's arms felt strong and she could smell the clean, soap smell of him mixed in with sweat. It wasn't unpleasant.

Finn made no move to let her go. Finally, she could feel his tight grasp around her loosening. She took a half a step back and looked up at his face. Unbidden, tears welled in her eyes and started down her cheeks. "I thought I might die," she whispered.

Pen had expected to see Finn's face looking like steel, as it usually did when something like this happened, when something went wrong for people he cared about. Instead, it held a look of such relief, such caring, that Pen looked away and moved back into his arms. It felt safe. But a different kind of safe. They had never touched like this before.

Finn said, his voice sounding husky, "I thought someone had taken you. After I went in through the open door to the dining room, I checked all the rooms. You weren't there. I thought the worst."

Pen nodded into his chest.

He continued. "I'm so proud of you, Pen. You hit the button to call me and you figured out a really good hiding place where there weren't many." He stood back and looked at her. "You did good, kid," he said, smiling slightly for the first time.

"Thanks," she said in a small voice. Then, anxiously, "Shall we go back inside?"

Upstairs, most everything looked the same. Except that one of the sliders to the porch was broken, the pieces everywhere. "Be careful where you walk," Finn said. "Lots of glass." Using the code, he turned off the alarm system and the loud blaring stopped.

"Praise God," Pen said, rubbing her temples as a headache began.

"The police will be here in a few minutes," he said. "I beat them because I was doing an estimate half a mile away."

"Thank Goodness," she said.

"But I think we shouldn't mention the other break in. There's no way to tell them about it without giving away the hiding place in your closet. And I'm not ready for that to be common knowledge."

"Me, neither."

"While we're waiting for them, do you want me to make some other calls about getting this door replaced? And maybe putting in some other safety features?"

Pen nodded her agreement.

It took the police thirteen minutes to get to the house, faster than Pen would have thought. She stored that knowledge for future use. Two cruisers and three officers arrived with sirens blaring. They went over and over what had happened. Finn made up a story about dropping by to pick up Pen for an early lunch and finding the damaged house and her in the back of the Highlander. It sounded plausible.

The officers had a million questions, many of them about the alarm system. What had triggered it, could they tell? Had it been damaged? Wires cut? Finn explained that he had remodeled the house and subcontracted the alarm system, and that he had a working knowledge of it because his company often installed similar ones. The panel that ran the system was intact inside the front closet. They walked the outside perimeter of the house, looking for any tampering with windows or doors. One of the younger officers, who introduced himself as Jimmy McLean, summarized what they all were thinking. Whoever the intruder was, he just bashed and broken the glass slider in order to get in. "Probably thought no one was home," Jimmy said, and Pen and Finn, who had reason to feel differently, nodded at this.

"Must have been fuckin' surprised when that alarm raised holy hell," another officer said. He must have seen his boss's face, because he immediately said, "Sorry, Ma'am," to Pen.

"Heard worse," she said, smiling.

They were there for forty-five minutes, leaving forms for Pen and Finn to fill out and return to the police station. When they asked about securing the broken slider, Finn said someone would be there that afternoon. Having done all they could, they began to leave.

"Thank you for coming," Pen said.

"It's what we do, Ma'am," he said, and then the men left via the back porch and headed toward their cruisers.

Chapter 23: Contingency Plans

Pen brewed tea for them both while Finn checked in with the foreman he called earlier and who was on his way with materials to secure the back entrance. "He'll be here in thirty minutes," he reported as he ended the call.

Minutes later they sat on the porch. There was something else between them now; something had changed with that hug, but neither was willing to address. "I can't stay here right now," Pen said. "Later, yes. Now, too scary. I'm too freaked out." Finn nodded.

"As soon as I feel calmer, I'll call Vivi and see if I can stay with her for a few days."

Finn continued looking out at the waves as if he hadn't heard her. "I have another suggestion," he said. After a few seconds he added, "Why don't you stay at my house?" Pen looked at him as if he'd lost his mind. "Just for a day or two...until you feel better. It's a safe place, and you don't even need to talk to anyone if you don't want to."

"But I've always stayed at Vivi's when I needed a place to stay," Pen said, realizing as she said it how lame it sounded.

"So, it's the law now?" Finn asked, a half smile on his face.

"No, it's just what I've always done." She shrugged. "I guess I could stay at your house." She sounded uncertain, both of what she wanted to do and what he was asking.

"Look," he said, as if reading her mind. "I have plenty of room, three bedrooms, living room, dining room, kitchen, three baths...and a study. We won't get in each other's way." And then, as if to seal the deal, he added, "And I, too, have a deck overlooking water, only it's a bay, not open sea. Great for tea drinking and reading." He must have been encouraged by what he saw on her face, as he added, "You can bring your laptop or even use my computer to write."

Pen had no adrenaline left, no energy. She was drained. Even making this decision was a lot for her. "Fine," she said. "For a few days." Then she spoke her thoughts aloud. "If I go to Vivi's right now, she will get all fired up. She'll want to know all about what happened and try to figure it out." She paused. "I just can't do it right now."

"Glad that's settled," Finn said, drinking the last of his tea. "Now let's make some decisions before Sam comes. Do you want some form of bulletproof glass in the sliders and any other easily accessible windows in the house? It would mean that no one could break them. But it's very expensive. Think about it. I can make recommendations, but it's your house, your decisions."

"Do we have to talk about it now?" Pen, who almost never whined, heard herself whine.

"Yes. You have to make some decisions right now, so Sam can get the crew in here and started. We may have to special order some stuff as well."

"How long will the whole thing take? The girls will be back on Sunday night from Peter's."

Finn looked thoughtful. "If you want to be gone for the whole process, you'll be out of the house for a minimum of a week." Pen's eyes got larger and Finn noticed. "I can have Sam board up the area today. Even with delays in materials, he could probably replace the slider and do the upgrades within a week."

"But Galen and Aggie come back on Sunday."

"I don't know how you could possibly explain the boarding up without telling them what happened and scaring them to death," Finn said.

"Right. I really can't have them here until the house is fully protected." She put her hands to her face and sighed. She forced herself not to sink back in the chair and relax, to focus. "OK. Go to Vivi's for a week or a short-term rental?"

No one spoke. The only sound was the one made by the waves pounding on the shore in back of the house. "It's June on the Cape. There are no short-term rentals," she said aloud, answering her own question. She sighed, a weary sound. "Plus, the girls would be full of questions. It wouldn't make sense."

Pen rubbed her neck. She could feel the tension gathering there and it ached. "Maybe we can go to Vivi's for a week. We did that for a lot longer when I was getting my divorce. God knows that house is huge, and she just told me the other day that she missed seeing us."

"Assume that will work. Sam will be here any minute. I suggest he put in motion-sensitive perimeter lights around the house, too. Are you ok with that?"

"I'm too tired to think. Whatever Sam and you think is right, do it."

"One more option," Finn said, sounding serious. She looked over at him. "You could just call it a day and move. Not do all these security upgrades. Move to a less isolated house, with closer neighbors. Maybe near town. You'd get a pretty penny for this place, based on the location and land itself, and you'd be able to customize a new house to meet your needs." Before she could answer, he added, "And it would be safer."

At that, Pen sat up and seemed to rally. "This IS MY PLACE! My house, my sanctuary. I bought it myself, with my own money, already had it customized. It's perfect. NO ONE will make me leave." The last sentence came out louder than she had intended.

"Hold on. I just wanted to cover the obvious and that wasn't one of the options we discussed. If you want to stay, then you'll stay. Sam and the team will fix the damage and do some upgrades."

Then they sat on the screen porch and drank tea until Sam's truck pulled in and the restoration work began.

Chapter 24: On the Way

While Finn talked to Sam and walked him around the house planning the work that needed to be done, Pen called Vivi. She didn't know why, but for the first time she could remember, she wasn't entirely truthful with her. She knew that if she told Vivi what had happened, she would get emotional. She'd want to try to figure out who had set off the alarm and why, even though it was a futile task. That was what Vivi did; she barged into war without a thought, even if it wasn't clear who was the enemy. It was endearing, but exhausting. Pen didn't have the energy to deal with her own trauma and then calm Vivi down as well. Plus, she knew Vivi well enough to project that she would insist that Pen come to her house. Now. And Pen couldn't explain to her that Finn's house would be more restful, that his presence would be restful. And that hers would be loving and caring, but not restful. It would all be too hurtful, so she lied.

Pen told Vivi that she was upgrading her alarm system and having some other work done at the house, and that it would be too noisy and busy for her to live and work there. She asked if she and the girls could stay over on Sunday night until Wednesday morning when they went to school. And of course, Vivi agreed. She was happy to have her friend and goddaughters visit, if only for three days.

Pen lay down on the couch in her office upstairs, the beginning of a headache just starting.

She awoke after what seemed like twenty minutes but was actually an hour by the clock on the wall over her computer. Finn was standing before her. "What do you say, sleeping beauty?" he asked. "Time to hit the road."

"I guess," she answered, groggy from her nap. At least her headache was gone.

"Sam is going to board up the window today," Finn said. "He thinks he can bypass that zone on the existing alarm system, so there will still be some protection for now. Not great, but better than nothing."

Pen sat up and nodded.

"Once we get to my house, I think you just need to chill out. Maybe sleep some more."

"Grab some clothes and whatever else you need, and let's go." As soon as he turned away, he turned back. "Have you reached Vivi about staying with her?"

"All set," Pen said, standing near her desk now and gathering her laptop and notes.

A half hour later she was on route 28 following Finn to Cataumet. He wanted her to leave the Highlander in the garage and let him drive. Said she could use his car if she wanted to go out; he would take his truck. But Pen insisted she take her car. She didn't know why. She trusted Finn and she knew he would give her free use of his car. But she wanted her own.

As they made their way down the winding road that took them to Cataumet, Pen hardly noticed the old houses alongside, or the lush vegetation that made this area so green. She didn't drive this route often, but when she did, she often marveled at the old Cape houses, with their flower boxes full of red and white and coral geraniums. Even the new houses, usually in a tasteful beige or grey, were done in a classic but casual style. No glamour or gloss here, just an understated charm that blended with the old growth rhododendrons that bloomed in extraordinary numbers along this stretch of road.

But her mind was not on the scenery. She kept thinking of Galen and Aggie. Last night she called and spoke to them both. The conversation with Aggie was brief and centered around how excited she was about an upcoming art show at school and what she and Galen and Peter would be doing this weekend. Then Galen took her phone to the bedroom she shared with Aggie when they were at Peter's house. "How's it going at school?" Pen asked.

"Weird. Good. I dunno. Kind of a mix."

"OK, what was the weird part?" Pen asked.

"I can feel some kids staring at me, on and off, most days. Like I'm a freak. Not as bad as at the beginning, right after the fight. But still happening."

"I'm sorry, sweetie," Pen had said, hurting for her daughter who had done nothing except be herself. After a pause, she asked, "And the good?"

"Two kids I barely know sat at the table with Grace and Nora and me. It was a little strange, because by now most kids sit at the table they've been at all year. It was kind of like a statement ... of something. Not sure what. Tolerance, acceptance? Maybe they're gay? I don't know. But they were nice. Susie something and Ava Greenwood. We talked about summer stuff after school gets out, and which beaches are best."

"Sounds good."

"Oh, I forgot. Susie told me about a great camp down near Truro. Lots of arts, sports, some theater. Apparently very tolerant of 'different lifestyles.'" Pen knew this was code for acceptance of LGBTQ+ campers. "I'm really interested, mom."

"But Galen, you're already enrolled in Camp Merrimore. For the month of July. It's what you said you wanted."

"Mom, that was then, this is now. But I get that you and dad already paid for Merrimore. I checked online. Camp Merrimore has two-week sessions, so does Camp EverArt. Maybe we can make that work. I already checked their websites, and they each have openings in the two-week programs." Pen didn't have an answer to the implied question.

"We'll see. Get as much of the information as you can online. Then we'll decide."

"Yeah, I'm already working on it."

"Have you talked to your father?"

"Nope."

Finn was exiting to the right now, on a street Pen had never been on before. With no idea about where she was going, she started paying more attention to her surroundings. The street meandered for a while and Penn was aware of large houses on either side, mostly older ones. The ones on the right faced a body of water, a bay, though she didn't know its name.

After about five more minutes, Finn put on his blinker for a right turn and Penn did the same. She followed him and travelled about fifty yards, passing an old farm on the right. The road narrowed and she saw a small bridge in front of them. It had barely enough space for two cars, and Pen imagined that people waited on either side for their turns to cross. There was a sign on each side of the bridge: the one on the left said, "Residents Only" and the one on the right said, "No Trespassing." Finn moved forward and Penn followed. It appeared they were on a peninsula, as she could see water through the gaps between houses on each side of the slightly widened road.

The road was rocky and went uphill. There were a number of old mansions, some in a bit of disrepair, some meticulously maintained, and some of newer construction. The newer homes appeared to be a variety of types, but all of them had been sited so they fit seamlessly on the land. Tall deciduous trees and smaller scrub pine separated them. Green lawns surrounded some and underbrush and pine needles surrounded others. Pen could see the sun winking off a huge number of windows.

Finn drove to the end of the peninsula and parked just before the last house on the street, in front of a free-standing three car garage. She pulled in next to him, then got out. *Well, well,* she said to herself, as she looked at the house next to the garage. It was constructed largely of rounded stones and had both a front porch and a turret. It was not what she had been expecting.

Chapter 25: Sanctuary

As they walked toward the house, Pen was immediately struck by how old it was, but also how new. For the most part, the house and porch were constructed of stones that looked ages old, held together by grey concrete. But the windows across the front looked new, each surrounded by wooden trim of deep red. As they crossed the front porch, she noticed two brown Adirondack chairs. The floor to the front porch was also deep red, the same color as the window trim. Finn pulled his keys out to unlock the front door, which appeared to be a full-sized Hobbit door, rounded on top with a stained-glass cutout a third of the way down. It was pretty amazing.

Turning the lock and pushing the door forward, Finn waved Pen ahead. "Welcome to Sanctuary," he said.

"Sanctuary?" Pen asked, not sure of what else to say.

"Yup, my sanctuary," he said. "Resting place, haven, peaceful place."

Pen nodded. "I can see why."

In front of Pen was a space she could not envisioned from the outside. The first floor appeared to be one large space, not the warren of small rooms she had expected from its exterior appearance. To the right, against the wall in front of them, was a mostly white kitchen, sun flowing into it from the two large sliding doors at its end. Across from it was a comfortable living room, with a taupe L -shaped sofa and several deep brown leather chairs. The rug that defined most of the room was oriental with combined tones of black, brown, beige, white and grey. The walls were a warm shade of white and they matched the floor to ceiling curtains that flanked the wall of windows. Outside the windows, Pen could see the twinkling of the sun on water.

"Wow," she said to Finn. "This is lovely...."

"I guess I'd rather you said "manly," Finn replied, laughing.

"Yeah, that, too."

"Come out here," Finn said, moving ahead to the bank of windows. He unlocked the sliders on the left side of the wall. She followed him out to a huge deck. The first part of the area was enclosed in a screened porch and there was a tasteful dark grey table and chairs on one side with two white Adirondack chairs and a small grey table on the other.

"I mostly live out here," Finn said, moving through the room toward the door on the other side and beckoning her to join him.

"I can see why. It's beautiful and it feels so restful."

"And if you want an unobstructed view, this is the place." Before him was a tan outdoor sofa, flanked by two small teak tables. "I sit out here sometimes, just watching the boats and the sunset."

"When you're not rescuing me," she said ruefully.

"Yeah, that has seriously cut into my sitting-watching-the boats-and - sunsets-time. For sure."

Until he laughed, Pen wasn't exactly sure of whether he was kidding. "Joke, Joke," he said laughing, after catching the uncertainty on her face.

"This is...I don't know...amazing. All of it. So peaceful, well thought out."

"Well, I do houses for a living, remember? Took me a while to find this one and gut it. And now, for the first time in my life, I have a sanctuary..." She knew exactly what he meant. She, too, had finally found her own sanctuary. Only it had been threatened, twice.

"Thanks for sharing it with me," Pen finally said, aware for maybe the first time that she was standing in Finn's personal space, where he lived his life. Before then, he had always just materialized. From somewhere. From outer space, maybe. Or some small cramped cabin. But now she was in his territory.

Just then, Finn pivoted, from his stance on the deck. "I'm a jackass!" he proclaimed.

"Because?"

"Because it is way beyond lunch time and you must be starving. What a bad host I am. Let's go in and get some food into you. Where would you like to eat, madam?" he quipped as they re-entered the house. "Kitchen island, screened porch, dining room?"

It wasn't until then that she noticed the dining room, in the front of the house, on the left as you entered from the main door. She had been so mesmerized by the kitchen and the vistas on the right that she had not even noticed it. It was dominated by a reclaimed wood table that would easily fit twelve and equally long benches, topped by grey and white and brown plaid cushions. "Love the dining room," she said. "But how about eating on the screened porch? Room with a view."

"Good choice. You like pizza, right?"

"Right."

"OK, gourmet pizza, straight from the freezer, coming up. In the meantime, how about a cup of tea and some crackers and cheese?"

"Yes, please," Pen said, suddenly aware of feeling slightly tongue-tied. And hungry. So, so hungry.

Half an hour later, the pizza Finn had brought out to the porch was gone. They had eaten between sentences, feeling the goodness of the cheese and sauce and vegetables as the food hit their empty stomachs. "We must have been starving," Pen observed wryly looking at her empty plate.

"Obviously," Finn said. "I feel better now."

"Me, too," Pen agreed, yawning. "Sorry," she said, covering her mouth and yawning again.

"Think you need a nap."

Pen yawned again. "You're right. I can barely keep my eyes open." All the emotions of the day, from the terror when the alarm went off to the relief when Finn found her, coalesced into a wave of exhaustion.

Gathering up the plates and cups on the tray nearby, Finn said, "C'mon inside. I'm going to do some quotes in my office. You can use the guest room to take a nap if you want."

Pen followed him in, watching him put the tray on the counter and head for the stairs that curved upward at the end of the dining room. "Go ahead," he beckoned her and she was soon on the second floor. She waited for Finn at the top and he turned right, down a hall illuminated mostly by skylights. "Here's your room," he said, pushing open the first door on the right. It opened into a small rectangular room furnished with a queen-sized bed and a dresser. A rocking chair and small table sat near the windows facing the street. A door to a small bathroom presented itself half open at the back of the side wall. Finn crossed the room and pulled down the linen shades. "Now, then," he said, commanding her but with a smile in his voice, "Sleep."

As he was passing her, he stopped and faced her. Leaning in he put his arms around her and pulled her in for a very short hug. Then he released her and stepped back. "Sleep tight, sleeping beauty. See you whenever you wake up. I'll be next door in my office if you need anything."

"Thanks," Pen said, sitting down on the bed while she shook off her canvas deck shoes. She watched the door close as she dropped onto the bed and pulled up the light throw on the bottom until it covered her. The room was pleasantly cool. Her mind was racing with the details of the day and she was unsettled by the surprise hug, but neither of these conditions kept her from falling asleep almost as soon as she was prone.

Chapter 26: Late Afternoon

When she awoke, Pen didn't know where she was at first. Then, as she opened her eyes slightly, she remembered: Finn's house. Sanctuary. As she looked around, she noticed the light had changed; it was definitely later in the day. *How long have I slept?* A quick look at her watch gave her the answer. She guessed she had gone to sleep around 1:00. Now it was 3:00.

Getting up and stretching, she noticed that Finn had brought up her navy duffle bag. It sat in the back corner of the room, next to the door of the bathroom. Her pocketbook sat next to it.

After using the bathroom, she looked in the mirror. Not her best, she thought, but not bad considering the morning she'd had. After brushing her teeth, she applied some lipstick and left the room.

In case Finn was still working in his office, she started quietly down the stairs, intending to sit on the porch and watch the waves until he came down. Partway down the staircase, she heard a voice behind her. "So, you're awake," Finn said.

"I am. Didn't intend to bother you while you were working..."

"No problem. I'm finished for the day."

At the bottom of the stairs, there was a moment of awkwardness. Neither knew what to do. The two hugs had changed something, had taken away some of the bantering ease they had before.

"Would you like to see the rest of the house? Continue the house tour, as it were?"

"Yeah, I'd like that."

"It's not all that big," he said, opening a pocket door on the wall along the dining room and the kitchen.

"I didn't even notice that."

"That was the idea." Once they were through the door, Finn noted, "These are the functional, not artistic, touches." There was an open-shelved pantry on the left of the wide hall, filled with canned good and cereals. Next to this was an extra refrigerator flanked by a large freezer.

"That's impressive," Pen said, taking it all in.

"It's handy, is what it is. And I can close the door and no one has to look at it."

"Nice."

"It works." Then he pointed to another door on the right. "Guest bathroom," he said.

Pen opened the door. Before her was a lovely room, filled with light. The sink, toilet, and vanity were all white and the floor was covered by tiles of turquoise, white, and grey. Turquoise towels hung on the silver towel racks. To her surprise, there was a huge shower on the right side.

"Gotta have a first-floor shower," he said after noticing her expression. "Especially after swimming."

Pen tried hard not to gush. "It's really pretty," she said. Again, that awkwardness.

As they entered the living room, Finn suggested they walk out to the bottom part of his property, where the water lapped on large flat rocks when the tide was full. Now it was low tide, he noted, and they made awesome seats.

Sitting on the rocks, with the late afternoon sun shining on them, Pen felt renewed. Her nap had helped, and the surroundings were peaceful. She knew from hours of sitting on her own screened porch that time spent near the water, watching the ebb and flow of the waves, sometimes worked like meditation. Worries were erased for the moment, and it was easy to just be.

"How is Galen doing?" Finn asked.

"Pretty well, considering." She told him about the end of school weirdness for Galen, but also about the new girls who had joined their table and about the new camp Galen wanted to try.

"She's looking for 'her people,'" Finn said.

"What do you mean?"

"What we all want: people around us who respect us when we are totally ourselves, who affirm us. Who understand us and let us grow.

Everyone wants that." He paused. "But for Galen it's harder. Most kids tend toward mediocrity, the middle ground. But not her. She's ahead of the game. She's being herself; other people be damned. And now she's looking for 'her people,' the ones who will accept her and expect acceptance in return. Real friends."

"I guess," Pen said, musing to herself about what Finn had said and about who 'her people' were. She wasn't sure she knew anymore. They watched the boats go by in companionable silence. She thought about the many people she kept up with, clicking "like" on Facebook pages, keeping in touch by text and email.

And then a memory from third grade arose, clear as a digital replay. She and a girl named Joyce Barkley were engaged in a kind of popularity contest. Four girls were running around during recess asking the kids in her class who they liked more, Joyce or Pen. Pen hadn't worried; she'd known all the kids in the class for a long time, and Joyce had just moved to town. When she was presented with, "Joyce won!" twenty minutes later, she'd been stunned. Maybe that was why she hung onto people who didn't really have a place in her life anymore, people who sometimes didn't even seem to like her. Maybe she clung to the idea that more people in your life, the better; then you'd win the contest.

She thought of Mary Scanlon, once a book club friend. Mary had voiced concern about Pen's divorce since the beginning. "But it will be hard alone, won't it?" she asked. "And Peter's not that bad, really. No worse than Bob." She laughed, referring to her husband, a local surgeon known for his biting wit and wandering eye. And then there were Lucy, Donna, and Barbara, carpool friends from when the kids were small. She still saw them from time to time, almost always after she'd reached out. The phrase, "not my people" ran through her head and startled her. *Truth?*

And along with that new thought was a another one. She and Galen were both engaged in the same quest. They were trying to find out who they were now, and who would support and embrace them. She hadn't seen it that way until Finn had started talking. She mentally named Marta and Vivi as her two real friends, adding Finn as he began to talk.

Then, Finn asked, smiling, "Where were you?"

Pen looked at him, bronzed in the late afternoon sun. His hair was unruly, and it was starting to curl around his ears and his neck. She was brought up short by how lovely he looked. In that moment, Pen decided to be honest. Maybe that was a part of finding your people, being truthful. "Far away," she said. "Far, far away. Pondering."

"Pondering?" Finn raised his eyebrows and looked at her. His eyes were clear and light blue.

Do I dare? she thought. And then she did. "Pondering about what it means to be your friend."

Chapter 27: Beginning the Story

Finn's eyes seemed to darken as he looked into hers. "That's quite a topic you've been pondering."

"Yep," Pen said. "I know."

"Well," Finn said after a minute, "that might require quite a really long story."

"Really?" Pen said, "I thought it might be more straightforward than that." She was surprised by both her boldness and the slight edge in her tone.

"My past, right now, the future...it's all related. There's a massive backstory that connects it all."

"I'm all ears," Pen said, smiling, but not willing to be put off.

Finn responded by looking at his watch. "Here's the problem," he said. "It's almost five o'clock. My story is long, and I want to tell it in one sitting. But if I start now, we're both going to be hungry part way through."

Pen raised her eyebrows in a question. "It's that long?"

"Probably. Let's grab something for dinner now, then there won't be a timetable." Before she could answer, he added," Grilled cheese sandwich or frozen dinner from the Quarterdeck."

"How did you swing that?" Pen asked.

"Whenever I have dinner there — and that's often — I order two and take one home for the freezer. Then when I'm running late or I'm beat, I have a good dinner when I need it most."

"That works for me."

After a minute, he added, "So frozen it is. Chicken picatta, steak tips, or spaghetti and meatballs.?"

Forty-five minutes later they were sitting on the screened porch, eating chicken picatta. Finn poured them wine, Savignon Blanc for him, Moscato for her.

"You actually have Moscato? How is that even possible?"

Finn had a look on his face she couldn't decipher. "I heard you say once that you liked it."

Laughing, Pen said, "So you bought some and stored it at your house on the chance I would be here sometime?" It seemed unlikely...until she looked up at him.

He met her eyes. "Something like that," he said softly.

The air felt different, the light, too. Pen could feel the difference, though she couldn't name it. Maybe Finn felt it, too, because no one spoke for a few minutes. Then Finn asked, "So was it a good idea to eat first?"

"The best. The food was to die for. Thank you."

As Finn gathered up the plates to take inside, he said, "You're welcome." From the kitchen he called, "More wine? Or coffee?"

"Coffee," Pen replied, as she watched the late afternoon light shift on the water and the birds swoop up and down in long arcs.

Five minutes later Finn put the tray down on the small table in front of them and handed Pen her coffee. "Here you are, Madam, Milk, not cream, two sugars." She laughed as he picked up his own steaming cup of black coffee.

For a moment they just enjoyed the sounds of late day, car doors slamming somewhere nearby, kayakers talking as they passed Finn's dock, voices carrying across the water, bird songs, both near and distant, and the waves breaking on the nearby rocks.

"So," Finn said, breaking the silence between them. "I guess I should begin."

To Pen, it didn't sound like something he was anxious to do. But a certain set of his jaw told her he was going to do it. "For starters, I lied to you."

That was not what Pen had been expecting. As she looked at Finn, she raised her eyebrows, as if to say, "What the hell?"

"It wasn't my intention," he said, meeting her eyes without flinching. "But I wasn't ready for the question you asked. And the answer was too long, and too early, to give. So I lied." He paused. He looked

133

vulnerable to Pen, different from his usual self-sufficient and confident self. He continued, "I'm sorry. You deserve the truth."

"Which is?"

"I was married once."

"Not now?"

"No."

"What happened?"

"She died." The words had the ring of honestly and finality. And she could hear that they were hard for Finn to say.

No one spoke. Then Pen broke the silence. "Do you want to talk about it?"

And Finn gave an honest answer. "No, but you need to know what happened, so I will."

Pen could feel Finn's reticence to start, as if it were a door he didn't want to open. He sipped his coffee, cold by now. Then he began. "I know this story so well that I'll probably skip parts or not explain others. Feel free to interrupt me, to ask questions if something isn't clear."

"OK."

Pen wanted to reach over and touch him. His arm, his hand, something. To say, "It's all right. I'm here. It'll be fine." But though she longed to do it, even if just to move closer to him physically, she knew it was the wrong thing to do. He didn't need her closeness, even if she did. He needed to be separate, to be back in his past, to own that part of his life. He needed to be able to tell his story. Closeness would only distract. And they needed to get this out and behind them, if they were even going to be friends. She sat still and listened.

"I met Rachel Santorelli in high school. Noticed her as a freshman, watched her as a sophomore, dated her as a junior, and committed to her as a senior."

"What was she like?"

"She was the smartest person I had ever met. Took advanced classes, aced them, never even broke a sweat. Laughed a lot. God, how she laughed. She had a really big laugh for a little girl, and it often startled people. Made her laugh even more." His mouth curled upward in the very smallest of ways, a tiny smile full of both nostalgia and pain. "She was pretty, of course. But not Barbie doll pretty. Her nose was a little too big, and she hated that her ears stuck out when she had a pony tail. She had dark brown eyes, almost jet black, and brown hair with sun streaks."

"We both knew it. One love, this was it. She went to nursing school on the South Shore; I went to Boston College. We managed to be together most weekends. My buddies used to rib me, tell me I was pussy-whipped, that I should make more time for them. But I didn't care. For me, there was only Rachel."

"We got married four years later, right after we both graduated. I can still see her walking down the aisle on her father's arm, long white gown, dark brown hair flowing over her shoulders, some kind of veil attached to a headpiece with pearls on it. It's like a snapshot in my brain. Her big, hard-nosed Italian father's tears streaming down his face as he handed her off to me at the altar. It was like a movie, only real, everything bigger, brighter than life."

Chapter 28: The Story/Interrupted

Pen had a million questions to ask, but she didn't know what to say.

Before she could sort it out, Finn continued. "It was perfect," he said. "We got a little apartment near the hospital where she had gotten her first job. I was working for my dad then, across town. I couldn't believe this was my life. We spent a lot of time with her family and sometimes mine. Ate lots of spaghetti, drank a lot of wine. Hiked on weekends, hit the beaches into September." He took a deep breath, then let it out. "Life was good."

Quietly, Pen asked, "What happened?"

Finn shook his head slightly, as if to stop the memory from being true. "In late April, Rachel went away for a long weekend with her nursing school buddies. They'd made a pact to do it every year, no matter what. I think there were six of them in the group: Dottie, Sara, Donna, Trudy, Ann, and Rachel. 'The Six Sisters' is what they called themselves." Abruptly, he stood up. "Want more coffee?"

"Sure," Pen said. Once back, they sipped coffee for a minute or two. Pen could feel how hard this was for him. She wished it were over, or even that he would stop. But she knew he would continue.

"The Six Sisters went to New Hampshire, somewhere north of Plymouth. Near Waterville Valley. On Saturday, they went for a hike, climbed some rocky slopes. On one of them, Rachel slipped and bounced straight down a really steep slope, hitting rocks as she went. Broke her left leg in three places and shattered her right elbow.

"Oh, Finn," Pen said.

"The Sisters got her stabilized and she was taken to the nearest hospital, then airlifted to Mass General. She was in a lot of pain. It was unbearable to see, but I visited her every day. It was all I did then, work and visit, work and visit. Eventually she was released, came home. Lots of rehab. Eventually her body healed. She went back to her job at the hospital. But the 'perfect' was gone. Something was different. I thought I was smart, but I guess not because I missed it. Everyone missed it."

"It?"

"The drugs..."

Pen frowned, not understanding.

"Rachel had been really messed up by the fall. Between the leg and the shattered elbow, the pain was unrelenting. The "normal" drugs, like Naproxen or Tramadol didn't touch it. The doctors used a stronger one, oxycodone. With that, she was so much better. She could talk and even laugh sometimes. Oh, the sound of that laugh after so much time. It seemed like a miracle to have her pain controlled while she healed." Silence. "To have her back again."

No one spoke. Finally Pen ventured softly, "She was addicted?"

"Oh, yeah. But no one saw it. She worked hard, loved being a nurse. Life was almost perfect again. Not exactly the same for some reason, but I wasn't splitting hairs. Rachel was healed and we were both still in love. We even started joking about having a baby."

He sipped his coffee, now cool. But then she started calling in sick sometimes, and coming home a little too late from her shifts at work occasionally. I started to panic, accused her of having an affair. She said that was ridiculous. But when she was accused of taking drugs from patients and giving them only half doses, the secret was out. Nothing was proven, and no charges were pressed, but her goose was cooked. They let her go. We spent hours, days and nights, talking. She finally confessed to her addiction. She was so ashamed I thought that alone might kill her.

"I loved her through the whole thing. Her family and I found a great rehab place for her, the best. She came out clean. Didn't last. More rehab. She was ok, then not. We tried another one, in Nevada. We thought the change of scene might make a difference. She was there for three months. Cost a fortune. But that one was different. We all had hope for the first time. It seemed to work. She came back clean, got a job in a local landscape and garden center. Her nursing career was over, but she seemed ok with that. The main thing was that she was clean and sober. She looked healthy, looked great, actually. Felt good, too. "

Pen wanted him to stop, somehow not finish the story that she knew had a horrible ending.

He continued, propelled by a need to finish and to have the story over. He was talking faster now. "We talked in earnest about having a child. She was ready, she said. And Lord knows, I was. By that time, she'd been sober for over a year. She still attended Narcotics Anonymous meeting several times a week, and she was adamant that she would always do that."

Then he stopped, and for a moment Pen thought he was finished, or at least for now. His face in the late afternoon light looked cut out of stone. He did not look at her, but at the water. She wasn't sure whether he would continue, but she sat quietly, ready to hear the end of the tragedy or not, whatever he could manage.

"And then," he said in a voice so low that it sounded unfamiliar, "and then she relapsed. One last time, or at least that's what we think she planned. Her boss found her in a potting shed at the back of the property. She was gone."

"Jesus, Mary, and Joseph," Pen said without meaning to, as Finn's pain flowed over her.

"Yeah, well, I don't think they had much to do with it," Finn said, his voice flat.

Pen had absolutely no idea of what to say that wouldn't sound trite.

They sat watching the light slant into early evening and listening to the water break on the rocks for several minutes. It felt companionable, not awkward, but the very air seemed heavy with the weight of the story just told.

Finally, Finn began speaking. "I buried Rachel in my family's plot. I visited every day. I was a mess. And, of course, I blamed myself for missing the signs. For being complacent."

"But," Pen said.

"I know...wasn't my fault," Finn cut in wearily. "But I was still destroyed. I was literally sick with grief. I was working for my father then, sometimes for people he knew in the trades. I learned to roof, to frame a house, to make fine cabinets. All I did. Work, visit Rachel's grave, sleep. I lost thirty pounds. My dad was pissed off because I didn't want to do cement work much anymore, but he held his tongue because he could see that the learning of new stuff and the hard work was engaging me in a way that nothing else did. And it kept me sane. After a while, I started to feel more normal."

Just then Pen's cell phone rang. She looked at it and said quickly, "I'm sorry, I have to take this. It's Galen."

Finn said, "Of course," and gathered up the coffee cups to take into the kitchen.

Even though the timing couldn't have been worse, she was still glad to hear her daughter's voice. "What's up?"

"I got all the information about Camp EverArt. But they only have two openings left for the second session. And we would need to cancel the second two weeks at Merrimore. And we need to put a deposit to hold the space at EverArt."

"Wait!" Pen said, "Slow down! One by one, please."

Pen heard Galen sigh. "OK, Mom," she said. "There are two openings for the second session of Camp EverArt. They had two cancellations. Susie Garabedian is already enrolled and Zoe is going to try to snag a spot. Anyway, I want to grab the last one asap."

"Sounds good to me."

"Yeah, me, too. But how do I do it? I need a credit card for a deposit. And I'm at Dad's. I don't want to get into the new 'camp thing' with him, you know?"

Pen did know. Explaining the whole thing to Peter sounded like a nightmare of drama and yelling. She thought for a moment. "OK, Galen," she said, "here's what you do. You tell your dad that Merrimore is ok, but it's getting a bit old hat and boring for you. You don't mind two weeks, but four is too much. Tell him that you heard about Camp EverArt at school and it is supposed to have the most amazing art program, with theatre arts, sculpture, painting and pottery.

Tell him that your friends Susie and Zoe are going and that I already said it's fine with me."

"That's ok?" Galen asked.

"You betcha. None of what I said is a lie. It's all true."

Silence. Then, "You're right, Mom!"

Pen could hear the relief in Galen's voice. "But what if he won't pay for it?"

"Our divorce agreement says we split a month of summer camp," Pen said, "so he will. He won't care where you go."

"But what if he won't give me his credit card for a deposit to hold my spot?" Galen didn't sound convinced that the plan would work.

"Worst case, call me," Pen said. "I'll either talk to him or I'll give you my credit card. Either way, you'll be ok."

"OK, Mom, sounds like a plan," Galen said, sounding happier. "I'm going to call tomorrow. When I talked to Ms. Rebello at Camp EverArt today, she said she would pencil in my name in one spot today, provided I called tomorrow with a deposit."

"See, it's almost all set." And then, as if reading Galen's thoughts, Pen added, "I'll call Camp Merrimore and cancel the second two weeks. We haven't put down the whole amount yet, so we won't lose any money. They can just use the larger deposit, the one for four weeks, toward the first two."

Galen didn't immediately respond. "Thanks, Mom," she finally said in a quiet voice. "It really means a lot."

"It was an easy problem to solve."

"No, Mom, that's not what I meant. I meant, thanks for understanding and for...everything."

Pen could feel the emotion in Galen's voice and her own became slightly hoarse. "You're welcome," she said.

Then Finn was back, probably drawn by the sight of Pen putting down her phone. "Everything ok?" he asked.

Pen told him about the camp situation and the problem with telling Peter, getting the open slot, and getting it paid for.

"He won't balk at the cost, will he?"

"No, I don't think so. He's a bastard in so many ways, but limited as he may be, he does love his girls." She smiled a mischievous smile. "Plus, he knows I would go after him in court if he reneged on the agreement. And tell the world in general that he had. He's very proud of what he thinks is his upstanding reputation in the community, Peter is. Wouldn't risk it."

Finn smiled back. The mood felt slightly lighter now; dealing with Galen's problems, serious as they were, seemed easier than dealing with the darkness about which they'd been talking. "Glad to hear that Galen is so involved in finding a place where she'll feel good," he said. "And with finding 'her people' as well."

"Me, too," Pen said. "Me, too."

Chapter 29: The Next Chapter

Finn sat down on the porch couch again. "So," he said, "are you up for the rest of the story, or have you had enough for one day?"

Pen looked over at him and thought she had never seen him look so tired. "Do you want to wait and finish another time? You look exhausted."

His eyes met hers. "No, I'd rather tell you the whole story once, and be done with it." He turned his head from side to side and then massaged his lower neck. "Can you stand to hear more?"

"Sure," she said, bowing to his wishes, not hers.

"During that time, I didn't have friends, really. People reached out, but I didn't want any friends, or ties. I'd go out with a group of guys from work sometimes to grab a pizza, but that was about it."

"No girlfriends?"

He looked at her as if she were mad. "No. None. Over and done with that."

"But I needed a distraction, once I'd learned all I could at work. Took about two years for me to figure it out. I floundered a bit, then decided to be a cop."

"Because?" Pen said, raising her eyebrows slightly with the question.

"I wanted to do something I thought had meaning. My regular life seemed to have none. I think I had a crazy idea of putting the bad guys away. Fight crime. Like in the tv shows."

"And it wasn't like that?"

"Oh, it was. For a while I loved it. It engaged me fully. I didn't need to feel anything. But we lost as many as we won. People suck. They lie. They cheat. I went to too many domestic abuse scenes, saw too many abused kids and drunken brawls."

"Then what?"

"I tried undercover work. I liked the idea that it was dangerous. That it was possible that I might get killed. I probably had an unconscious death wish. Anyway, I didn't look like a cop, and I worked in a different town, in New Jersey, actually, and I was good at it. Did that for three years."

"Why'd you stop?"

"One day I noticed that I felt good. Enjoyed some time with friends I'd met. Liked working out. I decided that I wanted to live. I wasn't as effective in my undercover work. When I started it, I actually did not care if someone stabbed or shot me, but now I did. I lost my edge, started to be too careful. Bad for me, bad for the team. A setup for disaster. So, I resigned. Best for everyone."

"Was that hard?"

"Not so much. It was time; I could feel it. I started doing jobs for some construction companies, using my old skills. Took on some side jobs for family and friends. It turns out I love to build things. More of the same, fast forward, and here I am. Have my own business, more work than I could want, even some good work friends."

"Well," Pen said slowly, "congratulations."

"For?"

"For finding your passion. For finding a way out of the nightmare you were living."

"I didn't find it, really. It just kind of evolved. 'One step in front of another' is my motto."

They looked at each other. Pen could feel Finn making some sort of decision. She wondered if this was the end of the discussion or whether there was more. He hadn't answered her question about what it meant to be his friend, but she was emotionally exhausted and half hoped they were done.

Finally, Finn said, "I can see, and feel, that we're both tired." He smiled ruefully. "Sorry for that." He paused. "But the story's not complete. And you are probably wondering how this relates to you or your earlier question about friendship."

She nodded.

"OK, then. 'In for a penny, in for a pound.' Also, since I seem to be full of aphorisms, 'No time like the present.'" He stood up. "It's getting dark and it feels chilly out here. Let's go in. I'll turn on the gas fire and get out some wine and begin the next chapter...the one that answers your question."

As Finn got up to get the wine, Penn went upstairs to get a sweatshirt. She put on some lipstick and ran her fingers through her hair to fluff it up. "You look like shit," she said softly to the image in the bathroom mirror. Then she turned and joined Finn in the living room.

Now the gas fire was blazing. Finn handed her an incredibly soft plaid throw along with a glass of Moscato over ice. "Make yourself comfortable," he said as he settled on one end of the couch facing the fireplace and she settled on the other. "Or I could say, "Buckle up."

"Rough ride?"

"Could be," Finn said as he watched the flames dance in the fireplace in front of them.

He took a deep breath. "Now for the connection between my story thus far and our friendship. I told you that from the time of Rachel's death, I put up a shield with people. I worked with them and interacted with them when I had to, but I didn't engage with them in any meaningful way."

"Go on."

Finn took a deep breath. "This is hard to say."

Pen was surprised at how unlike his usual cool-and-collected persona Finn was right now.

"From the minute I met you at Vivi's, something changed for me. "

Pen noticed that Finn was watching the flames and seemed to be purposefully not looking at her.

"I don't know what happened. For starters, I felt something. I felt interest and I wanted to get to know you. I was as surprised by it as anybody could have been. I hadn't cared about anyone for such a long time. Hadn't had even a flicker of interest. And it scared the hell out of me. So I hedged my bets, let a kind of friendship develop. I tried to be there for you when you needed help or advice or someone to talk to."

"For which I am eternally grateful," Pen said. "But it was confusing, too."

"Because?"

"Because you seemed to be willing to go above and beyond to look after me, but you never seemed interested in me as anything but a friend. And you never asked anything of me in return." She shrugged. "It kept me kind of off balance, because I couldn't read you or your intentions."

More wine?" Finn asked, offering to refill her glass from the bottle on the coffee table.

"No, thanks," Pen said. In spite of her bone deep weariness, she felt a kind of hyper alertness taking over and she didn't want to blunt that with wine.

"You were right to be puzzled," Finn said. "It didn't make sense. Because I was acting in a way that was not aligned at all with my feelings." He smiled a kind of melancholy smile that made his face look softer in the firelight, then shook his head ruefully. "I was so damn afraid." There was a kind of crackle in the air between them. "Pen, I knew from the first time I saw you, knew on a visceral level that had nothing to do with my brain or logic...." He stopped abruptly.

"Knew?" she said, encouraging him to continue.

"That you were one of 'my people'; that we were related, connected in some sort of ordained way. It was like fact, not debatable. Just there."

Pen was staring off into the fire now, trying to take in Finn's words.

"I couldn't act on it; I was too afraid. Afraid you wouldn't reciprocate. On my end, the feeling was immediate and intense. But that can feel threatening, even creepy, to someone if they're not ready for it. And you weren't; I could tell. Your divorce was barely over. Peter had eroded whatever trust in men you might have had. You would have been wary, and rightfully so. I was afraid if I made even the most benign move, it would have spooked you. You would have closed down...and that would have been that."

"Probably true," Pen said. Then, "So now? What's changed?"

"Having you threatened. Knowing that I could lose you before I'd even had a chance to see if you could care for me." He sipped his wine and the room was quiet. Somewhere the sound of a loon reverberated over a distant pond. "This last thing with the alarm...not finding you in the house, then finding you hiding in the car...put me over the edge."

He downed the last of his wine and put the glass down. "I just can't do it anymore, Pen. Pretend." His voice had a hoarseness she had not heard in it before. He looked at her now, directly into her eyes. "What do you think? With all the cards all on the table?"

In the silence that followed, the loon sang out its plaintive note once again.

Chapter 30: The Answer

When she awoke, she was disoriented at first to find herself in a bed. Someone was lying next to her; she could hear the in and out of his breathing. But before she could panic, she remembered where she was and what had happened. A warmth flooded her face at the memory. Finn had closed the slider door downstairs and taken her upstairs by her hand. She trailed behind him as if pulled by an invisible force.

And then they made love. Not tearing each other's clothes off as twenty-year-olds might do, but gently and insistently, both aware that this was a momentous decision that would change their lives. He touched her hair and her neck and then all of her. She stroked the face that she had unconsciously wanted to touch for months and then she pulled him close and loved him in a way she never could have imagined. Later, they lay together entwinned, breathing slowly now, savoring the closeness. They did not talk. Eventually, they fell asleep.

And now she was awake with the memories pouring into her brain. She regretted nothing. From the light coming into the room from the small rectangular windows above the French doors, she estimated that it was about five in the morning. She relaxed, taking in the sound of the waves hitting the shore and the near sound of Finn's breathing. She fell asleep again.

When she woke later, even before she opened her eyes, she could feel that she was alone in the room. But the smell of coffee wafted up the stairway and into the bedroom, so she slid out of bed and moved toward the guest room that had been hers only the day before.

Part of her wanted to run down the stairs and see what she'd find. *Was last night real? Did it carry into this morning?* The other part of her looked in the mirror: *not until you clean up and look presentable.* She listened to the second voice.

She surveyed the results fifteen minutes later, after having set a record for her fastest shower ever. Her hair was still damp, but she had towel dried it right away and it didn't look too bad.

After putting on cropped jeans and a blue sleeveless top, she surveyed the results in the full-length mirror in back of the door. Not bad, but...different. She might have said she glowed, but that sounded ridiculous. Suddenly, she felt incredibly self-conscious. She wanted to look great today, to greet Finn looking her best. She dug around in her makeup bag for moisturizer with sunscreen and then for makeup. A few minutes later, with the addition of lipstick, eyeliner, and eyebrow pencil, she decided she looked as good as she was going to get. She dabbed on a bit of perfume, brushed her teeth, and headed downstairs.

Finn was standing at the stove in the kitchen when she first saw him. He looked up and his face lit up. "Sleeping beauty," he said as he walked toward her, his arms outstretched.

Pen walked into them, and let herself be enveloped again by the same wonderful feeling of safety and caring she had felt last night. "You smell so good," she said.

"But of course," Finn said, joking, as he walked her into the kitchen. "I got up earlier and showered and changed down here," he said by way of explanation. "I didn't want to wake you. Especially after the long day you had yesterday." His eyes sparkled and he sported a partially suppressed smile. "Hungry?"

"You have no idea," Pen said, watching him start to get food ready. God, she thought, how could anyone look so good without even trying? He hadn't shaved yet, and he was wearing old cutoff jeans and a still older T-shirt, and he still looked good enough to eat. She smiled.

She had worried that the morning might bring awkwardness for either one or the other of them, but she needn't have. As they ate breakfast on the screened in porch, with the dappled sunlight streaming through the lilacs on one side, they might have been a long-married couple. Not much had changed, she thought. She smiled inwardly. Except for the memory of last night and the charge that ran between them even as they sipped their coffees and talked about the day to come.

They easily arrived at a plan. Finn would drive out to inspect two properties that his crew was renovating. Pen would throw herself into her writing for four undisturbed hours. She thought she was finally starting to get into the flow of the plot. And in four hours, she should really be able make a dent in both character development and description. The last time she'd written, the words loosened a bit and for the first time she started to believe that she might have a rough draft finished in time to appease her agent. If she could make some real progress today, it would go a long way in alleviating the gnawing anxiety that had been plaguing her this time around. She'd had several tension headaches in the last week or two and once she'd felt herself on the edge of a panic attack. It would be such a relief to not feel so much pressure.

The plan was to grab lunch locally at noon and to head out to Provincetown for a walk on the beach and a gallery crawl. After an early dinner at Napi's, they'd head back.

"Well," Pen said, "that sounds like a perfect day!"

Instead of quipping "Sure does," or "right you are," Finn looked at her, as if studying her for the first time. "It sounds like the kind of day I've waited half my life for."

Then he came over and pulled her up and into his arms. "We don't need to start the plan right away, do we?" he whispered to her.

"Absolutely not," she whispered back.

Chapter 31: Sunday

They left at 1:00 for Provincetown after a lunch at Seaside Jack's. Unlike her feeling only a day ago, Pen didn't care who saw them together. They talked about Finn's new projects and some old ones and Pen discussed her latest novel. And how her first one had changed her life. She recounted what Peter had told Finn in the bar earlier, only from her perspective this time. The way she had miraculously gotten an agent (the son of an elderly neighbor, who was a hotshot agent in New York) who had sold her first and only foray into adult fiction. How she had signed a contract for an enormous amount of money and published under the pseudonym Katrina Savage. And how she had offered to waive alimony from Peter if he would waive any right to the profits from her writing. Since Peter and his lawyer both believed she 'dabbled' in writing, they saw this as an amazing offer made by a very foolish woman and signed it right away. It was some time after the divorce was final that Peter began to question where she was getting the money to buy and renovate her waterfront home. She never told him, but he had used his connections to do some digging and found out the truth. While everyone knows the saying, "Hell hath no fury like a woman scorned," Pen discovered one of her own. "Hell hath no fury like a proud man who has just been scorned by and then financially screwed by his former wife."

"He was angry?" Finn asked. Remembering the bar scene with Peter, he added, "He was sure angry when I talked to him. Like furious."

"I can laugh now," Pen said, "but he was out of his mind with the whole thing. That he had so misjudged me as a rather financially stupid woman, that he had no idea about my writing success, that I was moving on without him."

"Here's to Peter, your amazing abilities, and the future," Finn said, eyes laughing, holding up his soft drink for his toast and clinking glassed with Pen.

"Hear, hear," Pen said, laughing aloud.

They passed the rest of the day walking Herring Cove Beach and looking at art on Commercial Street. At a gallery near the center of town, Pen fell in love with a large abstract seascape of turquoise, cerulean, and cobalt blues with touches of white, green, and purple. She decided to buy it, telling Finn and the artist it was perfect for the blank wall in her office.

"No, "Finn said."

"What?" Pen asked, puzzled by his tone. By now, she was used to buying what she wanted without asking anyone for permission. And she knew she would never be that subservient person again. She looked at Finn with a frown.

He took her by the arm to a little nook in the back of the gallery. "I want to buy it for you. For us." Then he redeemed himself by saying, "IF that's ok with you, of course."

"Oh," Pen said, clearly unused to being asked if things were all right with her and touched by the gesture.

Finn cut into her thoughts. "If you agree, I'll buy it to commemorate this day. Whenever we look at it, we'll remember...." They both understood the rest of the sentence.

Later, they tucked the large painting in the back of Finn's SUV and took themselves off to Napi's for dinner. The eclectic and brightly colored space was filled with diners and there was a jazz group playing in a small alcove to one side. The smell of freshly baked bread permeated the air. "I could get used to this, "Finn said.

"You better," Pen answered, meaning not only the restaurant and the ambiance. For the second time that day they toasted.

After dinner, they drove to Race Point Beach to watch daylight wane on the waves. It was summer, so they were surrounded by people and families doing the same thing. But it felt to the two of them that they were alone and that they owned the beach. And the future.

Aided by the lack of traffic, the ride home passed more quickly than the ride there. Mostly, they drove in companionable silence, punctuated here and there by conversation. It was eleven o'clock by the time they got to Finn's home and fell into exhausted sleep.

After breakfast and lots of coffee, they agreed to spend the morning reading the Sunday Globe, then work on their separate projects: Finn would check out a site for a new job and Pen would work on her book. After a false start yesterday, when she had to rewrite an entire chapter, things finally started to fall into place. She'd worked feverishly after that until Finn interrupted her at lunchtime. Another four or five hours today might put her within spitting distance of the end. Granted, it would still be a rough draft. But that was correctable; blank paper was not.

At four o'clock, Pen packed her things. She needed to go back to her own house. Peter was dropping the girls off at seven and she wanted to be unpacked and ready for them before they all went to Vivi's. Finn was going to her house as well, in his own car. Dan, his crew master, told him that the work there was progressing well, and he wanted to assess it for himself.

Pen let them in through the garage. The upstairs looked much as it had when she left. Someone had cleaned up the glass on the dining room floor. The slider area was still boarded up, awaiting its new door with safety glass. The other upgrades weren't obvious. "I don't think this will freak Galen and Aggie out too much," she said. "I can tell them something like the seal wasn't right, it was leaking and needed to be replaced. And that some other windows needed replacing as well. I'll say it was too loud and aggravating to have workmen in and out."

Finn nodded. "Sounds reasonable. Seeing Vivi again will probably sweeten the deal as well."

"Yeah," Pen said, smiling, already wondering how much of her recent adventures she'd share with Vivi.

Finn left at five and Pen worked in her office while she waited for Peter to come with Galen and Aggie. She was beginning to feel some of the ease that she'd felt when writing *Two Suitcases and a Cat,* and was happy to feel sentences coming out of her mind fully formed. When she read what she'd written earlier in the day, she exhaled. Except for needing edits here and there, it wasn't bad. She was happy to have a few hours to expand it further and to lose herself in the fictional world she'd created.

As suspected, the girls were not bothered by the work going on at the house, but they were excited by the idea of staying with Vivi for a day or two.

"We haven't seen Vivi in, like forever!" Aggie exclaimed happily, as she walked into her room to get clean clothes for the visit.

"Yeah, Mom," Galen said. "Great plan. I miss her. And I LOVE staying at her house."

Mission accomplished, Pen thought.

Vivi greeted them all with hugs and squeals of delight on the front porch. "It is SO wonderful to see you all, "she said, shooing them into the huge interior of the house." Do you girls want the same rooms you had the last time you stayed with me?"

There was the ring of two loud "Yesses."

"OK, why don't you take your things upstairs and get settled in. I want to talk to your mom for a few minutes. You know, grown up talk?"

Galen and Aggie rolled their eyes good naturedly at the phase "grown up talk" and started up the grand staircase to their right. They were already giggling with the excitement of being back.

"And as for you, Missy," Vivi said in a mock-angry tone. "You come out on the back deck and catch me up. It's been waaaay too long!"

Pen moved her bag and laptop case to the area just inside the door. "Bathroom break first," she said, smiling. "Maybe coffee?"

"On it," Vivi said, moving toward the kitchen. "Meet you on the porch."

As Pen was washing up in the small bathroom to the left of the great room, she glanced out the window and was surprised to see the white truck she'd seen on earlier visits driving away from the house. Vivi must be selling paintings like crazy. She was glad.

Chapter 32: At Vivi's...

Vivi was waiting for her on the deck. They sat on the chairs overlooking the ocean and Pen could feel herself relax. Everything was going well for the first time in what seemed forever. She sipped her wine. "Vivi, what's up with the white truck again?"

"What do you mean?"

"Just saw it go up your driveway," Pen said. "They work even on Sundays?" It seemed strange to Pen, even here on the Cape where it seemed that everyone worked every day in the busy season.

"Yeah," Vivi said, "they work all the time. I gave them the code for my garage, and I lock the door from the house to the garage all the time now. I leave the art and the paperwork on a pickup stand and they come and get it whenever they want, at least once a week. I don't care, as long as the paintings go to their new owners asap, so I get paid."

"Great system. All you have to do, really, is concentrate on painting."

"That's the whole purpose. I'm more productive now, and I don't have to drag myself out of bed to do the parts of the business I hate. I just get to paint." She paused for a moment and they both took in two boats moving from opposite sides of the horizon as well as the huge white and grey clouds hanging over them. A picture-perfect scene. Then Vivi said, "Do you want to see some recent work? Paint's not even dry."

"Nothing would make me happier," Pen jumped up. The next half hour found them in Vivi's studio. Large canvases were stacked against the walls.

"Different," Pen said as she inspected one canvas covered with black with white lines cracking the dark surface in an abstract pattern. Paint strokes of gold and silver were subtle to the point of disappearing, but the more you looked, the more you saw them. It was mesmerizing and unlike anything Pen had ever seen before.

"My new thing. Variations on a theme." She pointed to the other paintings surrounding them. "I love painting them and at the moment, people seem to like buying them."

'Well, congratulations!" Pen said, hugging her friend. "They are astounding." She couldn't help but compare these dark and stunning works to the one filled with sea and sky and color that Finn had bought her earlier. She knew her friend would be surprised if she told her that Finn had bought a painting for her. She might have done so anyway, but she was afraid it would hurt Vivi's feelings, because it wasn't one of hers. And it might lead to discussing other things. She couldn't right now. It was too new and too private.

Then the girls came down and Vivi got them drinks and snacks. They begged for a Monopoly game with Vivi and Pen, but Pen said, "I'm really beat. Raincheck for tomorrow?"

"Even if it's sunny?" Aggie asked, cracking herself up.

"Yes, silly," Pen said, "even if it's sunny tomorrow."

And it was sunny the next day, one of those days that you live for if you live on the Cape. Warm and sunny, white clouds, high seventies. She went with the girls to the beach a short walk from Vivi's and set up a chair and beach umbrella so she'd have shade in which to work when she wasn't watching the girls. What a treat it was, she thought, to see them so happy. Aggie was thrilled to be out of school. She had several friends in the neighborhood to hang with and she was excited to start camp the next Saturday. One of her friends, Maggie, would be going with her. Galen looked, not exactly happy, but more settled, more content. She seemed to be enjoying riding the waves into the beach with a sense of abandon Pen hadn't seen from her in a while. Pen knew she wasn't thrilled with going to Merrimore but was buoyed by the promise of Camp EverArt after that. It had all worked out. For now.

As she watched the girls share their boogie boards with two other girls, she pulled out her cellphone. She needed to call Peter, though she had been putting it off for a while. She still wondered whether he might be the one behind the break-ins at her house, and there was only one way for her to tell. She needed to tell him what had been going on at the house. He had no idea she could read him as well as she could. But she hadn't survived all those years married to him without learning to read his every frown and facial expression. She knew if she did a face-to-face discussion, she would be able to read his micro reactions. Like surprise, or not quite. Or outrage that someone would do that. Or maybe complicity. She was confident that if she studied his reaction to the break-ins and to her being terrorized, she would have her answer. But while she badly wanted closure on the unknown source of her recent misery, she was fearful of the answer she might get.

Peter answered, a surprise. "Hi, P," he said, sounding almost cheerful and using the nickname she hated the most. Some things never change.

"Hi, Peter. I was wondering if we could meet tomorrow night to talk about some things?"

"What things?" he asked, sounding slightly annoyed.

"I'd rather speak face-to-face," she said," if you don't mind."

There was a minute of silence on the phone and she wondered briefly if he had hung up on her. It wouldn't have been the first time. Then, "What time? Where?"

They made arrangements to meet at seven the next night at the Boathouse, a low-key restaurant they had once both loved. Soon, Pen thought. She would know soon.

Chapter 33: Meeting with Peter

Vivi agreed to watch the girls while Pen went to meet with Peter. "It'll be interesting to see what he's like," Vivi said. "Remember I told you when I last saw him that he was actually quite human and polite? I still wonder what's up with that."

"Well," Pen said, gathering up her keys and her purse, "we'll know soon enough. Thanks again for watching the girls."

"Are you kidding? Best offer I've had in a week. The monopoly game is already set up in the dining room."

The air was heavy and the sky overcast as Pen drove toward town and The Boathouse. It looked like it might rain before she got there. Her stomach was unsettled. The thought of telling Peter what had been going on, the ways in which she'd been terrorized, did not appeal to her. In fact, she had to fight the urge to turn the car around and go back to the safety of Vivi's house. But her desire to know if he was the perpetrator was stronger than her need for safety, so she continued.

He was already at a table when she arrived. And, Peter being Peter, it was the booth they used to reserve when they had come here together as husband and wife. She slid into it and stowed her purse next to her. "Hi, Peter. Thanks for coming."

"Yeah," he said, "No problem, but what's this about?" She appraised him quickly, noting to her surprise that he looked good, fit and tan. He appeared to have lost at least fifteen pounds, which also surprised her. He loved his wine and his scotch and had been in the habit of eating out almost every night since they separated. She wondered how he'd managed it.

Before she could answer, he continued talking. "Wine?" he asked. When she nodded, glad for some time to gather her thoughts he said, "What was it you drink? Something sweet, right?"

158

"Moscato," she answered, watching his reaction. He himself drank only expensive red wines and thought anyone drinking a wine like Moscato might as well be drinking drain cleaner.

She watched as he beckoned the waiter and ordered.

Her plan was to begin by talking about the new camp that Galen was going to attend, talking about it in the broadest terms, and explaining how its 'artsy' offerings appealed to Galen. She wished she could have begun by saying, "Let's talk about the fact that Galen is gay," but she wouldn't betray Galen's wishes that way. She made a mental note to talk to her daughter about disclosing the secret to her father sometime this summer. In the meantime, she answered Peter's question with one of her own. "Were you ok with Galen's decision to go to Camp EverArt after two weeks of Merrimore?

"Sure. Why wouldn't I be?"

"No reason. It's a fine camp. I just wanted to check in and make sure you were all right with it. It does cost four hundred dollars more."

"Which we'll split," he reminded her, smiling.

She was running out of things to pad out their small talk, and wasn't sure how to introduce the topic on her mind, her nightmare living at 29 Wild Oak Drive. She made up her mind. *Now.* "Actually, I have something else I want to talk about." She took a deep breath, willing herself to continue.

As she did that, she noticed that Peter looking over toward the entrance to the restaurant. It would be embarrassing but not the end of the world if a mutual friend or former neighbor walked in. She watched as Peter nodded to someone and made a subtle 'come on over' motion with his hand. From her angle on the opposite side of the booth, she couldn't see who it was without craning her neck in a way that would look weird, so she just waited and mentally braced herself for whoever was going to show up.

To her surprise, it was no one she knew. The woman appeared to be about 35, much younger than Peter's 43 years. "Sit down, sit down," Peter encouraged her solicitously, beckoning to the seat next to his in the large booth.

Pen checked her out, as women do with other women, and did not find her wanting. There was a lot to admire across the table. She was thin, very thin, something that Pen had never been. She had dark hair, styled so it sat on her shoulders, and there were very fashionable blond streaks running throughout. A big shock of that bright blond ran across the front and was tucked nonchalantly behind her ears, which were small and close to her head. She was wearing a tight white dress with a deep V neck and small cap sleeves of lace. It looked expensive.

"Hello," the woman said to Pen, reaching out her hand. "I'm Heather Flannery."

Pen extended her hand. "Penelope Elliot," she said. "Nice to meet you."

"I'm a lawyer and I work with Peter," Heather said with a pleasant smile. Peter beckoned the waiter over and ordered a scotch for her.

"And," Peter said, looking back at Pen like the cat that swallowed the canary, "her other title is...." He paused for effect, and Pen considered what he might say. "My fiancé." He looked very pleased with himself.

Pen was glad for the poker face she'd developed while married to him. Her expression remained in neutral while her mind went blank. She'd had no inkling. He'd not given her any hints that he was even dating. Not that she minded. It was just so sudden and she felt blindsided.

As if reading her mind, Heather said. "We met at work, began dating two months ago. And now, we're engaged."

Peter said, "When it's right, it's right. Why wait?" Pen herself was happy and didn't begrudge Peter some happiness, either. He just looked so smug and full of himself that she wanted to vomit. Or tell Heather what a prince she'd be getting. Instead, she said: "Best wishes to you both."

Peter and Heather murmured "Thank you" at almost the same time.

"Have you told Galen and Aggie yet?" Pen asked.

"Not yet," Heather said.

"Heather and I are taking the next two days off from work to spend with them, before they leave for camp. We want to have some bonding time, then we'll tell them, probably on Friday," Peter said.

Pen almost choked at Peter's use of the term "bonding time." He'd had amazingly little of that with his children when he was married to her. She imagined that Heather had brought that phrase to his attention, because he sure hadn't known it before. She tried to keep her emotions in check as she said," I think it's great that you have a plan for telling them and that you'll do it together. But do you think the day before they leave for a month of camp is the best time?"

"What do you mean?" Peter asked, slightly irritated. He clearly didn't know what she was getting at.

"Well," she said, "it will be a lot for them to adjust to, especially since they have no idea that you were even dating. If they have a hard time getting used to it, or for some reason they are upset about it, they won't have anyone to talk to about it. Pretty sure they won't mention it at camp. And they can't process it between themselves, because their sections at camp are separated by age."

Heather looked thoughtful, and for this Pen gave her credit. Peter said, rather brusquely, "They'll be fine. Kids are adaptable. You worry too much is your problem. Always has been."

Instead of saying what she was thinking, which was "you are a fucking asshole," Pen willed herself to be civil and calm. "Well, I think you'll do what's best for the kids." Not that she did think that, but Peter had them for the next two days, and he would do whatever he wanted. There was nothing she could do except "damage control" after the fact. But that was not today's problem.

Heather, who had been quietly sipping her Scotch, finally spoke. "We wanted to meet with you today because we didn't want you to hear the news from the girls. That felt disrespectful. Plus, I wanted you to have a chance to meet me, see what I was like. I'll be Galen and Aggie's stepmother, and I thought you should have a sense of the new person with whom they will be spending days and weekends." This was all very well, even nice, but it was clear from what she'd said that Heather thought that she and Peter had called this meeting. Peter hadn't told her it was a meeting that Pen had requested.

Pen nodded as she replied, "Thank you, Heather. I appreciate your thoughtfulness. And it does make me feel better to have met you." Mentally she gave Heather points for trying to be gracious and do the right thing.

"Do you have any questions, about anything?" Heather said. "While we're all right here?"

"Do you have a wedding date?"

"Not yet," Peter answered. "But probably by the end of summer." "Just a small wedding," Heather added. "Family. A few friends."

"Sounds just right," Pen said.

With that, Peter called the waiter over for the third time and handed him his credit card.

Heather finished the last sip of her drink and Peter downed the last half of his wine. When the waiter came back with the bill, Peter signed it, and said, "Well, we need to go. Lots to do to get ready for tomorrow. And the wedding, of course." He and Heather exchanged smiles, and for the second time that evening, Pen thought she'd puke.

While they slid out of the booth, Pen slid out, too. She offered her hand to Heather. "Thank you for coming" she said. "I'm happy to meet you." Which, if she was honest, was the truth.

She shook Peter's hand as well. "Congratulations."

"Thanks, Pen. I appreciate it."

"Oh," Pen said, "before you go. It's my weekend and I'll take them, of course. But it's also the weekend the girls go to camp. Do you want to follow us up and get them settled, like we usually do?"

"No," Peter said quickly. We'll see them over the next two days. We'll say our goodbyes then. Maybe we'll go on Parents' Day."

"OK, then," Pen said.

She watched them walk out as she slid back into the booth. There was half a glass of her wine left, and she intended to sit here and gather her thoughts. Her mind was whirling. Now she understood why Peter had been so nice to Vivi. He was leaving grudges from a past life behind. As she sipped, she found herself feeling relieved.

Before she started to bemoan the lost opportunity to tell Peter about the recent terror, and to get his reaction, he walked back over to the booth and slipped in across from her.

"Heather's gone home to do some work on a big case," he said by way of introduction. "But I have a question for you."

"OK, shoot."

"Before I get any further into this wedding planning stuff, I have to ask you one last question."

"Fine. Ask away," Pen said after swallowing the last of the wine in her glass.

"Think carefully," he said, looking into her eyes, and she could feel a sense of foreboding she knew all too well.

"I have to ask," Peter began. "Is there any chance, even the slightest chance, that we could get back together? You know, be a couple? Be a family again?"

Pen looked back into his eyes and shook her head almost imperceptibly. "No. No chance. Not now. Not ever." She spoke softly, trying to be kind. But the truth was what it was.

"Well, then," he said abruptly, sliding out of the booth. "I guess I'll go now." After three steps he turned around and spoke. "I think you'll live to regret that decision."

"Glory be to God!" Pen muttered under her breath, as she waved to the waiter and pointed to her glass. She really did need another glass of wine now.

Chapter 34: Wednesday

After the girls had gone to bed, Pen rehashed the night with Vivi.

"So," Vivi said, "just the same old Peter after all."

"Yep. I actually feel sorry for Heather."

"Not your problem," and Pen knew she was right.

Several times Pen almost brought up Finn and what was going on. It felt wrong to withhold such a major change in her life. But she needed to know how much she could share about Finn's background story before she did that. So, she bit her tongue. There would be time soon enough.

Upstairs in one of Vivi's huge guest rooms, Pen settled into a chaise that looked out through a floor-to-ceiling window onto the sea. She called Finn. It rang for what seemed a few minutes, then, to her relief, he picked up. She could hear in his voice that he was glad to hear from her. "I didn't want to intrude on you and the girls or horn in on Vivi's time with you," he said, explaining why he hadn't called earlier. "Some good news here."

"Do tell."

"Your house renovations are almost done. Should be ready late Friday."

"That is good news. I've missed having my own space." She realized at once how ungrateful she sounded and added, "Though I loved sharing yours."

"I know. No offense taken. No place like home, and that's a fact."

"Thanks for rushing the renovation job."

"And how do you know that I did?" he asked, and she could hear the smile in his voice.

"I just know it."

"You're welcome. What's your schedule like the next three days?"

"Tomorrow I'll drop off the girls and then spend some time with Vivi. Thought we'd do some shopping and hang out. Then on Thursday, she wants to check out some galleries on Martha's Vineyard and I agreed to go with her. Friday, in the late afternoon, Peter will drop off Galen and Aggie and I'll get one last night with them before they leave for camp. They'll be laundry to do and lots of packing to get done for the morning, so it'll be a busy time." She sighed. "I wish camp weren't right now. I'd like some time with them to hang out and see movies and swim."

"After camp you'll have the rest of the summer."

"I guess."

Finn could read her mood. "You'll have Friday evening and the ride to camp on Saturday with them. And some sort of Parents' Day can't be too far away."

"Yeah, you're right. As usual. But with Peter getting married, they might be feeling upset or abandoned."

"Say WHAT?"

She soon recounted the evening she'd just spent with Peter and Heather. Finn was quiet, then said when she was finished, "Boy, he sure has impeccable timing, huh? Nothing like springing it on the kids."

"Yeah, that's what I thought. But I'll have some time to talk with them before camp. See if I can tell whether they're ok or not. Who knows? They might be fine."

"Probably will be. But I, on the other hand, will not be fine unless I see you fairly soon."

"I miss you, too," Pen said softly.

"Shall I meet you at your house late Saturday afternoon, once you get back from camp? I could bring some steaks and wine and the stuff for salad and we could grill and eat on the porch and watch the sunset."

"Been there, done that...loved it." She could almost see Finn smiling on the other end.

"OK, plan in place," Finn said, sounding happier than when the conversation had started. "Enjoy the girls and Vivi. And don't fret. Everything'll be ok."

That was her final thought as she dropped into sleep.

After breakfast, the girls packed and they all headed off to Peter's.

Vivi came with them, as she and Pen were going to go clothes shopping several towns over after the drop off.

As they pulled into the driveway to Peter's townhouse, Vivi said, "Wow, check out the geraniums!" She gestured toward the truly massive coral geraniums surrounded by variegated ivy in two large grey urns on either side of the brick walkway leading to the front door.

"Yeah," Pen said. *Heather's obviously supplying the homey touches now.*

"Looks nice," Aggie said, and Pen agreed. "Yes, it does."

"I like ours better," Galen said, getting out of the car, her preference for all things Pen apparent.

At the top of the stairs, she hugged the girls and told them that she'd see them on Friday and reminded them to make sure that they checked the camp list online for anything they might be missing."

"I can pick up anything extra you need."

"Mom!" both girls said together.

Galen added, "We already did this with you. We're all set. Relax." They hugged again.

"Call or text if you need me," she said, just as the door opened and Peter appeared.

"Thanks for the drop off," Peter said.

"No problem," she said, turning away and starting down the stairs to the car. Her eyes were filling and she didn't want any of them to see that. She would miss them. But she also knew what they didn't; their lives were about to change in a very real way, and right now, they had absolutely no idea. Though she had no recourse, she felt like a criminal for leaving them like this, clueless. No, not a criminal. Just a very, very bad mother. Part of her knew there had been nothing she could have done to make it easier. But as she walked down the steps toward the car, she noted, not for the first time, that emotion was no respecter of logic.

Chapter 35: Time with Vivi

Pen was glad she had Vivi with her and happy to be distracted by shopping. There were only a few shops on the Cape where Vivi would buy her clothes, and Pen loved going to them with her. They were what she would call "high end," and on her own she would have been too intimidated to shop in them. But being with Vivi made all things possible. Since Vivi had no problem dropping hundreds of dollars if she liked an item, salespeople tended to fawn over her and to make them both feel comfortable. Within two hours, Vivi had bought taupe palazzo pants and a multicolored tunic of red, orange, and taupe silk to wear with them.

Pen had been served two cups of coffee in her role as fashion consultant and was finishing up the second one as Vivi paid for her purchases.

"Now what?" Pen asked as they got into Vivi's cream colored Audi.

"Are you up for more shopping?" Vivi asked. "We can stop now if you want."

"Your wish is my command," Pen said and soon found herself singing to sixties music along with Vivi as they zoomed off to the Purple Hen in Chatham. It had been a while since she had had a full day with Vivi and she noticed now how much she had missed her company. Vivi found four more items that met with her approval by the time shopping was completed, and they moved on to lunch. Sipping iced tea on the patio of the Sand Castle Inn, Pen felt a contentment that had eluded her for months. For the first time in a long time, her shoulders didn't ache.

They spent the afternoon at Vivi's. Vivi painted and Pen concentrated on her book. Jessie, her agent, had called her on the way back to Vivi's and prodded her to finish the book within the next three weeks. "It needs to be at the publisher. I know you can do it, kiddo."

The words had literally made Pen's stomach flip. True, she had been on a roll for a little while now. But she was nowhere near done. And she was only on the first draft. Even if she stayed in the kind of writer's zone she was in now, it seemed almost impossible for the book to be in condition to submit in three weeks. She would have to commit more time, that was all. And work harder. But at least she had the feeling, which she hadn't had at the beginning, that it was doable. She was anxious, but not panic stricken. The next four hours flew by as she immersed herself in the world she was creating.

As they sat on the deck after a dinner of frozen pizza and wine, Pen thought about bringing up Finn. She thought she could do it without mentioning his personal history. But even as she tried, she couldn't make herself do it. Her relationship with Finn felt too real to subject to the scrutiny they had always imposed on new beaus. She didn't want to hear any negatives. Besides, she thought, finishing up her first glass of wine, something was up with Vivi. She didn't know what it was, but there was something bothering her. In the past, before Georges, this had indicated a new love interest, so Pen decided to let her own romance story stay a secret and to focus on Vivi's possible involvement with someone.

Vivi," she said, when her friend came back to the porch from the kitchen, "what's going on?"

Blunt had always been better with Vivi.

Vivi looked at her strangely. "What do you mean?"

"Feels like something's going on with you." There was a pause. Silence.

Pen broke it with her next question. "Is there a new man in your life?"

"Why would you think that?"

"It's me, Vivi, remember? I've known you forever. You seem a little preoccupied, not much, just a little. And that means...usually...a new man."

"Yeah, there is someone. I'm surprised you could sense it, but you were always good at that."

"Do you want to tell me about him?" Pen asked, watching the greyish cloud scud across the sky over the ocean in front of them.

"Not really," Vivi said, startling Pen. This was unlike her friend, who loved to dish about any and all relationships.

"Because?"

"Guess," Vivi said.

Pen thought for a moment. "He's married?"

"Bingo."

"Oh, Vivi," Pen said, trying not to be judgmental, but wanting more for her friend.

"I know, I know," Vivi said, sounding weary. "Can we drop the subject?"

"Sure," Pen said, both surprised and slightly uneasy that they both had secrets from another. She wondered what this meant for their friendship, but then gave it up. Time would tell.

They spent the next day on Martha's Vineyard, at the galleries Vivi was checking out. She loved to look at the competition, she said, see what was selling and for how much. And she was always scoping out new places that might take her on as an artist. Walking around the Vineyard was like reliving the past. They had come here so many times over the years, when they were younger and carefree and poor. They had felt the same breezes and seen the same streets. Even the ferry ride over had been an exercise in nostalgia, where they traded tales of other days like this one and gossiped about the people they'd known then.

Neither seemed to want the day to end, so they took the last ferry back. It seemed like the old days, and it felt good to Pen. She made a decision not to worry about Vivi. Whatever was going on, Vivi was a strong woman, and she always ended up on her feet.

They went their separate ways in the morning. Vivi had appointments with her primary care physician for her yearly physical and with her accountant to discuss the tax consequences of some recent sales. Pen was grateful for the free time and hunkered down. She'd made real progress the other day, and while she knew she'd have to seriously revise her first draft, she could feel the story flowing from her imagination to the paper. Once she'd accepted that the first draft would be very rough one, something had shifted. She'd let go of her need to have it be great and settled for "done." The words seemed to come easier now and she let her innate sense of pacing and character take over. Revising she could do. Could work a few days straight if needs be. Could probably even beg another week or two from Jessie for the revision. But the creative part, the actual spinning of words into a world, had to happen now. With expectations lifted, Pen was finding the joy in writing again. After she downed a glass of water, she reread the last page she'd written and began typing again. After three hours of work, she felt like she was on track. Making progress. Getting up only to use the bathroom and to eat a banana, she kept at it for another hour. She hardly noticed when the tide turned or the light changed until she typed the last word of the first draft. Then she massaged her neck and shoulders.

"Done. Rough, but done." She savored the sounds she had spoken out loud and smiled. Life was good. It would get hard again very soon as she began to beat the first draft into submission, but the arc, the story, and the characters were alive now. Life was very good, indeed.

Chapter 36: Camp and After Camp

Pen heard the front door open and the sounds of talking; then she heard bags drop with a thud. The next thing she knew the girls were hugging her in the kitchen.

"We're back." Galen said.

"And glad of it." Pen said back, smiling at her daughters. "You both need to pack for camp really soon, but let's sit on the porch and you can fill me in on your weekend." She was wondering how the wedding announcement went over, but she didn't want to ask specifically, in case Peter and Heather had not told them. "I missed you."

A minute later, with sodas in hand, they marched to the porch. "Did you have a good time at your dad's?"

"Yeah," Aggie answered. "Better than usual."

"Really? Why?"

"Well, for starters, "Galen said, "he hardly yelled at all. It was a little weird."

"Weird?"

"Like he looked the same, but he acted really different."

"Why do you think that was? Do you have a clue?"

"Might have been because of Heather," Aggie said.

"Heather?" Pen asked, knowing who she was, but wanting to hear what the girls said.

"Yeah," Aggie continued, "she's the lady that dad is dating."

"Oh, really?" Pen asked, not happy to be so disingenuous, but also not wanting the girls to know she knew about Heather.

Galen said, "Her name is Heather Flannery and she's a lawyer. She's pretty nice, actually."

Aggie added, "And dad is like a different person with her around. No yelling. Plus he took us all out to dinner and to the beach the next day. He NEVER goes to the beach."

"So, it was a good visit?"

"Yeah," the girls said together.

"Oh," Galen added nonchalantly, "I think they're going to get married."

"What makes you think that?" Pen asked, trying to sound surprised. This acting gig was killing her.

"Because they told us." Aggie said, sounded excited. "At dinner, the first night."

And before Pen could ask how they felt about that, Galen said, sounding serious, "Probably a good thing. He sure was nicer to us with her there. Plus, she seemed pretty nice herself. Even boogie boarded with us on Friday at First Beach."

"That was fun" Aggie added.

And just like that, Pen's worries about the girls being upset by the impending marriage of their father dissipated. It seemed they viewed it as a good thing, bringing them both a nicer father and a woman who wanted to spend time with them. *Who would've thought?* she wondered as she shooed the girls into their rooms to pack their bags for the next morning's trip to Camp Merrimore.

They were on the road the next morning at nine. By 12:30 they were at Camp Merrimore having lunch and getting Galen and Aggie set up in their bunks. Both ended up in cabins with two campers they knew, so when she left at 2:00, she was leaving two very happy girls.

"Bye, Mom, see ya," Aggie said after a brief hug. Then she and a girl named Sara went back into the cabin, chatting excitedly.

Ten minutes later, Galen hugged Pen tight. "Bye, Mom," she said. "I know I'll be happy here, so don't worry. See you in two weeks," she added. They looked each other in the eye. "Love you," Galen said.

"Love you, too, sweetie." Pen could feel a big wave of sadness attempting to overwhelm her, so she said, "Go hang out with your cabin mates. I know the way back to the parking lot by now."

Halfway down the long slope to the parking lot she turned once and saw Galen watching her. Pen waved and Galen waved back. Then she found her car and headed south toward Cape Cod again. For the first five miles she felt a heaviness born of knowing that the girls were gone for weeks. But then she put on the radio, and after another fifteen minutes she started to feel better.

It was five thirty when she pulled into her driveway, totally beat. She had forgotten what a long ride it was to the Berkshires. Though she had been there many times, this was only her second time alone, and it seemed much longer than she remembered.

Pulling up to the garage, Pen was heartened to see Finn's car there. She had just gotten out of her car when he appeared.

"I've been listening for your car," he said. He held out his hand, which she took, and they went up the back stairs to the deck.

"It's really, really good to be home," she said, as she hung her purse on a dining room chair. "Lotta driving."

"Yep, but you got the girls where they had to be and where they'll be happy for the next few weeks. Now you get to relax." After a bit he added, "How about some wine and cheese and crackers on the porch? I brought the promised steaks, and I've already got the baked potatoes cooking and a salad made."

"Oh, Sweet Lord," Pen said a minute later, sinking into the chaise on the screened in porch. She was sipping some wine and had already devoured three crackers with cheese. "This is heaven! I feel better already."

"Shall I start the steaks now," Finn asked, "or do you want to wait a while."

"Let's wait awhile," she said. "I just want to sit and enjoy the view and the wine." After a moment she added, "And talking to you, of course."

Finn filled her in on the three local projects he was doing and their respective problems. With one, the owner had changed his mind three times. New plans and new materials each time. "And he has to pay for all of it."

"Must be nice to have that much money."

"Foolish, is what it is. I wouldn't have signed on if I had known he was so undecided about his plans. Wrecked the schedule. But that's the

173

nature of the business. Crazy home owners with more money than brains. Materials unavailable in the sizes you need. Workmen who sometimes quit." He sighed. "But it's what I do. And mostly, I love it."

"Yeah, I get it. I get stressed by deadlines, and sometimes I get stuck, but I love to write. To make up people and situations and to weave them together into a world. Nothing better."

"We're lucky to have found our passions," Finn said, finishing off one of the beers he'd brought.

"And the people we're passionate about," Pen added, looking over at him.

"That's the one I'd toast to," Finn said, smiling.

"And we will," Pen said, eyes twinkling as she smiled over at him.

Pen told him about finishing her book "Hear! Hear!" Finn said, and she said, "I'm starving." Then added, "My stomach is growling, too."

"Yeah, I was going to talk to you about that." Then he got up. "You've done your work for the day with the driving. Now I'll do mine with the cooking. How do you want your steak?"

When Pen said, "Medium rare, please," he headed off to the kitchen saying, "Coming up" as he exited.

Pen reveled in just sitting there, watching the waves, the light starting to slant toward evening. It seemed like a long time since she'd been able to sit on her own deck and enjoy the silence overlaid by birdsongs. It was like a balm to her spirit. Ever since the last break-in, she'd been hypervigilant, never really relaxing. It was exhausting. But now, with the modifications to her house made, and Finn nearby, she felt safe for the first time in a very long time. She closed her eyes for a moment.

And then, "Pen, Pen," a nearby voice said. She opened her eyes lazily. "Dinner's ready," the voice said, and she recognized it was Finn and slowly sat up.

She noticed that the light had changed significantly and that it was in full tilt toward evening.

"How long did I sleep?"

"Doesn't matter. We're not on a schedule. You seemed beat, and I didn't want to wake you. I turned the potatoes to low a while ago, and I just started the steaks. I would have let you sleep longer, but I was afraid if you slept too much, you'd have trouble sleeping tonight."

"Too true," Pen said, rubbing her eyes. "But what time is it?"

"Eight o'clock."

"Eight o'clock!" Pen all but shrieked. "You must be almost starved to death by now, poor thing." She couldn't believe he'd let her sleep so long.

"Relax!" he said with a laugh. "I've been fortified with beer and crackers and cheese. Let me flip the steaks, and we'll be ready to eat in ten minutes."

As they sat in the dining room and looked out at the ocean, Pen thought she'd never enjoyed a meal more. Thank you," she said. "This is manna from the Gods." Then she added, "Just what this tired body needed."

"You're welcome," Finn said quietly between bites. "It's about time someone looked out for your wellbeing."

"Are you volunteering?" Pen asked, wondering when she started to speak without evaluating every word.

"I most certainly am," he said, leaning over and kissing her gently on the cheek.

Pen stopped eating for a moment as she felt her throat close. It had been so long, so long, since anyone had cared for her like this. No, she amended her thought, it had taken a lifetime for this to happen. No one had ever loved her this much.

Chapter 37: Night

After dinner, they sat on the porch. "Oh," Pen said, "I forgot to tell you about the ending to my visit with Peter." She proceeded to tell him about Peter's coming back in after Heather had gone and his question about whether they could ever be a couple, and a family, again.

"And you said what?" Finn asked. When Pen looked at him oddly, he added, "Just wondering how you worded your answer. I think I know what it was."

"No. I just quietly said 'no'. I didn't get histrionic, didn't raise my voice, or go over the many ways I might kill myself if I had to get back with him. Just a simple 'no'." She paused. "I did add, 'not ever.'"

"And he accepted that?" Finn asked.

"Well, "she said, "he kind of had to. I mean, it's hard to argue with 'no.' But he didn't take it well."

"Meaning?"

"When he left, he turned and said 'I think you'll live to regret that decision.'"

Finn didn't immediately respond. Then he said, "That sounds like a threat, don't you think?"

Pen sighed. "It does. I wish I could have asked him about the break-ins and if he was involved. I know I could have read his reaction, and then I would have known." She laughed. "He fancies himself such a player and negotiator. And yet, if you know him well, his tells are so obvious. At least to me."

"Do you think you should try again? To tell him what's been going on and watch his reactions?

"I do, but I don't look forward to it." She paused. "But I have to know. I can't imagine who it could be if not him. I don't have enemies, at least none I know of."

"I agree. Maybe next week you need to set up another meeting, but specify that you want to see him alone."

"Well, that will certainly feed his fantasies."

"All the better. He will definitely meet with you then. Make it a public place. I can be outside in my car, if that will make you feel better."

"Yeah, that would make me feel better about seeing him at all."

They were quiet for a moment or two, then Finn said, "Speaking of feeling safe...how do you feel right now? Here, in the house?"

"Right now, I feel fine." She ticked off all the safety features that had been added to the house: "all the easily accessible windows and glass doors have been replaced with unbreakable glass, the locks are changed, the motion detector lights are set up. So yes, now that I think about it, I do feel safe. Plus," she added, waving her wrist in the air, "I always have on my step counter." She smiled at Finn and felt her shoulders relax even more. "And, of course, I have you here, my own personal bodyguard."

"There is that," Finn said and smiled broadly back at her.

She was just thinking how incredibly handsome he looked in the waning light, with his tan skin glowing against his white shirt and his blue eyes still reflecting the light, when he said, "Time for bed?"

Pen thought she might have blushed, because she could feel her face get warm all at once. She met his eyes and nodded at him as he took her hand.

He opened the door from the porch to the house and beckoned her in. She could hear him locking the door.

Before they made love, they showered together, something Pen had never done with anyone. It felt intimate in a completely different way to be soaping up Finn's muscular body and to let him wash her body as well. Pen thought it might have been the most exquisite foreplay she could have imagined, and she was ready to love him once they had rinsed and toweled off and tumbled into bed. She didn't care that she had no makeup on and that her hair was still tangled and wet. Nothing mattered except loving Finn.

Later, they feel asleep in each other's arms, sated, contented, happy. Once when she woke groggily for a second, she wondered idly if life could really be this perfect. Then, without waiting for an answer, she fell asleep again.

Finn sat up in bed a split second before the alarm went off. Pen woke to the horribly loud sound of the alarm. Finn was already bounding out of the bed, yelling to her to get up. "Pen," he yelled, "Get up! Get out!"

It was only then that she noticed the flames on the porch outside her bedroom, reaching upward and spreading.

"Where's the fire extinguisher?" he yelled above the screeching alarm as he pulled on shorts.

"Bedroom closet and kitchen closet!" she hollered back, grabbing the robe at the end of the bed and moving toward the bedroom closet as he ran toward the kitchen.

In a very short time, Finn was back. He showed her how to activate the extinguisher and then he opened the door to the screened porch. The flames were higher now and had moved over to the deck as well. Pen followed his lead and sprayed the fire closest to the house, hoping to beat it back before it could attack the house proper. It worked for a bit, she noted, but the fire was eating the dry wood of the porch, devouring it ravenously. She could vaguely hear the licking of flames from another direction but didn't stop working on the porch.

"That's it!" Finn shouted at the top of his lungs. "We need to get out!"

At the same time, she heard the unmistakable sound of sirens over the screeching alarm, and she dropped her extinguisher.

Finn took her hand and pulled her toward the front of the house. He went to pull open the front door, then inexplicably stopped. Putting his hand tentatively flat on the front door, he recoiled. It was then Pen realized that she could hear the sound of racing flames from this side of the house as well. Finn pulled her away from the door. "Not this way out," he yelled and moved her away from the hall.

For one second, Pen felt complete and total panic. The two back doors were blocked by flames, and now the front door was as well. The windows at the side of the dining room didn't open and they had unbreakable glass in them. She could barely breathe or move.

Finn pulled her after him, but she had no thought as to where he was going. She had lost the rational part of her brain and would have stood still had Finn not been pulling her. Now they were near the door to the cellar. With her mind a blank, Pen watched Finn put his hand on it, then pull it open. He pulled her behind him down the stairs.

Through the small cellar windows, she could see red and orange and yellow. The next thing she knew, they were downstairs in the cellar, and Finn was moving them toward the garage. Again, he tested the door, then opened it. As they stood at the far end of the garage, she felt tendrils of fear run through her body as she realized they might well be trapped here. If the wiring had been affected, the garage doors wouldn't open. They would be stuck in a burning house.

Idly, with no emotion, Pen watched Finn push the button to open the garage doors. Nothing. Pen didn't react. She knew they were going to die. Here. In the house she loved.

Before Pen had any idea what he was doing, Finn moved quickly away from her and toward the front of the garage. She could barely see him as he got to the middle of the large door, bent down, and reached upward. "Pen," he shouted. "Here!" She followed his dark outline and voice.

A second later, Finn opened the garage door manually and they raced through it to fresh air.

There were three fire trucks outside, and firemen running everywhere. Water was being pumped from the trucks to a myriad of hoses manned by yellow-clad men in helmets and boots. It was if she had landed on another planet. Or in the worst nightmare of her life.

She was aware that Finn had not left her side. That he was moving her away from the house toward a bench in the front garden. She couldn't remember walking, but now she was sitting there, with a blanket wrapped around her. Someone was handing her a bottle of water and urging her to drink. She took a large drink from the bottle and a minute later vomited it up. She was hot, burning up. But then she was shivering, too, and she wrapped the blanket around her more tightly. After a minute or two, she noticed that her breathing was rapid and that her heart was beating out of her chest. Without being worried, she wondered if she might be having a heart attack. But she wondered from a vast distance away, and she didn't really care.

Chapter 38: Aftermath

When she woke, Pen didn't know where she was at first. She was in a bed and there was light coming into the room; she could tell that even with her eyes closed. Languidly she opened them. Vivi's house. Her room in Vivi's house. She shifted the pillows, one in front of the other, so she could sit up. Through the large windows, the sea swelled before her, with large waves breaking into whitecaps.

Images from last night flooded her brain: flames, fire engines, Finn leading her to safely. Sitting on the bench. Shivering. Her house, in flames. Ruined. Burned. She shook her head as if to shake the memories out. It couldn't be true, but it was. She could feel that the memories were real, not from a dream. And the despondency that fell on her last night fell again.

She didn't know how long she'd been sitting there when Finn walked in. As he pulled up a wicker chair from the corner of the room, she noticed that he looked tired. "How are you feeling?" he asked, taking her hand.

Pen shrugged. She had no idea. She had no feeling.

"I thought Vivi's house would be the best place for you to stay right now," he said, "and Vivi agreed. Is that all right with you? Just for now."

She nodded, a slight movement of her head. She wanted to be home, in her house, in her own house, sitting on the screened porch, watching the sun and the waves. But all that was gone. Someone had finally won. She had finally been forced out of her special place. Where she had once felt empowered and safe.

"If you want me to, I can meet with the Fire Marshall. He's going to want a statement about what happened. I can tell him you aren't feeling well, if you like."

Again, the slight nod. *Whatever. None of it mattered.* She wanted to sleep again.

"I've been over to the house. We don't need to talk about that right now. But I wanted you to know that it's been secured, locked up and boarded up. The flames didn't move past outside walls, so the inside is mostly intact. There's some minor water damage, but not a huge amount of smoke damage, because most of the flames were on the outside." He paused. "I was thinking I could bring your clothes and maybe some of your office things...."

He stopped talking when he realized that Pen was watching the waves and not responding to his words. "Pen," he said more urgently, "Pen!"

He reached over and gently wiped the tracks of tears from under her eyes. She hadn't known she'd been crying.

She removed the extra pillow in back of her and slid down into the bed, pulling the light blanket up to her chin. Her eyes were closed.

One of the last things she heard was Finn telling Vivi that he was on his way back to the house to get Pen's things. Then crashing waves. Then nothing.

Hours later, she woke up, probably driven by hunger. She hadn't had anything to eat since dinner last night, and now the clock on the bedside table said it was two o'clock in the afternoon. She was a bit more lucid now, and her mind fog seemed to be clearing. Since the divorce, she'd thought of herself as a strong person, and she was upset by what last night's horror had revealed about her resilience. She felt better now, but she could feel she was working at about thirty percent of her usual speed.

The fire at the house had been the last straw. She'd bounced back from the first break-in, when she'd hidden in the space behind her closet wall. She'd taken precautions to make the house safer and moved on. Then she and Finn had traced the trashed garden ornament to Joe, gotten justice, and she'd moved on. Even the last break-in, when she'd hidden in the trunk of the car, hadn't broken her. She'd just made the house even safer. And with the help of some kind of delusional magic thinking, she'd convinced herself that she'd returned it to its sanctuary status. *Ha. What a joke.*

No, this last episode had pushed her over the edge. There was no safety. It was all illusion. The house was gone, would never be safe, even if it was made whole again. She didn't feel she would ever be safe again, either. Someone wanted to hurt her. Maybe Peter. But she had no more fight left. She had given up, whatever that meant.

Just then, Vivi entered the room. She brightened when she saw that Pen was awake. "How about some lunch?" she asked.

Pen smiled a wry smile. "How long have I been asleep?"

"Eleven hours," Vivi said, adding "Sleeping is good. And, believe me, you needed it."

"I guess." Pen was starting to feel like going to sleep again, but then her stomach rumbled, reminding her of how long it had been since she had eaten. Remarkably, she wasn't very hungry, but evidently her stomach was.

"Food would be good," she said, starting to get out of bed, but sitting down abruptly as she realized how weak she felt.

Vivi noticed. "What if I bring up sandwiches for us both and we eat on the upper deck?" Noting the frown on Pen's face, she added, "If you feel like it, that is. Otherwise, we can just stay where we are. OK?"

"OK," Pen agreed, falling back into the bed. As soon as Vivi left the room, she closed her eyes.

The next few days passed in much the same way. Pen thanked God several times every day that the girls were in camp and protected from the horror of the fire. She felt marginally stronger, but still floated in some neverland where she did not have to deal with the aftermath of the fire. Finn delivered several trash bags of her clothes and Vivi washed them and filled the closet and drawers of the room for her. He'd brought her computer as well, and set that up on a desk in one of the many unused upstairs bedrooms.

Remarkably, Jessie, her agent had not been bugging her for her edited manuscript. Pen wondered if someone had told her what had happened. Sometimes she had a vague memory of sending off her completed first draft, and maybe that was why she hadn't heard from Jessie. At any rate, she was grateful not to have to think about it.

Writing this last novel felt like something she had done a million years ago, when she was a different person and the world felt safe. Now it was polluted by malice and fear. And she had changed from superwoman mom and writer to a frail version of herself who napped a lot.

Finn had been incredibly patient and kind. He went back and forth between his house, work, and Vivi's. He was often there for meals, bringing delicious treats to temp her to eat. There were sandwiches, and pastries, and dinners from at least three of the local restaurants. While she still hadn't regained her appetite, she did eat some parts of them, mostly to make Finn happy. It seemed to cheer him up when she finished even the semblance of a meal.

Today, for the first time in a week, Pen noticed she felt some parts of herself waking up. She had gotten up, showered, and put on clothes. All in time for breakfast, a first. And she'd combed her hair and even put on lipstick. She felt like a pale replica of herself, but at least she could feel a self again. Finn had mentioned last night that he'd like to talk about the house's condition sometime today, and although she hated the thought of it, she knew she was ready to at least listen. She could nap afterward if she needed to. And she knew Finn wouldn't push her beyond where she could go. He was the one thing in her world that was unchanged. Along with Vivi, of course. And the kids, safe at camp. They were her people, her sanity. She thanked God again for their healing presence in her life.

Greta had come by at least three times, and Pen was aware of how much of her healing was due to her therapist's wise counsel and listening. Greta had gotten her thorough a rough and ugly divorce and now was helping her navigate a world that had shifted precariously from light to dark. She knew she'd be seeing a lot of Greta in the weeks to come and the thought gave her comfort.

Chapter 39: Marcus

Several days later, on Wednesday, Pen started to drive again. She had felt so out of it that a week ago she'd given Finn her car keys. "What's this?" he'd said, holding her keyring in his hands like he'd never seen one before.

"The keys to my car," Pen said. "I feel weird. Floaty. I don't want to be tempted to drive until I feel more normal."

Finn had given her a hug. "That's my girl, full of common sense."

Now she had them back and was on her way to see Greta. They'd decided to meet on the bench at the end of Shore Drive, near town. Pen was secretly hoping that the sun and water and Greta's good counsel would somehow blast her back to herself. Or at least move her toward that place. Or, an even smaller goal, make her feel better this afternoon.

She arrived to find Greta already there. The bench was set far to the left of the beach and back from the water, and the bathers and beachgoers were mostly down near the water, so they had at least the semblance of privacy. For the next hour Greta listened to Pen pour her heart out, tried to help her make sense of the life she had right now. And by the end of the hour, Pen felt lighter, as she always did, holding onto a seed of hope that things wouldn't always be so bleak. Greta was a gift, she thought, not for the first time.

On her way back to Vivi's, she stopped and parked at the beach about a mile away. It was filled with bathers and kids running and playing beachball. In short, life. It was good for her to see it. No darkness here, just sand and sky and water. She thought it might be good for Vivi to have her house to herself for at least a few hours. Pen had been there for ten days now. And while Vivi always seemed delighted that she was there, and the house was big enough that they weren't in each other's pockets, she wondered sometimes if Vivi didn't find it a burden to have such constant guests. Maybe she was wrong, but giving Vivi a few hours by herself couldn't hurt.

She stayed at the beach for two hours. For the first one, she just sat and took in the scene. She was glad she had found the red straw hat that was in the back of her car; it would have been killer hot if she hadn't been wearing it, and it shaded her eyes so she could enjoy the scene in front of her. She never tired of watching people: the dads holding little babies, the pregnant mothers dipping their feet in the water, the toddlers racing the waves that chased them onto the beach as they screamed in mock terror, the teenagers flirting, and the grandmothers reading their summer novels.

Eventually she felt the urge to put her own feet in the water, and she walked the shoreline for an hour, waves crashing around her ankles and seagulls screeching and wheeling overhead. She forgot her problems in that hour, lost in the present sunny day. After a while, she realized she was quite a distance from the parking lot and she started back.

Once she was behind the wheel of her car, she could feel a nap coming on. But she felt a good kind of tired, more like what you feel after a busy day than you feel when you are sinking into a depression. She was happy to note that she could tell the difference. "Change comes on little cat feet," she said aloud, mangling Sandburg's poem, and making herself smile.

Until she turned the key in the car, that was. *Nothing.* She tried again. *Nope. Might need gas,* she thought idly. *Or, maybe something was wrong. Well, Finn would deal with that.* In the meantime, she'd just walk the mile to Vivi's house. She walked down to the shoreline again and turned left, toward Vivi's house. After a while the boulders half in and half out of the water made it difficult, and she cut up the slope near Vivi's house, weaving her way through the brush and scrub pine.

As Pen entered Vivi's grand entry, she called out, "Vivi!" The sound echoed in the massive space, but there was no answer. She was either out or painting, Pen thought as she climbed the stairs to what was her temporary bedroom. She stepped out of her sundress and hung it in the closet. Quickly she donned the t-shirt and jeans shorts on the nearby chair. Then she lay down on the bed, feeling drowsy and comfortable. A minute later she was asleep.

She woke hearing voices, and she was disoriented at first; they seemed near, in the house, but they were so unusual and loud that she wondered if they were part of a dream. She got up gingerly and opened the door. The voices were definitely coming from downstairs, near the foyer. She edged toward the railing that ran along the hall upstairs and allowed a view of the great room below. Keeping just out of view, she saw that the argument was between Vivi and someone else. Vivi was calling him Marcus.

She almost ran down the stairs to join Vivi in forces against him, but something held her back. Now she was hearing actual words. Vivi heard Marcus say, "So we're moving out for now, probably be back in late fall." He chuckled. "We had a 'successful fire', as they say, and we're good to go at another location."

Even from here, Pen could see Vivi's face drain of all color and all emotion. She looked grey. "What do you mean, you had a 'successful fire'?" she said with an edge in her voice.

"Nothing, nothing," the man called Marcus responded. "I've said too much. It's not your business."

"What do you mean you had a fucking successful fire?" Vivi shrieked. "The one at Wild Oak Drive?"

"Not your business," Marcus said angrily. "Let's settle up for the season; I have places to go."

"You set fire to my friend's house?" Vivi yelled incredulously.

"Yeah, so what?" he said back. "It's business. Sorry it was your friend's, but it was business. "

Pen was shaking. She was having trouble breathing. She was rooted to her spot in the hall. She knew she needed to move, but she couldn't make her legs follow her directions. Almost without her volition, she hit the button on the step counter she wore every day. It made her feel like nothing bad could happen. But something was. *Breathe*, she thought, *breathe. Finn will come. He will come.*

That thought gave her the energy to back slowly into her bedroom. Picking up her phone from the end table, she hit "Message" and then "Finn." She texted, fingers moving frantically over the keyboard: "come quick man downstairs with vivi said he started fire very scared vivi in danger."

A second later, a return text: "where are u?"

"my bedroom"

"get under the bed NOW"

"ok"

"PROMISE"

"yes"

Pen slid under the queen-sized bed, toward the middle. The floor underneath was hardwood, easy to slide on.

She tried to control her breathing, making her breaths quiet and counting in for seven seconds and out for seven seconds. It was Greta's calming mantra from long ago, and she hoped it would work now. She closed her eyes and concentrated on counting breaths. Finn would be here soon. She didn't know what would happen. That thought scared her almost as much as the creepy Marcus guy downstairs

Chapter 40: Some of the Answers

She couldn't stand it any longer. Pen's breath had slowed, but the panic was still threatening to overcome her. It wasn't helped by lying in the cramped space underneath the bed. She had to get out.

Once on her feet, she moved toward the door. She could still hear Vivi and Marcus, but now there was a third voice, Finn's. "Arms up!" he shouted. "Both of you!"

Then Vivi screamed and there was a loud thud. As if in a trance, Pen walked to the edge of the railing and looked over. Marcus was on the floor and wasn't moving. Finn stood facing Vivi, something metallic in his hand.

"Where's Pen?" he asked her.

"Not home," Vivi said. "She went out to meet with Greta and I haven't seen her since."

"Nope," Finn said. "Wrong! She's upstairs."

At this they both looked up and saw Pen standing near the railing above.

Finn said, in a softer tone than before, "Can you come down, Pen?"

Vivi said, "I'll go help her."

"No," Finn said. "You will not!" Then to Pen, "It's OK. I'm here. C'mon down."

Slowly Pen descended the massive stairs, holding tightly onto the railing as she would never have done before. She looked toward the right, at the body lying on the floor and Finn followed her gaze.

Seeing her horrified look, he said, "He's tasered, not dead. I had to use the taser; he was about to shoot. He'll be awake soon." Pen saw the gun on the floor in back of the prone Marcus. Finn picked it up and put it in waistband of his jeans.

Then to Vivi and Pen both, "Sit down." He pointed to Vivi. "You sit on the couch." Then, "Pen, sit over here." He indicated a leather chair to his right. "Now stay there for a minute; I have some work to do."

They both watched him with huge eyes as he removed plastic ties from his pockets and proceeded to use them to secure Marcus' arms and legs. "Old tools of the trade," he quipped to Pen as he finished. "Always have them in the car."

He asked Vivi, "Do you have duct tape?" She nodded. "Get it," he said, and then followed her as she went into the kitchen wing to the right of the stairs. When they came back a minute later, he tore off a piece of the black tape and secured it over Marcus' mouth.

"Now then," he said, after pulling our Marcus' wallet. He sat on the loveseat next to Pen, facing Vivi. "What the hell is going on?"

Vivi didn't answer immediately and Finn had lost his patience. "Now! Goddamnit!" he roared at her in a voice Pen had never heard before.

Taking a huge breath and letting it out, Vivi began to talk in a quiet voice. "It began a long time ago," she said. "Before I met Georges. Only I didn't know it then..."

"OK, good start, keep going," Finn said in a voice devoid of emotion.

"I married Georges and I moved into this house, which was his," she said. "We had a wonderful life. We had friends, and we socialized a lot. We flew around the world, took cruises. It was like I was living in a dream. And we were so in love." Pen couldn't look away from her friend, who looked infinitely sad. "And then, when things couldn't have gotten better, Georges got sick...and...and then he died." Thus far, everyone in the room knew the story.

"And then what?"

"One day, several months after Georges died, two men in suits rang the bell. When I opened the door, I was sure at first that they were lost, had the wrong address. But then they said, 'Hello, Vivi. We need to talk to you.' They scared me, and I tried to close the door. But they were quicker and stronger than I was, and they came in." Pen couldn't take her eyes off her friend, obviously dumbfounded by this story she had never heard before.

Vivi needed no prodding. "They came in and sat down. Here, where we are right now. They told me that they'd had an arrangement with Georges for many years. That all his businesses had been struggling, were on the edge of disaster, and when they offered him a chance to avoid ruin, he'd taken it." She paused, looking at them, but no one spoke. "The deal was this. There is a peculiarity with this house that few people know. There's a cave in the middle of the rocks out back." She looked at Pen. "The one that you found.

"The cave has an entry into the cellar of the house. Don't know who made it, or when. But it offered a way to bring things in by small boat, take them into the house through a room in the cellar, pick them up, and distribute them."

"Things?" Finn asked. Pen looked at him and saw a steely set to his jaw. He looked like a frozen statue.

"Drugs."

Pen's heart almost imploded. This could not be happening. It must be a bad dream. She hoped it would end and she would find herself in her own bed, or in Finn's. None of this could be real.

"And what did you tell the men?" Finn asked.

"At first, I was so flabbergasted, I couldn't take it in. I just couldn't believe it. But they convinced me that it was true. Had been true for about ten years. That was where all the money for trips and cruises and new cars came from. There was literally no money coming in from the businesses, they said."

"And they demanded that you continue."

"Yes, but I said no. I knew that I would probably lose the house and that I'd have to get a job." She paused and swallowed. "I would have done that. I couldn't imagine allowing drugs to pass through my house or doing business with these two men."

"But?"

"They said their arrangement would continue, with or without me. If I opposed them, I would be 'removed.' They made it clear what that meant. They also said they knew I had two attractive goddaughters and what a shame it would be if they got hurt."

"Oh, Vivi," Pen said. She sprang up and sat next to her friend, taking her hand, and Finn didn't object.

"How did it work?" Finn asked.

"Someone would bring in the 'product', that's what they called it, by boat. There were always two men in a small boat. I don't know where they came from, what direction. They would get out and one would climb the rocks to the cave. He'd throw down a rope and the other guy would attach the packages; then he'd haul up the packages and take them into the cave and finally into the house. Then they'd leave by boat. They could do it in less than an hour. Usually in the middle of a dark night."

"Did they tell you when this was going to happen?"

"No. They told me to just live my life as usual and to ignore their coming and going."

Something clicked in Pen's brain. "What about the white truck?"

"That came later," Vivi said. "The most dangerous time for them was when they made pickups. I'm pretty isolated here, but I do have some neighbors and there's a beach not far away. Someone might notice a car or a truck coming at regular intervals. Once they found out I was a painter, a painter who sold art, they had their answer. The white truck was theirs, as was the art business: the framing and mailing of art. Looked legitimate and it actually did what they said it would do. But it was also a front for the drug group."

Just then Marcus started to moan and move. He was regaining consciousness. Finn jumped up and went over to where he was lying on the floor. "Are you awake? Look at me and nod if you are."

Marcus looked up at Finn, his eyes filled with contempt, but made no effort to communicate.

With horror, Pen watched Finn kick the man in the ribs. "If you want to live, nod at me."

Marcus nodded. Finn said, "I want to hear the story this lady is telling. Do not make me interrupt her. Lie still. I'll deal with you later. Do you understand?"

Finn looked ready to kick again, and Marcus nodded.

"OK, then, we understand each other," Finn said. "Continue, Vivi."

"Someone on the other end got the bright idea of framing my works in really chunky frames. Sometimes wood and sometimes metal. Somehow, that caught on and became my trademark." Pen thought of the many works of Pen's she'd seen framed this way. "And they could put packets of 'product' inside. Easily mail them all over the world. To my 'collectors.' A perfect, or nearly perfect, scheme."

"What changed?"

"Pen found the cave. I made the mistake of telling them that it had been discovered, that it was a matter of time before someone found out about the door that led inside. I thought that they'd just shut down the site and move somewhere else, that they would leave me alone so I could go on with my life."

"Not that easy, though, right?"

"They needed an alternative site, that's what they kept saying. One not near a beach, or nosy neighbors. Too many people using boats in the summer, too. They needed a more secure spot. I didn't care where they went, I just wanted them gone. They said they might come back in the winter, when the area was more deserted, but right now they needed a summer site."

Pen closed her eyes as it hit her. "My house."

"I didn't know that," Vivi said. She turned, taking her friend's face in her hands, "I didn't know that. I didn't know where the new site was. It could have been anywhere on the Cape." Tears began streaming down her face. "I swear, Pen! I swear!" she added, sobbing.

And Pen believed her. She knew Vivi was a good actress, had seen her in action at a million openings, talking to people she despised. But no one was as good as this. Vivi was sobbing full out now.

Finn tried another question: "Why Pen's house?"

Vivi shook her head. "I don't know! I don't know! I just found out it was Pen's house when Marcus came today. He mentioned they'd had a 'successful fire," and I figured it out. She looked directly at Finn. "That was what you walked into."

"OK." Pen could almost feel Finn thinking. After a minute he said, "Now let's hear what this tough guy has to say."

He looked with disgust at Marcus, lying on the floor with his eyes wide open, taking it all in.

Chapter 41: Endgame

Walking over to Marcus, and bending down to where he lay on the floor, Finn pulled the tape off the man's face in one swift motion. Marcus yelped with the pain and unexpectedness of the gesture. "OK, here's how it's going to go. I'm going to ask questions. You're going to answer them."

Marcus remained stone faced and looked at Finn with steely eyes. Even tied up, he looked intimidating.

"Why Pen's house? The one you tried to burn down? Why her property?"

Marcus remained silent. Pen could feel her muscles tighten. She was afraid that Finn would kick the man again, but he didn't. Instead, he said in a soft voice. "Maybe I can convince you that talking to me would be your best option. Do you know what a 'cleaner' is?" Marcus' eyes widened slightly; if Pen hadn't been watching really closely, she wouldn't have seen it.

Finn continued. "I can see that you do. So, here's one option. I can call for a 'cleaner.' I have contacts and favors to call in; I can make all of this go away. You. The truck. Any money or product you have. Any sign of your presence in this house. Gone. Our lives become simple again." Now the man was listening closely. "I have a few other options, but that is the easiest one. You might want to talk to me and see if there are other ones. Ones that would let you see those beautiful girls of yours grow up."

This time Marcus' face changed entirely, and he struggled against the ties that held him immobile. "Yeah, I checked your wallet. Cute girls. Pretty wife, too."

They sat silently, with the sunlight flooding the room and washing the oriental rug with white light. A Grandfather clock chimed the hour. Finally, Marcus said, "What do you want to know?"

Finn answered immediately. "For starters, why Pen's house?"

The man quickly began to speak. "Because of the property. The shoreline curves way in on the right side of the house. Then it curves out again, making a narrow cove. It would be easy to bring a small boat in and not be seen from either side. The woods are dense with fir trees, and the nearest neighbor has a wooded section of land that abuts it. It would be easy to bring in product, especially at night, and be almost invisible." Once he started talking, he couldn't stop. No doubt he was hoping for some other outcome than the one Finn had set out earlier. "There's also an old cemetery in those woods, halfway between the water and the street. Not many graves, but there's an ancient family mausoleum there. Looks like no one's opened it in twenty years. Has an old rusted lock. We can use that, with a new lock on it, of course, to store product and bring it in and out. A jeep can follow the old path down to retrieve the stuff from the mausoleum. It's a nice setup."

"So why not just use the site and carry on? Why bother to frighten Pen or to burn her house down?"

"Too dangerous," Marcus said, struggling to get in a more comfortable position

Finn got up and hauled him to a seated position against the wall. Marcus moaned with the discomfort of changing position. "Continue," Finn said.

"The main thing was, we could see that someone was in the upper rooms of the house. A lot, mostly at night. There was no pattern. And from that room, you'd have a perfect view of a boat moving across the water toward the cove. Especially on moonlit nights. And if you saw that a lot of times times, at say, three o'clock in the morning, you'd probably wonder what was going on. Maybe investigate. Call the cops. Whatever."

"You decided to hurt whoever lived there, to get them to move?" Finn's voice was quiet but there was an edge in it that was chilling.

"Not hurt. Just scare. He shook his head in bewilderment. "The guy never could figure out how she got away."

"And if he'd found her?"

"He would've tied her up." He looked at Finn to see if that would fly. It would not.

"And that's all?" Finn asked, his voice even softer this time.

"He might have hit her a few times," Marcus said, aware that a lot was at stake if he lied. "Enough to scare her and make her move. For a lot a people, one experience like that would do it."

"Yeah, but not for Pen. Of course, you had no way to know how stubborn she is." He continued, "And the second break in?"

"Same."

"Tell me about the fire."

"Last resort," Marcus said. "Figured at the least it would require months to rebuild, if the owner even wanted to. Would take until September at least, and by that time the crowds near Vivi's would be gone, and we could move back here if we needed to."

"Did you even think that there might be people inside the house? That someone could have died?"

Marcus looked at the floor. It wasn't clear if he was embarrassed or just didn't want to meet Finn's eyes. "It wasn't personal. It was just business. If we'd wanted to kill someone, we wouldn't have just done the perimeter. Would've used a Molotov cocktail or two or three. House would've gone up in flames in twenty minutes." When no one spoke, he added, "Just wanted to scare them away, is all."

"I need to think. I'm going out to the back deck. Vivi, make me coffee. Black and strong. Pen, stay here and watch Marcus. Yell if he so much as hiccups." Pen nodded. The fog she had been in since the fire had lifted; now she was hyperaware of everything: the dust motes in the sunbeams piercing the living room, the ticking of the clock at the end of the room, the man sitting fifteen feet away from her, staring straight ahead.

When Vivi brought Finn's coffee to him on the porch, he said, "Sit down, Vivi. We need to talk."

She sat on the chair next to his. "No, on the footrest in front of your chair. Look at me. I want to see you while we talk." But he didn't talk.

He looked past her, at the ocean, for at least ten minutes. Abruptly, he said, "Need some answers. No embellishment. Just answer what I ask."

"OK."

"You have to make some decisions. Right now. And they will be hard ones." He sipped the coffee. "If we take Marcus to the police, the whole story will come out. Including your involvement. I know you inherited the problem, and that will work in your favor. But you did go along with it." He saw that she was ready to argue but stopped her, holding out his hand palm up. "That's the way a jury would see it. You were a victim, too, but you profited from it. They might feel bad for you, but they'll also feel that there has to be some punishment for being involved in drug running."

She burst forth, "That's not fair."

"It's not about fair. It's about real. Do you want me to help you or not?"

She closed her mouth and nodded once.

"So, a jury will probably find you guilty of something, some part of this. Even if you couldn't have done anything, they will think you should have. Truth." More coffee. "You might get a fifteen to twenty-year sentence, maybe do five to ten with good behavior." He looked directly at her. "Can you do that?"

Her eyes filling with tears again. "No," she whispered. "I don't think so."

"You could start your life again once you got out. And, of course, maybe I'm wrong and they'd find you innocent."

"What are the odds?"

"Slim to none," Finn answered. "But there's always a chance."

"If they find me guilty at all, for anything, will they take all of my money?"

"No question. That would be a given. Any money they can find in your bank accounts, they'll take. Probably the house. Securities, whatever can be traced to the time period when the drug running happened. Even if it was under Georges' watch. They won't leave you with anything that might be part of the drug running profits."

"You're saying I might come out of jail after five or more years, penniless, with no home?"

"It's a possibility. The prosecution will be looking for what you did with your share of the money. And they will search like mad dogs until they figure out where it went."

Finn paused here. Vivi had gone white. "If you have any off shore accounts, and I'm going to assume you do, they will try hard to access them. Might not find them. But they will watch you for the rest of your life for anything that looks like money that can't be accounted for, new luxury car, travel."

"I don't think I can live like that," Vivi said in a choking voice. "Is there another option?"

"There is, but I doubt you're going to like it a much better."

"Try me."

"You have to leave now. Take nothing. Not your purse, license, nothing." He paused, then asked, "Do you have a passport?"

"I have two."

"Two?"

"Georges got extra ones for us both, with different names and pictures. I found them in the safe after he died. By then, I knew what he was thinking. He knew what he was doing was dangerous. They were his escape plan."

"Well, that makes things easier." Finn, now energized, drained the rest of the coffee.

"Do you have any money in the house? How much?"

"Fifty thousand, in the safe."

"Are you all right with leaving? Everything? Everybody? Life as you know it?" Finn paused for a bit, then added, "Maybe not forever. You never know. Things change. But you'd have to leave knowing that it might be forever."

Vivi remained looking out at the waves, and he could see tears running down her face. "Yes," she said finally, wiping them away with her hand.

Chapter 42: Plans

Finn walked back into the house with Vivi. "I need to talk to Pen for about ten minutes. Why don't you get some paper and a pen and make a list of things you need to remember." He looked over at Marcus. "Watch him, OK?"

It wasn't until Vivi was all set and making her list that Finn took Pen's hand and said, "Let's go out to the deck."

"What's happening?"

"We need to have this conversation, Pen. And fast. It's about Vivi and what we do next."

"OK."

"You heard her story about the drug running."

She nodded.

"OK, now we need to have a talk about what to do next. I've thought of a way to help her, but it means we'll be breaking the law. Big time. If we help Vivi get out of the country, we're helping someone who broke the law get away. That makes us culpable in the eyes of the law. Aiding and abetting."

Pen exhaled loudly. She looked scared.

"I've already figured out a way to get her safely away, but I won't do it without your permission. My life will be in jeopardy and your life as you know it will be in jeopardy, too. I know Vivi is your friend. But I need you to think hard about whether you can be part of this and whether you can live with it afterward."

"What's your plan?"

"Essentially to get Vivi safely to another country. Too long for details right now; time is running out."

Pen stared at the rolling sea for about a minute. "I'm in. I trust you. Vivi is my family. She's always been there for me. Now I'll...no, we'll...be there for her." They locked eyes, agreeing to this crazy plan, agreeing to put everything on the line to save Vivi: their new love, their future plans, everything.

"OK. If we're going to pull this off, we're going to need some really good plans. Why don't you go and change places with Vivi. I need to give her directions and we all need to get moving."

A minute later Vivi was back on the deck. "Listen carefully," Finn began. Vivi looked grey and her eyes were flat. "First, put $5,000 from the money in the safe into your wallet. Take mostly big bills and use smaller ones for purchases along the way. Leave $5,000 in the safe and give the rest to Pen. We'll get it to you at some point way down the road."

"Why leave $5,000?"

"It has to look like you were taken, not like you left and cleaned out the safe."

She nodded her understanding.

"Leave your old passport here, take the new one and any other documentation for that identity." He stopped for a second of two. "Do you have a license to go with it? "

"Yes," she said.

"OK. Put it in your purse with the money and passport. Make it a big purse, put a sweater on top. Take a carry-on with additional stuff you need, underwear, change of clothes, whatever. As if you were going on a normal trip. You know the drill." He looked at her sharply. "You're going to leave your phone and purse and license and wallet downstairs, as if you got taken unexpectedly. You have to leave everything. Got it?"

A slight nod.

"Do you have another phone?" Finn asked suddenly.

"I do," Vivi said quietly, sounding defeated. "One I used for contacting Marcus. That was the only way we communicated."

"OK, I need that right away. I'll dispose of it. For a while, you won't have a phone. Until you get to your final destination, set up bank accounts, and all that. Speaking of which, I assume you have accounts somewhere with the money you've been paid?"

Vivi could see the disgust on Finn's face, thought it was obvious he was trying to hide it. She looked down and took a deep breath. "Can you access if from anywhere?" he asked.

"If I have the codes."

"Do you have them?"

"They're in the safe. I'll put them in the old wallet I'll be carrying."

"When you get to your final destination, use cash for a bit, then set up a banking account with an international bank, using a few thousand. After about a month, wire some money to the account, never more than five thousand at a clip. Never at a regular interval. OK?"

Again, "Yes."

"I don't have enough time right now to explain all of what we have to do. We need to move fast." He looked Vivi in the eye. "Do you trust me?"

"Of course."

"I'll tell you more later, then. We can go over it in the car on the way to the airport. Basically, once you're at the airport, book the next flight to anywhere. Doesn't matter where, just out of Boston. Using your fake passport. On that flight, you need to decide where you want to end up."

Vivi started to talk. "I already know—"

Finn put up his hand. "No!" he said. "I don't want to know. If they ask me where you might be, I want to be able to say, 'I have no idea' and sound believable." He continued, "When you get to the first destination, book another flight, this one to the general area of the end target. Like to Ireland for England, or Portugal for Italy. Understand?"

"And then, book one to the final destination."

"Exactly. You can wait a few hours, even a day, between flights. No more than that. You'll be using the cash you're carrying. It's a little weird, but some people still use cash. Remember that you can't leave the country with more than $10,000 in cash without declaring it, but you're only taking $5,000, well below the limit." Finn took a deep breath. "The hardest part is going to be going through customs in a foreign country. You need a good story as to why you're traveling there and why you're carrying some of your assets in cash. Your mother is sick and living wherever, and you need money right away. You don't trust banks, never have. You're fleeing an abusive boyfriend. Something plausible. After that, you should be ok."

As she tried to take in all these directions, Vivi looked ashen. She knew the rest of her life depended on her getting them all right. And some luck. It was a heavy burden, but she had already made up her mind that it was her only choice. She felt like she was carrying bricks on her back.

"I don't know how to thank you," she said softly, looking at Finn.

"Not doing it because of you. Doing it because we both love Pen, and you've always been there for her. That's all."

"Thank you, anyway."

"Get packing." As she stood up, he said, "Do you have any of Georges' shoes in the house?"

An unexpected question, Vivi thought, but answered, "I kept one pair."

"Size?"

"Twelve and a half."

"Perfect. Bring them down with your purse and carryon."

Chapter 43: Pick One

Finn followed Vivi back into the house. Pen was still sitting on the same chair where he'd left her and Marcus was still propped against the wall.

"I'll be right back," he said to Pen as he walked toward the kitchen. "Want a water?"

Pen said, "Yeah," and he was soon back with two bottles.

"Now, then, Marcus," he said, sitting on the velvet couch on the other side of the room. "What are we going to do with you?" The question hung in the air, adding more tension to an already tense situation.

Marcus looked at him with steely eyes.

"We already talked about the "cleaner" option as the easiest one. Let me throw out some others. I could call the cops and turn you over to them. You could ask for a plea deal and probably get one if you could help them shut down this whole drug ring." Before Marcus could say anything, he added. "You might get put in witness protection program. Best case scenario for sure. Or not. If you go to jail, though, for any length of time, you're pretty much fried. Really fried if you talk to the police. Nobody likes a rat. Equally fried if you don't. Longer sentence if you don't talk. I'm thinking twenty years, maybe out in ten or fifteen." Finn stopped then, gauging the effect this was having on Marcus. He continued, "Of course, your girls would be grown by the time you got out, and who knows if your wife would wait around." He shrugged.

Finn drank his water and let that information hang in the air. Pen knew enough to be quiet.

After letting that hang in the air, Finn began again. "I could let you go, and you could report to your superiors that you had royally screwed up this incredibly profitable gig. That people knew how it worked. Or you could not tell them and let them find out for themselves. Not good.

If they let you live, unlikely from my standpoint, you'll be carrying their coffee and cleaning the bathrooms for the rest of your life." He shrugged again. "Don't see many viable options here."

Marcus was still staring at Finn with those steely eyes, but Pen, who had been watching him carefully noticed the look of fear playing just below the surface of his features.

"And finally, the last option. I could just let you go. And you could take off."

The words hung in the silence. The AC quietly droned on, and a dog barked somewhere nearby.

Marcus broke the silence. "Why would you do that?" he asked in a husky voice that had none of the bravado he'd shown before."

"Two reasons," Finn said, standing up and massaging the knots of stress in his neck muscles. He moved closer and faced Marcus. "Reason one, it suits my purposes. That's all you need to know about that." He cleared his throat and drank from the bottle of water still in his hand. "Number two. I happened to see the picture of those three girls of yours. And your wife. Hell of a life for them if something happens to you."

For the first time there was some real emotion on Marcus' face. He looked shattered, Pen thought. As if, in the arrogance of his earlier life, he had never looked at or weighed the consequences of his choices or actions on those he loved. And now he was.

"So, here's how this option would work. I let you go. You call your wife and tell her to pack up for a month-long vacation." He stopped himself for a moment, thinking. "Does your wife know what you do for a living?"

"Partly," Marcus answered, no delay in his speech now. He was paying desperate attention to this last and only chance for a life.

"Well, she's about to learn more. Tell her the bad guys are after you and life is about to change."

Finn had no idea how smart Marcus was. He had met some pretty stupid criminals before, and he didn't have time for an IQ test. He decided to spell out everything for Marcus, so he wouldn't make a

205

dumb mistake and blow the plan all to hell before he even had a chance.

He continued his direction. "Tell her to pack for a trip, and to take anything of value in the house with her. That includes cash and jewelry. You won't be going back."

Marcus was hanging on Finn's every word and Pen could almost see him taking notes in his mind. He was envisioning a new life. He had hope. Then Finn added a new wrinkle to the deal. "Of course, to let you fly free like that, there would need to be something in it for me."

Marcus looked warily at Finn. "What?"

"You'd need to provide me with information about how the "business" worked. Names, dates, pickups, phone numbers." Marcus started to shake his head. "Not a lot of options, buddy. You give me the info, I let you go with a head start before I pass the information to the feds. Time for you to move far away and to live peacefully and watch your girls grow up."

Silence filled the room. Then Marcus said quietly, "They'll kill me."

"Not if they can't find you. And they won't know it was you who ratted. There will be lag time between now and when some kind of follow-up operation by the feds happens. Maybe quite a bit of a lag time." Marcus's face was grey. "And if you stay here and face the music for fucking up this beautiful operation, they'll kill you anyway." Finn paused for several seconds. "Look on the bright side. With my plan, I get the info I need, and you get to have a normal life with your family somewhere. Seems fair."

Marcus nodded.

"OK, let's get cracking. Time matters. Send me the contact list on your phone. Here's my cell; start talking into the memo section. Times, places, who's in the operation, how it works. I want it all. Go over to the back of the room, now. Start talking. I'll listen before I let you leave. If it's not complete, no go. Understand?" Again, Marcus nodded. "You have ten minutes."

While Marcus recorded the information and Vivi was upstairs packing, Finn went and sat on the couch next to Pen. "Are you still OK with this?" he asked. "You can see that we're putting ourselves on the line here. We have to make it happen or we'll be arrested for aiding and abetting."

Pen looked serious. It was clear that reality had set in for her. "We don't have a choice, do we?" she asked, sounding grimly determined. "If we want to help Vivi get away?"

"No, we don't. Not one I can think of."

"OK, then. We have to do it. Vivi could have gone to the police in the beginning, when she found out about the operation. I think she would have, if she were the only one in danger. But when they threatened the girls, she wouldn't take the chance that they might be hurt. She did what she could to protect them, not herself." Taking a deep breath, she added, "So now it's our turn to protect her."

Finn nodded. "That's the way I see it."

They sat quietly for a few minutes as Marcus talked into the phone. Finally, he looked up. "I'm done," he said, holding the phone up to Finn.

Finn took the phone, sat down again, and hit 'play.' Marcus voice could be heard documenting the way the drug operation worked, including all the information that Finn had asked for. When the playback was over, he hit 'stop.' "Good job. That's exactly what I needed."

Pen looked at him quizzically. "I have some friends in undercover work, from my old days there. At some point, I'll send all of this their way. They'll know who to contact and how to proceed. My name won't come into it." Pen said nothing. "It's one thing to help Vivi. I see her partly, not totally, but partly, as a victim in all this. And she's part of your family. And she protected the girls. But this is drug running. The kind of drug running that killed Rachel. And there is no way I can let that go. So, this is my ethical compromise. We save Vivi and the bad guys get taken down big time."

"What about him?" Pen said, pointing to Marcus.

"Small potatoes. Way down in the chain of command. Have to let him go to protect Vivi right now. Plus, once I saw the damn pictures of his kids..."

Pen smiled. "OK, I get it."

Finn turned his attention to Marcus. "Let's get rolling," he said. "Do you have more pickups due today?"

Marcus nodded.

"Call them and tell them you had trouble with the truck and you'll be a few hours late. Say something like the timing belt went, so they'll know it'll be a while. Where do you live?"

"Marion, just over the bridge."

"That's good. Close by. Before you go home, steal some plates from the Steamship lot on Gifford Street. You want people who are away for a few days, who won't report the loss immediately." He looked at Marcus. "You've done that, right, stolen plates?" The look on the man's face gave him the answer. "Put them on your car later. Then drive home. Do not exceed the speed limit. When you get there, put the stolen plates on your car. Your wife drives the car, you drive the truck. Leave the truck at a busy mall as soon as you can. Then hit the road. You have to get as far away as possible before anyone realizes something's wrong."

Pen was listening to Finn set up the escape plan for Marcus with the same sense of unreality she had had since she'd heard Marcus and Vivi arguing earlier. She knew Finn must have been calling on his experiences as both a cop and an undercover agent, but it seemed unbelievable to listen to him plan an escape route for a criminal. She got immediately why he was doing it, so the police would have no knowledge of the drug dealing or Vivi's role in it. But his acumen in planning the evasion of Marcus' superiors was unsettling. As was the gun tucked into his waistband.

Finn continued, hardly taking a breath. They all needed to be out of here very soon.

"Aim for Georgia, or somewhere South. Get as far as you can today and tonight. Stay in a motel when you need to stop. Continue down to the keys. Find a rental for a month. Make sure it has a garage for your car. Settle down and make believe you're on a vacation. Do things with the kids, act like a family on vacation, look normal. Figure out where you want to go next. Questions?"

A shake of the head was the answer, and he continued. "While you're in Florida, buy new identification documents for your family. I'm sure you can figure out how to make that happen. When you have them, buy a new vehicle, used if possible. Pay cash." Then, as if the idea had just occurred to him, he asked," Do you have money in the truck?"

"Quarter of a mil," Marcus said.

So, like I said, "Pay cash. For everything. While you're being a family on a vacation in Florida, decide where to go. Somewhere far away. Oregon. Minnesota. Doesn't matter, just small time America. When you get there, find a little house. Settle in." A shadow like a black cloud passed over Finn's face. "Don't even think of trying to get into the same kind of work. Death sentence. They'll find you. The network is efficient. When they find you, they will kill you all. Remember that. Work in Home Depot for a while, start a small landscaping business, something ordinary like that. Blend in to middle class America. Don't spend a lot of money, a rookie mistake you could never fix."

The only sign that Marcus gave of his inner state was that his breathing rate had increased. Pen could see his chest moving in and out.

"How much money do you have at home?" he asked.

"Half a mil," Marcus said.

"Great." Finn said with a false smile on his face. "A saver." Then he got serious. "That should be enough. Spend it slowly. Small house, small business if any. No showiness of any sort. Got it?"

Marcus nodded.

"Number one reason people get found. They stand out. Can't avoid being showy, calling attention to themselves." He looked at Marcus to see if he got the message. The man looked grey. "Then BAM!" Finn yelled, and Pen and Marcus flinched at the loud sound. Finn continued, "They're dead!"

A minute later, Finn was massaging his neck again. He picked up the man's wallet and handed it to him. "Do not use your credit card, never, not even once. Oh, by the way, ditch your phone and your wife's after you take out the sim cards. Maybe throw them in the ocean or a swamp. Buy a few burner phones as soon as you can." He assumed the man knew all this, but felt compelled to say it. At this point, they all had a stake in Marcus' ability to follow directions and evade his bosses and the police.

Marcus put his wallet in his pocket and faced Finn. "I don't really know why you're doing this, man," he said, looking Finn in the eye. He took a deep breath, as if the next words were stuck in his throat. "Thank you." Suddenly he stuck his hand out toward Finn. Finn at first made a tentative move to take it, then stopped. He had almost forgotten the man was a drug dealer. Had caused havoc, and pain, and tragedy. But in spite of all his bad life choices, he was a human being.

To a departing Marcus, who had turned quickly once he realized he was free to go, Finn said, "Be careful."

Chapter 44: Action

As she watched Vivi bring down her carry-on luggage, purse, and
Georges' shoes, a thought flashed through Pen's mind and she said,
"Oh!" Loudly.

Finn looked at her. "What?"

"I left my car at the beach!! When I went to leave, it wouldn't start.
That's why I walked here and went upstairs."

Pen could see Finn take in her words and the situation. It no doubt
screwed up the plans he had for the next step, but he gave no indication
of that except to sit down. "Give me a minute," he said, and Pen
watched him. Not even a muscle twitched, but she could almost see his
mind whirling at some unimaginable speed. "OK, "he said. "Here's the
next step. Pen, are you wearing what you had on earlier, when you went
out this morning?"

"No," Pen said right away.

"Then go put on the same clothes again. It has to look like you've
been there all this time. Take a big purse, with a book and a sunhat.
Beach stuff."

"OK," Pen agreed, leaving the room quickly and heading upstairs.

When she came down a few minutes later in a coral sundress and
sandals, he looked at her carefully. "Are you all right?" he asked,
maybe sensing her inner turmoil and uncertainly.

"No, not really. I'm kind of a mess. But I'm ok enough to follow
directions."

Finn began talking again almost immediately. "This is the one tricky
part. You need to get to the edge of the beach, where the big rocks end,
so you can blend in with the other people on the beach. The ideal
situation is that no one sees you coming from Vivi's house right now;
that would not square with the timetable we're going to make up. Any
ideas about how to do that and not be seen from the street?" He

stopped for a minute and no one spoke. "I can't think of a foolproof way," he added.

Pen smiled. Finn frowned, confused. "It's the way I came here from the beach earlier. There's a path that leads from the big rocks along the beachfront up through a small hill of scrub pine to the house. It's overgrown and brambly. But it's not too bad, and it's almost hidden from the road by the oak and evergreen trees that grow on the side of the house."

"That's perfect."

"That section of the beach isn't used much, because the slope into the water has lots of rocks. Hard walking. There are more people further down, where the sand extends thirty feet into the water. I'll settle in close to the sandy beach, sit on a towel and read my book. I wasn't too far away from the water when I was there earlier and I walked the shoreline for a while. Some people may have seen me there before and hopefully think I've been there this whole time."

"OK, that's good. Let's get ready to go," Finn said to Pen, "and I'll make sure Vivi's stuff's ready to go."

Fifteen minutes later everyone was ready. Finn explained the next part of the plan. "Pen, go to the beach. Sit and read. Or write. When I can, I'll call you. Don't answer. I'll leave a voice message asking you to meet me for coffee if you're free. Call me back a few minutes after that; say you turned off your ringer to get some peace and quiet and just checked for messages. Agree to meet me in town at Killer Coffee. Then walk up to your car. Try to start it. When it doesn't work, call me. Leave me a message saying the car won't work. We want a record of where you were and where I was around this time. I'll text back saying I'm on my way. Hopefully I can get the car to start."

"What if you can't?"

"I'll think of something."

"Where will I be?" Vivi asked.

"Underneath beach towels on the floor of the back seat of my truck," he answered. Vivi's face was impossible to read.

"Pen," Finn said, moving toward her and giving her a hug, "time to go." And then she was gone.

"Give me your things," Finn demanded of Vivi. "Georges' shoes as well. Stay here, I'll be right back." Outside the house, where his truck was parked behind a line of arborvitae, Finn put Vivi's carry-on luggage and large purse on the back seat. He picked up a smaller tarp and a large beach towel he always carried and covered them. He got another tarp from the truck bed and allowed himself a small smile. When Vivi was on the floor of the back seat, it would cover her nicely.

Back upstairs, he looked at Vivi, trying to assess her mental state. She was going to need a lot of strength for this next step. "What?" Vivi said, as she saw him looking at her.

"Ready to rock and roll?" He tried to give her a smile, to make his face less intimidating, help her relax. Everything was going to depend on how well she could act as she normally would. "Sit down," he told her, as he sat across from her on an ottoman.

"Here's the drill. You are going to disappear. It needs to look like you were here alone and someone broke in and abducted you. Like he, let's assume it's a he, broke in intending to rob you and was surprised to see you. You and he fought. Maybe he hit you too hard, or you fell and hit your head, or you had a heart attack. Something unexpected happened, and he couldn't leave you here because you'd seen his face. That's the basic premise." He looked at her pale face and hoped she wouldn't fold now. "You and I are going to reenact that scenario. I'll be wearing Georges' shoes, which will be a different type and size from anyone who's been here lately."

Vivi looked at his quizzically, like he'd lost his mind.

"I'm going to put my size eleven feet into Georges' size twelve shoes."

"Oh," she said. He couldn't tell if she understood or not. She seemed dazed.

Then the enormity of what they were about to do seemed to stun them both, and they sat in silence for a moment, only the ticking clock for company. It seemed preposterous to both of them that they were in the middle of this insane scheme. That only this morning each had gotten up and thought they were about to begin an ordinary June day on the Cape. Unexpectedly, Vivi broke the silence. "I'm ready," she said with a strong, determined voice. "Let's go."

"I'll go downstairs and put on Georges' shoes outside. I'll give you a few minutes. Then I'll pick the lock in the small entry door to the garage and make it look like someone broke in that way. I'll come through the garage, into the cellar, and up the stairs. You wait in the kitchen. Maybe take out a mix and some eggs as if you were going to do some baking. Turn on the oven. There's already a pot of hot coffee on; you can throw that at me later. Just act as if it's not me but some strange and scary stranger who had entered your kitchen. Ask me to leave. Try to hit me. Try to protect yourself." Her eyes were large. "I won't hurt you, but you have to believe I would. Your reactions need to look authentic."

Vivi swallowed. "What if I hurt you?"

"I'll see your moves coming. I'll be fine. But try to hurt me. That's the whole idea."

She nodded.

"Fight for your life."

Then he went downstairs with the shoes and Vivi went into the kitchen to make brownies.

Chapter 45: The Fight

Vivi heard the door to the cellar open and felt herself freeze. She willed herself to fight for her life, realizing that in some ways, she was actually in that fight right now.

She looked up and saw Finn standing in the doorway from the living room to the kitchen. He looked huge, and hulking and his eyes were steely. The way he was standing, very still, with his hands at his sides, felt menacing. For a second, she felt shivers of fear run up her back. She faced him, turning and backing up a step or two. She positioned herself near the end of the island, where the knife rack sat prominently.

"Surprised to see you here," Finn said, in a deep voice. Even though her rational mind knew this was not real, it felt real.

"What do you want?" Vivi answered, sliding her hand closer to the knife rack.

"No sense making small talk. Money."

"I don't have much with me," Vivi said, perseverating. "But take what I have in my purse. Then go." He looked askance at her." She reached for the purse on the end of the island. Grabbing her wallet, she took out the cash and half threw it toward the other end of the island as they had agreed she would. "Just go. I won't even report it."

Finn laughed harshly. "Sure, like that would happen. Do you think I'm stupid? You'd call the police as soon as I was gone." They were doing a dangerous dance now; he was moving closer to her and she was moving around the island, further away from him. She surprised him by suddenly moving forward, and in that moment of surprise, she grabbed a knife and threw it at him.

If Finn had not had the training he'd had, it would have landed close to his ear. But he had ducked to the left as she saw her first move, and the knife flew harmlessly past, hitting the wall and bouncing off. As Vivi saw him duck, she moved closer still and picked up the coffee pot, lobbing it toward Finn with strength doubled by adrenaline. That did hit him slightly on the shoulder, and he felt some hot drops splash on his forearm. The shattering of the pot on the floor sounded almost simultaneously. "You bitch!" Finn shouted, making a move toward her. As Finn circled left, she ran the other way around the island toward the living room. Finn followed her, clipping her purse with his elbow on the way past, spilling its content on the hard tile floor.

Neither of them heard her wallet and makeup and keys fall, so intent were they on the battle. Vivi had almost reached the front door, in fact had touched the handle, when Finn came up in back of her and grabbed her by her shirt. She bounded away, shirt tearing, across the living room, toward the small bathroom on the far wall. She pushed over a chair as she ran, hoping to slow Finn's steps. Two steps more and she would have made it. Just as she reached the door handle, he tackled her, landing on top of her back and pinning her to the floor.

She squirmed and wiggled and fought to get out from under him, but his sheer weight was too oppressive. She could not move. She wondered if she were hurt. He wondered the same thing.

"That's it," Finn said, slowly pulling himself away from her and standing up. "Are you ok?"

Vivi didn't answer. She got up slowly, trying to gauge if there was any damage to her body. The wind had been knocked out of her by the tackle, and she stood, trying to suck in air for a moment.

Finn looked on intently, hoping that in his efforts to make things look real, he hadn't inadvertently hurt her.

Vivi rubbed her elbow. "Well," she said, flexing her shoulders and moving her arms around, "I think I'm basically all right." Then, unexpectedly, she shone a brilliant smile at Finn. "Stronger than I look, right?"

Finn was assessing his own body. It seemed to be fine, though he knew he would have at least one bruise from that tackle. So would Vivi. "Now," he said, "for the next part..."

"Wait," Vivi protested. "There's more?"

"Five more minutes. We'll make believe that you hit your head with that last bit, banging it really hard on the floor. Could have caused a concussion. You might be out cold. But he can't leave you here to come to, because he has a record and he knows you'll be able to pick him out of a lineup or book of mugshots. He's not thinking clearly, maybe he's high. He has to get you out of here. He's playing it by ear, no plan to follow."

"OK, now what?"

"I'm going to drag you across the floor, toward the steps to the cellar. At that point, he would probably just pull you bouncing behind him, down the stairs."

There was fear on Viv's face, so Finn quickly added, "But unless he was terribly impaired, he would have known that you might wake up during that trauma and he'd have more of a fight. He would most likely pick you up and carry you over his shoulders, like firemen do." She looked relieved. "Like I'm going to do," he said. "After I drag you across the floor to the stairs."

She nodded and smiled a small smile. "Proceed."

"Get down on the floor, the way you were a minute ago." Then he turned her over, as if to see if she were awake. He grabbed hold of her legs. "Try to lie limp," he said. "I'll be gentle. Shouldn't hurt."

For the ten seconds it took Finn to get her to the door to the cellar stairs, Vivi closed her eyes. She wished she could have just stayed prone on the floor. She was so tired, and half of the plan had yet to happen. She willed herself to be limp as she felt Finn move down the stairs with her over his shoulder.

Two minutes later, Vivi was under a tarp on the floor of the back seat and the truck was moving.

Chapter 46: The Longest Day

Finn drove into town. He pulled over in front of Killer Coffee and called Pen's cell phone. It rang, then went to voicemail. "Hey, Pen," Finn said, sounding very normal and upbeat. "Not sure where you are right now, but I'm wondering if you might want to join me in a coffee and a bear claw at Killer Coffee. Text or call me back when you get this." Then he sat for a few minutes waiting for Pen to call him back. He got a text in five minutes.

It said: "Sure. I'm at Old Silver Beach. I'll be there in fifteen minutes. Order me a bear claw and a large coffee."

Ten minutes after that, another text. "Car won't start. Can you help? Parked on left, not far from beach shack. Meet you there."

Finn's reply said: "On my way."

Pen's Highlander was right where she had said it would be. After greeting Pen, Finn got to it. Clearly, it wasn't starting. Opening and propping up the hood, he looked at the battery connections. Corroded. He got a rag, a wrench, and a screwdriver from his truck. After disconnecting the terminals, he proceeded to scrape corrosion off the connections, wiping the screwdriver with the rag from time to time. After a few minutes of this, he called out to Penn, who was sitting in the driver's seat. "Try it now."

Pen looked startled when it started on the first try. She got out of the car and walked toward the front, giving Finn a thumbs up and a smile when she saw him.

He smiled back at her, then closed the hood with a thud. "Back in business." he said. "Let's go get that coffee."

Twenty minutes later they were sitting in a booth at the front, eating pastries and drinking coffees. They tried to keep the banter light, as if this was another one of their usual coffee dates. They had picked the booth on purpose; it was near the front, and anyone entering would probably see them. Also, Penn had "accidentally" spilled her coffee as soon as she got it, so there had been a mopping up scene as well as a repeat order. Something to be remembered. After they'd been there about fifteen minutes, Finn suggested calling Vivi, to let her know where Pen was and to tell her she'd be at Finn's for the rest of the day and the evening. Pen complied, and when there was no answer, she left a voicemail. She tried not to think of the phone ringing over and over in the quiet house by the ocean or of her friend, hot and sweaty and scared under the tarp in the truck.

Before they headed out, Finn suggested they pick up some more pastries. "Never know when you might be starving for a fruit tart or a donut," he said, as he bought two of each at the cash register.

Once they were safely at Finn's house, they parked in front, with Finn's truck furthest away from the neighbors. Pen's Highlander was parked next to his truck, and when Finn opened the side door of the truck, Vivi was shielded from any neighbor's eyes by the body of the truck and by the Highlander on the other side. Finn knew from living some time in this neighborhood that it was unlikely that anyone nearby was at home right now. Also, the two houses nearby were angled for privacy, and so, while he had no clear sight lines of their homes, they had no clear view of his parking spots or front door.

Finn helped Vivi out of the car, and she kept her head down as she moved with him toward the front door. In a swift motion, he turned the key and opened the door. They were inside. Safe for now. Vivi and Pen sat down on the couch in the living room, spent. Finn got them all bottled water. Then he went back for a plate and handed Vivi the plate and the bag of pastries. "You haven't eaten for a while. Have one. I'll get you a sandwich. You need to be fed and hydrated for the next patch."

He returned shortly with a ham sandwich. Placing it in front of Vivi, he said, "I'll leave you two alone. Need to shower and change."

Pen looked at Vivi. "C'mon," she said. "Let's sit on the screened porch. No one can see us there." She helped Vivi carry the water and food outside and put them on the table.

Vivi was quietly sitting on the screened porch, drinking a glass of water, trying to choke down her sandwich, and watching the waves. Finally, she asked, "Will I ever see this again? I can't bear it."

"You have to bear it," Pen said, trying to couch the hard truth in a supportive tone. "There's no other choice."

"I know. I can't think about it. About leaving you, the girls, my house, my family." Looking at her friend, Pen thought she had never seen her so bereft. She looked the way you look when you leave a funeral after burying a loved one. She looked even smaller than usual, as if even her very bones were diminished. There were tears running silently down her face, and she didn't wipe them away. "I should have gone to the police as soon as they contacted me," she said in a whispery voice. "I should have been braver."

"Vivi, listen to me. You did what seemed right at the time. Hindsight is great, but in the moment, you were afraid. For yourself, for the girls. I would have been, too." She put her hands on either side of her friend's face and looked her in the eyes. "You did the best you could. Then. You'll do the best you can do now. You'll move on. You'll be ok." Then the two best friends fell into each other's arms and sobbed their goodbyes to the sound of the crashing waves in front of them.

Finn found them then and let them be for a few moments. Then he said, "Fifteen-minute warning. We have to leave soon. It's already three o'clock."

Vivi asked in a quiet voice, "Can I shower quickly? I'm sweaty and wrinkled...and a mess."

"You can if you can be really, really quick."

Pen said, "Your blouse is torn. I have extra clothes here; I'll leave you a clean one outside the bathroom." Then they scattered to make preparations.

"Some important points," Finn said, once they were all seated at the dining room table, dressed and ready to go. He wanted Pen to hear what he had to say, but he addressed Vivi. "You can't contact anyone for a year, minimum. No email, texts, letters home. After a year, you can write and tell us how to contact you, preferably at a PO Box that is not close to where you live. Tell us how you are with no identifiers. Use a different name. Write the letter with the kind of language that sounds innocuous and could have been sent from a friend traveling. Use plain paper, plain envelope. Or send a birthday card and write your message in code. Just so it looks normal. Use this address: 27 Old Pond Drive, Cataumet, MA 02534." Vivi scribbled it down in a small notebook.

And then they were on their way. Finn and Pen in the front seat, Vivi on the floor in the back of the truck. Once they were over the Bourne Bridge, Finn told Vivi she could get out from under the tarp and lie down on the back seat. Route 495 was crowded, the windows to the truck were darkened, and it seemed safe enough to Finn. He was cautious, but there was only so much they could do. He thought it would be enough.

"Are you ok?" Pen asked as they got closer to Boston. "Can you follow the plan?"

"Yes." Vivi was already somewhere else.

After twenty minutes more, they were approaching South Station. Finn had planned initially to take Vivi to Logan, but the more he thought about possible cameras recording traffic in and around the airport, the more he decided on another plan. "We'll let you off a block from South Station," he said to Vivi, glancing back at her over his shoulder. "Just go into the station and take the Silver Line to Logan. Then follow the rest of the plan." No answer. "OK with that?" he asked.

Vivi said, "OK" in a barely discernable voice. The future was now. And she was scared to death.

Five minutes later, Finn pulled the truck over into a miraculously open parking spot a block and a half from South Station. "We're here. I hate to be cold, but you have to say your goodbyes in the truck. Once you get out, Vivi, just start walking, blend in with the crowd." Even through the tinted windows, they could see the dense foot traffic flowing along the sidewalk next to the truck.

Pen was taking deep breaths, trying not to cry. She knew instinctively that to come apart now would jeopardize Vivi's whole plan, and she clamped her teeth together to prevent herself from actually wailing.

Vivi looked to be in the same shape. She reached forward and grabbed the arm that Pen had extended toward her. Leaning forward, and clasping each other in a mini embrace, they took in each other's scent, a scent as familiar to each as their own. Vivi said, in a stronger voice than Finn would have expected, "We WILL be together again, I promise."

Pen, choking back her pain, said, "I know we will. I promise, too."

Finn turned and offered Vivi a handshake. Vivi shook his hand, then kissed her own fingers and touched his. "Thank you," she said. Then she gathered her belongings and opened the back door. Seconds later she was part of the foot traffic moving towards South Station. Pen watched her back as long as she could see the white blouse moving. Then she could see nothing. Vivi was gone.

They sat in the truck for twenty minutes. Pen felt scooped out like a pumpkin. Her house had burned. Her best friend was gone, maybe forever. Her heart was empty and in its emptiness was an ache that hurt like a freshly broken bone. At that moment she could not take in her blessings: her girls, Finn, her career. She couldn't think, only feel a sadness unlike anything she had ever experienced.

She would have sat there forever, only Finn finally asked, "Think it's time to go?"

Without looking at him, she nodded, and he pulled out of the parking spot and began the long ride home.

All she wanted to do was sob, but as if he were reading her mind, Finn said, "You have to hold it together a little longer, Pen. We have to go out tonight, be seen in town, smiling and having a nice dinner." She didn't answer. "Do you understand?" he asked gently, eyes on the road.

"Yes," she said. They didn't talk again until they had crossed the Bourne Bridge and were on route 28. The late afternoon light was just starting its slant toward twilight when Finn pulled into a small strip mall on the right. The stores were small and old, somewhat shabby. Off to the far right, next to the last store, one obviously being renovated, was a dumpster.

Finn got out of the truck and took a plastic bag from the back. With a mighty toss, it sailed through the air and landed in the dumpster. "Georges' shoes," he said and got back into the truck. "I noticed the dumpster the other day, when I came up this way to pick up some customized shutters." He put the truck in gear and headed back onto route 28. "Handy."

They called Vivi from Finn's house and left a message. "Hey," Pen said, "Finn and I are going to catch a bite at The Flying Bridge. Wanna join us? It's six o'clock. Give me a buzz back."

Later, they sat on the outside balcony of The Flying Bridge, eating oysters, drinking wine. Finn had told Pen they had to look "normal," like they were out on a regular date. She understood this was necessary. And so, she made an effort to talk, to laugh slightly, to eat her shrimp scampi. By the second glass of wine she felt slightly better, a fact she attributed more to her food and the alcohol than to any mental adjustment she might have made. Finn leaned toward her across the table and she leaned close to hear what he had to say. "It will get better," he said, taking her hand. "I promise you."

The next day they would head off to pick up Galen at Camp Merrimore and take her to Camp EverArt in Truro. Early on the way up, Pen would call Vivi again, leaving a message asking if she wanted to eat a late dinner on Finn's porch once she and Finn were back from taking Galen to the new camp. Maybe around seven. Call back, please, she'd say. An hour before they got to Camp Merrimore, Pen would call and tell the police that she'd made three calls to Vivi's cellphone over the last two days and that none of them had been answered or returned. Pen would tell them that Vivi always returned calls, was almost always home painting at least part of each day, and that Pen was worried. If she were in town, she would explain, she would have driven over to Vivi's to check on her. But because she and Finn had to leave early to pick up her daughter at camp in the Berkshires, and then take her to another camp in Truro, she wouldn't be home until late in the day. She'd ask if the police could possibly send someone over to Vivi's to do a "well-being" check? Probably lost her phone, Pen would laugh. Again. "Sorry to bother you," she'd say, "but I'm worried. Thanks so much. Please have her call me, ok?"

But it was still tonight. A halfmoon had risen, and except for its pale light, it was full dark now. Finn paid the bill and they walked toward the truck holding hands.

"Time to go home," he said, opening the door for her.

Pen nodded and bit her lip, the tears still waiting. "Yes," she said softly. "It's time to go home."

She knew she would sob later tonight, and that Finn wouldn't try to talk her out of it. He knew, more than most, that sometimes sadness takes root in your heart and your bones, and you have to let it live there...until it doesn't. He would, she knew, help her move through it. He would be tough enough and love her enough to sit with it and tolerate her unhappiness. She also knew, in the way you sometimes do, that it wouldn't be forever. That she would be happier with Finn than she'd ever been in her life. Just not now. It would take time. And time they had.

Chapter 47: As time Goes By

They were cruising at 35,000 feet, the sound of the engines' purr relaxing her and almost pushing her into sleep. But the excitement swirling in her brain prevented that. For now, she was content to relax with her eyes closed.

She could feel Finn move around next to her as he tried to get comfortable; being six feet five was not an advantage in an airplane. She sensed that he was not asleep, either.

Vivi's first letter had come a year and two days after she'd left. On that day Pen had taken a break from working on her newest novel and gone outside to get the mail. On top had been a check from her publisher, something that always made her smile. As hard as it had been to write, her last book had saved her. After Vivi had left their lives, she had thrown herself into revising it as if her life depended on it. And that was how it felt. Her joy at its success was greatly muted by the absence of her friend with whom to share it.

Pen pulled out the publisher's envelope to put in her desk drawer and flipped through the rest of the flyers and junk mail. Underneath the whole mess was a piece of mail with a Dublin postmark. Pen's breath h caught in her throat; time seemed to stop. The envelope was addressed to her, but in a hand she did not recognize. Feeling oddly disconnected, almost floating, she carried it out to the screened porch and sat down heavily.

Finally.

The words inside were written in the same hand as those on the envelope, on the inside of a generic card that said, "Have a great day!" and had a picture of a sunflower on the front. It said, "I'm enjoying my time in Ireland. Such beautiful vistas everywhere. People have been nice, too. I've taken many photographs to paint from, if I ever get around to it. Hope all is well. Miss you." It was signed, "Love, Charlotte."

Pen smiled. Charlotte. Of course, she thought. Charlotte from "Charlotte's Web," a book they had both loved as children. Charlotte: "a true friend and a good writer" as Wilber says. Inside joke, as Pen was the writer. That sounded like Vivi. Turning the envelope over in her hands again, she noticed a Post Office box number as a return address, with the post office in Ennis, Ireland. Relief flooded Pen's heart. Vivi was all right.

Since then, there had been occasional correspondence between them, always carefully discrete. This trip was the result.

Pen tried once again to sleep, letting the drone of the engines lull her and trying a simple mantra to calm her mind. She did feel calmer, but still, sleep would not come. She could not stop thinking of all that had happened in the two years Vivi had been gone.

Galen had not gone to Falmouth High School as they assumed she would. Instead, she attended Tuck Academy in Marion, a school she'd found online. Its mission statement said it embraced both social justice and the arts, as ways of making the world better. For Galen, it sounded like home. She lobbied hard, and finally even Peter had gotten behind the idea of her attending the private school, willing to pay his share of the yearly $36,000 yearly tuition.

Since his marriage to Heather and the subsequent birth of his son Jasper, Peter had softened considerably. A blessing. He'd been brusque about Galen's eventual coming out, but accepted it with more grace than Pen could have imagined. She remembered her own mother saying "miracles never cease," and smiled to herself. There seemed to be many floating about.

One was the transformation of Galen. She was becoming the person she was meant to be. She'd gone to political rallies and marches and discovered photography, soccer, and poetry slams. She'd had three girlfriends, the latest of whom was Ethel (called El) who had flaming red hair and according to Galen a "wicked sense of humor." Pen carried two pictures that told the tale. In one, Galen held a black and white photograph of two shells on a beach, with a plastic bag and a dead seagull next to them. She was holding a blue ribbon. In the other, she and El were standing on a beach, silhouetted against a darkening sky, holding hands.

Aggie was doing well, too. She was as Jefferson Middle School, the same school that Galen had attended. Mr. Dockery had left of his own volition, and been replaced by June Sennot, who had transformed the school, bringing it up to speed in academics as well as the arts. It was surprising to Pen to see how much her mild Aggie liked a challenge; she took the toughest options and worked hard, her grades reflecting her interest and commitment. The picture she brought of Aggie showed her at the Falmouth Art Museum, standing before a wall of watercolors and collages. Hers. Even though she was only 13, she applied to be a 'visiting artist.' A bold move in Pen's opinion. She was the youngest person ever accepted in that capacity by the museum. In the picture, she wasn't slumping as she often had done in earlier times. She stood ramrod straight, and a half smile played on her face. She was still short, but she looked both confident and proud.

Next to Pen, Finn snored slightly, and she was glad he had finally been able to sleep. One of them would need their wits about them as they navigated the roads to Galway.

Pen stretched and tried to move into a more comfortable position. She badly wanted to sleep, but she knew that wasn't going to happen. Her mind just kept swirling around the past and what the near future would bring. She knew at some point Vivi would want to know what had happened to the drug dealers who wrecked her life and especially whether they were after her.

And the strange truth was, Pen didn't know. She knew only a few things that Finn had told her. He said he had passed all the information that Marcus had given them to his undercover contact and was certain that the man would not reveal Finn's name or part in the story.

But there had been no investigation, at least not a public one. Which was confusing to Pen. When she'd questioned Finn about it, he'd gotten unusually quiet. And solemn.

Then he told her. It had taken two years, he explained, for the information to yield results. It had all been done undercover. The underground operation had led to a huge drug network, bigger than anyone could have imagined, with contacts all over the country and in three foreign countries. It would shortly break open, with warrants for over a hundred and fifty people at all levels of the organization. Some of the top figures, the hardest to catch, would finally be arrested and stopped. It was a giant coup.

Pen could tell that Finn took a quiet pride in being a part of it, of passing along the information that began the investigation. He was happy being in the background, with no connection to the actual investigation and no glory, either. There had been, as much as there ever could be, revenge exacted for Rachel's death. It was not enough; nothing could ever be enough. But it was a hell of a lot better than nothing.

When she asked him if Vivi's name would come up, he was less clear. He'd looked her in the eyes and said, "I'm not sure. I'm hoping not. No way to be sure until everything explodes." And then, seeing the worry on Pen's face, he 'd stroked her cheek and added, "I'm pretty sure it won't."

As to Vivi's disappearance, that was entirely another story. It had made the papers all over the Cape. There was an extensive investigation. Pen and Finn had been grilled over and over again, but their information had not helped find any leads. They had been excluded early on as being culpable in any way in her disappearance. Their stories were identical, they had been seen around town, neither had any prior records, and the texts and calls on Vivi's phone confirmed what they said.

Their heartbreak at her disappearance appeared to be real. And indeed, it was. Pen was bereft; that did not have to be faked. And Finn, for his part, had shown deep sorrow at Vivi's loss as well. They were told the investigating was ongoing, but after two years, it seemed unlikely to be solved. Vivi's parents had power of attorney and were the beneficiaries of her will; they were living in the house temporarily, hoping against hope that she would miraculously return one day. Pen's heart ached for them, as she knew how unlikely that was to happen. She knew she would sugarcoat as much of this as she could for Vivi, who, she suspected, held enough guilt and sadness to fill an ocean.

The airport was much more crowded than Pen remembered from the last time she'd been here, on a graduation trip with her friend Clarice, the summer between high school and college. It was bigger and was teeming with tourists. She was glad she had Finn to help find the Hertz car rental and to drive out of the airport. Every few minutes, one of them would say, "Left! Left!" as a reminder to stay on the left side of the road. It felt foreign at first, then more natural as they blended in with the native drivers.

What she remembered correctly was the green. All shades. The countryside seemed to vibrate with it. As the clouds shifted, they would shade the land below and it would appear a deep, dark green. In the patches in between the clouds, the sun shone down and turned the green to a bright, almost florescent color. Chartreuse, she thought it was called. Because of the sun and the shade, the landscape of the hills and valleys surrounding them looked like a crazy checkerboard of color. Even stranger, the colors kept shifting as the winds blew the clouds rapidly across the bright blue sky. *Magic*, she thought. *This is magic.*

As Finn navigated the roads to Galway, Pen was reminded of another bright and sunny day a year ago when she and Finn had married on the rising rocky ledges in back of Quissett Harbor, hiking out with fifteen family members and friends through the woods to the high rock-formed platform at the end. She opened her purse and glanced at the last of the pictures she'd brought. In one, she and the girls, one on either side of her, stood against the backdrop of a clear cerulean blue sky and deeper blue ocean. The sun was on their faces and the wind was whipping their hair and they were laughing. It wasn't a perfect picture, but it was a joyous one. In the other, she and Finn faced each other, she in a long white sundress with a circle of daisies in her hair and he in a navy suit and red tie. They were looking at each other with both delight and astonishment, as if they couldn't believe what was happening. There was no mistaking the look that passed between them. Love. Finally.

There were no pictures of the latest news she brought. In fact, no one else was aware of it, not even Finn. She smiled at something he said about a stone archway they had just passed, as she unconsciously rested her right hand on her belly.